The Second Human Extinction Event

Scott S Neal

* * *

The Second Human Extinction Event is a work of fiction. Names and places are products of the author's imagination and do not reference any living person or place. Any resemblance to any person, living or dead, or place is purely coincidental.

Description of the book:

(Tolle, Eckhart, *The Power of Now: A Guide to Spiritual Enlightenment*, Namaste Publishing, 1997, Vancouver)

Used with permission of Namaste Publishing

Map Art: Adam Workman
Cover Picture: Loc Dang - pexels-timegrocery-1905054

Prologue

The first human extinction event has been estimated to have occurred around 5,000 BC. Humanity came very close to becoming extinct. The story of the Great Flood has been recorded in different ancient religious texts, with the story of Noah in the Bible as just one example. Now, a second human extinction event is occurring. A virus named COVID-24, unleashed by man, has spread around the world, killing almost every human on Earth. A few survivors have gathered in one special valley, protected by a young man with a common name. John Smith has been given the title of Marshal of the Valley. To do his job, he has learned to listen to the energy of life, the Chi, and earned the title of Chi Master. Using the guidance he receives from the Chi, will Marshal Smith be able to save humanity from extinction again?

PART ONE

THE VALLEY OF CHI

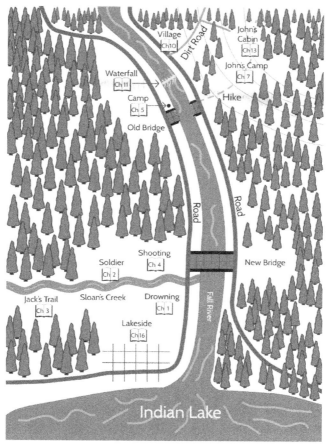

The Valley of Chi

1

Spring in the valley meant warm, wet weather was John's constant companion. Recent rains enhanced the scent of the earth and evergreen trees that dominated the valley, but today, the bright sunshine and calm winds brightened his mood. He would have appreciated a breeze to keep him cool as John's shirt, drenched in sweat, clung to his tall, slender frame. The importance of his mission kept him from stopping to cool off as he followed the trail of a man named Jack, who had molested a woman and then killed her.

As Marshal of this valley, John's job was to protect the valley's residents from people like Jack. The less violent ones mostly left peacefully, but John wasn't sure Jack should be allowed to roam free. He and Jack had lived in the same village for a month, which made this job much more difficult. He'd sensed an air of evil around Jack, but he never thought Jack would do the things he'd done.

Jack was last seen at a nearby campsite where John had picked up his trail. He wore hiking boots with a distinctive tread pattern, making following his trail easy. Ahead, John could hear the roar of a creek raging against its banks, swollen by the recent rains. Jack's trail led him to the creek's bank, where he paused to welcome the cooling mist as it drifted over him. Jack's trail indicated he'd not crossed the creek but had turned and headed upstream.

As John paused to read the trail, he heard voices from upstream. He looked up and saw a man and woman trying to cross the creek using a fallen tree. As Marshal, John knew he should stop and talk to them, giving them directions to a village in this valley.

The fallen tree seemed like an easy route across the creek, but the tone of the couple's conversation indicated how nervous they were about the crossing. As John watched, the tree suddenly shifted sideways as the water overflowing the banks eroded the soil anchoring one end. The woman was instantly thrown into the turbulent water while the man managed to cling to the branches of the tree. John saw the fear on the woman's face as she struggled against the current.

He dropped his pack and moved closer to the creek's edge, ready to offer assistance. The noise from the water crashing against the rocks was deafening, but he shouted at her anyway. She must have heard him because she looked up and saw him for the first time. A look of relief briefly flashed on her face as she realized help was nearby. She started swimming toward John, and he was impressed with how strong a swimmer she was as she handled the current expertly. She slowly made progress toward the bank, where John stood waiting.

Suddenly, she disappeared under the water. It happened quickly, like an underwater monster had snatched her from the surface. She didn't make any sound. One moment, she was there; the next, she was gone. John watched for a few seconds, hoping to see her reappear farther downstream. She didn't.

John immediately started wading into the creek, heading to where he'd last seen her. The water was cold, the current strong, and water kept splashing into his eyes, interfering with his vision. It took all of his strength to move against the current.

He saw her hand briefly rise above the water, only to sink again beneath the surface. His progress was slowed as he fought the swift current, and the water rose to the level of his chest as he waded deeper into the creek.

When he finally arrived where he'd last seen her, he reached beneath the surface, searching for her. He caught hold of some cloth and tried pulling it to the surface. It moved slightly but no farther. Something was holding her under the water.

John took a large breath and ducked under the surface. He could not see in the muddy water, so he used his hands to follow the contours of her body deeper into the creek. He found the problem when he reached her ankles. One of her ankles appeared to be wedged between the branches of a sunken tree and held there by the swift current pulling her body downstream. He anchored his feet against the sunken tree and pulled her body back against the current, trying to free her ankle. He made no progress at all. His strength couldn't overcome the force of the current pulling her downstream.

John started to get lightheaded because of the lack of oxygen, and his mind and heart were racing. He needed to calm down and not panic, as he was determined not to leave her. He stood up to get his head above the water, gasping for fresh air, before ducking back underwater to try again. He repositioned his feet to gain more leverage and focused all his strength on another attempt. As he pulled her back against the current, her ankle was finally freed from the branches.

John stood up again, filling his lungs with air, but this time with her in his arms. With her head now above the water, John could see she wasn't breathing.

John struggled as the cold water, swift current, and lack of oxygen took a toll on him. Now, with the extra weight of the woman, he was losing his fight against the current. John slowly progressed toward the bank as the current pulled them both downstream. When they finally reached the bank, he knew he had no time to rest. He lifted her body at her waist, letting her head hang down like a lifeless ragdoll. He watched as water drained out of her mouth from her lungs.

John laid her on the ground once water stopped draining from her lungs and started CPR. He wasn't sure she'd live after being underwater for so long, but he wasn't giving up easily. He prayed that she had a strong will to live.

As John continued CPR, he spoke to her, telling her not to give up. He visualized sending his own life energy into her to help her live. After several minutes of CPR, she finally coughed up more water and started gasping for air. John rolled her over onto her stomach as she continued coughing up water. He told her to breathe deeply to help clear her lungs, which brought on another fit of coughing.

The coughing finally subsided, and it looked like she'd live but would require some time to recover. As her breathing became more regular, she sat up and looked at John. He got his first good look at her face. She was a middle-aged woman with laugh lines around her eyes and gray streaks in her short chestnut hair.

But beyond her physical characteristics, she had a purposeful appearance, as if she wouldn't allow herself to be overcome by life. John had first seen this defiant spirit when she'd been suddenly thrown into the creek. She found the strength to fight the current and start swimming to the bank. Never for a moment did she give up. Only the unseen submerged tree defeated her. He took an immediate liking to her and was glad she'd survived.

The woman looked at her rescuer. He was very young and tall, with curly brown hair, olive complexion, and brown eyes. As she looked at John, her face beamed with a sudden look of recognition, and she smiled.

"You remind me of someone I knew long ago. My high school boyfriend was tall with curly hair like you," she said, but then her face clouded, and she continued, "But he probably died in the COVID-24 epidemic."

"Yes, ma'am, many people died with the virus."

"I knew him when he was about your age. How old are you? 18?"

"That's close, I guess," John replied, trying to sound convincing. "How do you feel, ma'am?"

"I've got a headache. I remember falling into the water, but I don't remember anything else. How did I get here?"

"I was on the creek's bank and saw you fall in. I was waiting to help you out of the water, but a tree snagged your ankle and pulled you underwater. I jumped in and pulled you out."

She looked down and started coughing but then looked back up at John and asked, "Did I drown?"

"Yes, ma'am, but it's common for people to forget the details when they have accidents. I knew CPR and got you breathing again. Your lungs will hurt for a while, and you'll also have some coughing spells until all the water is out of your lungs. After that, you should be OK."

"Thank you so much for saving me," she replied and then started coughing again. When she could speak again, she said, "I was lucky you happened to be at the creek when I fell in."

"Jill! Jill! Where are you?" someone called.

John yelled back, "We're over here."

"Your husband will be glad I was able to pull you out."

"Oh, he's not my husband; my husband died with the virus. That's Reggie, someone I met about a month ago, and we decided to travel together out of convenience. The hiking has been difficult for him, but he doesn't give up. He's become very protective of me."

Her expression saddened, and she continued, "At some point, he'll die, I'm afraid, and then I'll be left alone again."

John felt bad for her. She'd lost so much, and her future didn't look bright.

"Maybe I can help," John responded. "I know of a village some distance away. They'll take you in if you mention my name and say I sent you."

Her face brightened a little, and she thanked him.

At that point, Reggie arrived from somewhere upstream. He moved slowly and obviously had been hurt when the tree bridge had shifted. They were an odd pair, as he looked defeated in sharp contrast to Jill. His beard had a lot of gray, and he was bald on the top of his head. Few men shaved anymore since it was challenging to find razors. He looked down at Jill, and a look of relief spread across his face. His expression indicated he didn't want to be without her.

She explained to Reggie what had happened, at which point he reached out his hand to shake John's. "Thank you for helping Jill," he said.

After another brief coughing spell, Jill said, "Reggie, this is ... I just realized I don't even know your name!"

"I'm called Marshal Smith," John replied.

"Marshal isn't a name you hear much anymore," she offered.

John laughed and responded, "I'm sorry, ma'am, but Marshal isn't my first name; it's a title. I've gotten so used to everyone calling me Marshal Smith that I sometimes forget and use it as my name. My first name is John. I'm the peacekeeper in this area, hence the Marshal title. Right now, I'm following the trail of a man as part of my job."

"You look young for a peacekeeper. You don't even have a beard yet," Reggie said slowly. "Are you sure you have the skills to deal with this man? As an older man, I know how crafty we adults can be."

John smiled and replied, "Yes, sir, I can handle the situation even as young as I am. And I don't have a beard because being clean-shaven is part of my Marshal identity. It's like my uniform, so people will

The Second Human Extinction Event

know who I am when we meet. But I thank you for your concern.

"Will you and Jill be OK now? I must keep going after the man before his trail gets washed out from the rain. I'll return to this area in a couple of days when my job is done. If you're still around, I'll take you to a village that will take you in. Getting to the village is a long hike, but we can take our time and give you a chance to heal."

"How will you find us? Do we need to tell you where we will camp?" Reggie asked.

"No, sir. My job is finding people, remember? You couldn't hide from me if you tried," John responded with a wide grin.

John picked up his pack and turned upstream to follow the trail of the man he knew would never offer to change his ways. He was unsure how this situation would be resolved.

2

Several miles later, John suddenly smelled smoke. There was a slight breeze this morning, which meant the fire was not too far away. He proceeded cautiously, following the smoke, and finally saw a campsite up ahead near the creek. He removed his pack and slowly walked into the camp. He noticed the campsite appeared empty, even though a fire still burned. As John looked around the camp, a man suddenly emerged from behind a large tree. He was holding an AR-15 assault rifle.

He was a big, middle-aged man, slightly taller than John's 6-foot 2-inches and heavily muscled. His dark skin contrasted with the slight graying of his temples and beard. His hair and beard were cut short, and he looked like a seasoned military man. John slowly raised his hands. His throwing knife was his only weapon and was still in his pack.

"So, you've come back to steal again," the soldier growled. "That will be your last mistake. No one steals from me and gets away with it."

John could sense the man's frustration and desperation all mixing together. He was not thinking clearly, and this was a dangerous combination of emotions. John must handle this carefully.

"Hello, sir. I'm Marshal Smith, the peacekeeper of this valley. You're mistaken; I haven't taken anything from you. I was tracking a man when I came upon your campsite."

"You stupid kid. No one would believe that you're a Marshal. You should come up with a better story than that when someone catches you stealing food."

"You're angry, sir, I'm sure, but I didn't take your food, and I'm not looking for any trouble."

"Well, I don't believe you, and I'm going to show you what happens when someone steals food from me."

He leaned his rifle against a tree and slowly began walking towards John. He suddenly pulled a knife from behind his back.

John tried to project calming feelings toward him, but it had no effect. "You haven't hurt anyone yet, so this can be handled peacefully if you just agree to leave our valley."

"I haven't hurt anyone yet, but your presence here might change that. Taking someone's food is a serious crime these days," the soldier replied, calming down slightly. "I was a hand-to-hand combat instructor in the Army, so you stand no chance against me. You're just a young kid. If you turn around and leave, I'll let you walk away."

"I'm sorry, sir, but I can't turn back. You can't win this fight. You must leave this valley immediately."

The soldier smiled with a broad, confident grin and said, "You sure are cocky for a kid. I haven't had a good challenge in a while. This should be interesting."

He raised his knife and moved closer to John, circling him. He stopped at a point where the sun was in John's eyes, which he thought would offer him an advantage. He was wrong.

"You don't even have a knife. You're making this too easy for me," he said.

At that moment, the soldier moved in, lunging with his knife, but only as a feint. The point of his knife stopped an inch from John's stomach before he withdrew it. He seemed surprised John didn't fall back as he lunged toward him. John had correctly anticipated the feint, so he didn't react. The soldier grew worried that John seemed to be able to read his intentions.

The soldier's next move exploded toward John as he rushed in at full speed, hoping to overpower John with his bulk. John stepped quickly to one side to avoid the thrust of the knife. He grabbed the soldier's shirt and arm and used the soldier's momentum to rotate his body and slam him to the ground. The soldier landed flat on his back, and John heard the air forced from his lungs while his head hit the ground hard.

The soldier lay there in a semi-conscious state, fighting for his breath. John picked up the soldier's knife and rifle and set them beside his pack. As he returned to the soldier, John sensed that he wasn't yet done fighting.

The soldier was alert again but trying to make John believe he was still semi-conscious. He suddenly rolled onto his side, using his leg in an attempt to sweep John off his feet. John jumped up, letting the soldier's leg pass through the empty air beneath him, and stepped away.

The soldier quickly jumped to his feet and said, "I see I misjudged you. It won't happen again."

He walked to his firewood pile and picked up a branch about three feet long, intending to use it as a club. As the soldier stepped back towards him, John could tell the soldier was angry and more focused this time. He wouldn't stop until John was severely hurt or dead. The soldier poked the club's end at John twice in succession, forcing him to retreat. He continued coming at John with a spinning move, using the club like a baseball bat. The fight would be over if the club connected with John.

John correctly anticipated the soldier's spinning move and dropped to one knee. He ducked below the club's path and then delivered a fist to the soldier's midsection. He put all his strength into the punch to compensate for the muscle mass he struck. John heard the air rush out of the soldier's lungs again, but this time, he also heard the sound of ribs breaking. The soldier went down to the ground again.

John moved over to him, knelt, and looked into his eyes as the soldier struggled to breathe.

"Please, sir, stay down," he said softly. "You now have some broken ribs which will heal with time. I'll have to hurt you more severely if you get up and continue to fight. You may not survive those injuries."

"Who are you?" the soldier gasped, still trying to recover his breathing. "You fight like no man I've ever faced, yet you're just a kid."

"I truly am the Marshal in this valley and a Chi Master. I sense your every move before you make it. You were the one who stood no chance in this fight. I'm sorry I hurt you, but you gave me no choice.

"You have a decision to make now. Unless you can live peacefully, you should leave this valley and return to where you came from. But there's a second choice you can make. You can choose to help people rather than hurt them like you were trained in the Army. A village near here could use a strong man like you.

"But let me be clear. You must not hurt anyone, or I'll remove you from this valley. I worry that if I ever face you again in battle, you won't survive. Either way, I must take your gun, but you can keep your knife.

"Let me tape up your ribs before I go."

As John applied tape from his medical kit to the soldier's ribs, he said to him, "I sense a lot of good in you and a gentler side to your personality. It may be more difficult than your Army training, but I believe you can change if you wish to. It's the harder path to take, but in the end, it's the more rewarding one. And, just for the record, I didn't steal your food."

"I believe you now. I was so angry and frustrated that I let my emotions control me. I'm sorry.

"I've decided I'll go to your village. I was doing survival training when the virus struck. From the reports, I knew not to go into the cities. I've been traveling around the countryside for months, and nobody is left alive. From a distance, all the cities and towns look to be empty. Only bodies remain. You're the first alive person I've seen in months.

"By the way, my name is Fred, Master Sergeant Fred Maldonado. The way you fight, you would have been a good soldier. May I ask how old you are, Marshal? Are you even 20 years old yet?" he asked.

"Almost 20, sir," John replied as he returned to his pack and picked up the soldier's gun. He'd stop and bury it later today in a place no one would find. He handed Fred's knife back to him. John wanted to change the subject of his age, so he started giving the soldier directions to the village.

"Following this creek for about three miles will take you to a paved road that parallels the river. Follow that road north for about 35 miles, and you'll come to the village. Ask for Rob and tell him that John sent you. You don't have to tell him how your ribs were broken; he'll know. You and Rob might get along well since Rob was in the military, too, although he was in the Navy.

"I lived in that village for about a month, and it's a nice place to live. Please don't mess it up!"

"You said that you were tracking a man. I never saw who stole my food, but they've been at it for days. First, it was a freshly cooked fish, and then I had a rabbit on the fire. My thief was very good at sneaking into my camp when I had gone to the creek for water."

"That couldn't have been Jack since he's been constantly moving since I've been tracking him."

"So, you're telling me my thief may be back?"

"Yes, but it's my job to stop this sort of theft. Do you mind if I look around your camp for any clues? I might be able to help you catch this thief."

"Sure. I have nothing to hide, and with broken ribs, I need all the help I can get."

John started walking around the camp's perimeter. He could see that Fred had been there for several days. The tent had been set up in a sheltered location with a fire pit nearby. A large stack of firewood had been collected, and a rope for drying clothes was stretched between two trees. He spotted a blue baseball cap hanging from a tree branch. After several minutes, he returned to Fred.

"That baseball cap looks a little small for you," John noted with a laugh.

"You think?" Fred chuckled. "I found it down by the creek yesterday. I don't know why I kept it, but it is difficult to throw anything away these days."

"I've discovered that Jack didn't go through your camp. He walked around it so he wouldn't be seen. I did, however, discover another set of tracks leading into your camp. These tracks were made by someone smaller than yourself, who made multiple trips to your camp."

"Can you track them down and stop them from stealing my food?"

"Yes, but you stay here and rest. They're camping nearby, so they shouldn't be too difficult to find."

"No. I'm going with you."

John and Fred started following the thief's trail. Fred had picked up his club for a weapon, while John needed none. John came to a sudden stop about a mile from the camp. He sensed that someone was ahead of them and could feel their fear. He motioned for Fred to stay there while he moved off to his left around some large boulders.

John hoped to get behind whoever waited for them. After quietly moving around the screening boulders, he arrived at a small clearing. A pile of branches leaning against a boulder didn't look natural. It was a hastily constructed shelter, and John sensed someone was inside. John positioned himself near the entrance to the shelter and called out to Fred to join him. The two of them blocked any path of escape from the shelter.

After Fred arrived, John said, "This is Marshal John Smith. I'm a law enforcement officer in this valley. Please come out so that we can talk."

A dark-skinned boy, about eight or nine years old, emerged from the shelter. His clothes were ragged and dirty. His hair contained twigs and leaf debris. He had a bruise on his cheek, a cut lip, and scratches on his arm. His face was thin as if he hadn't been eating much lately. Even with his disheveled look, he was defiant. His eyes quickly scanned the area, looking for an escape route, but found none. He didn't say a word but turned his eyes to stare at John.

"Have you been stealing food from this man's camp?" John asked.

The boy just nodded.

"What's your name?"

"Willie," he replied.

"Are you with anyone, Willie?"

The boy just shook his head. With that question, John felt a wave of guilt and sadness radiate from the boy's Chi. Something dreadful had happened, resulting in this boy living in the wilderness. It was a deep scar that would take some time to heal, if it ever would.

Suddenly, Fred stepped forward and addressed the boy. "Willie, I didn't like it when you took my food, but I now understand why you needed it. I'm not mad at you, and I need your help. I'm hurt and must travel a fair distance to a village. That village will let us both live there. I'll teach you how to catch enough food for both of us if you help me get to the village. I can also teach you how to build a better shelter. We need each other, Willie. Will you help me?"

Willie first looked at Fred and then back to John.

John added, "If you help this man, I'll forget about the food you took, but you must stay with him until you get to the village. It will be a good life in the village, and you won't go hungry again."

"Will you teach me how to build a fire and a camp like yours?" Willie asked Fred.

"Yes, but I need a strong boy like you to help me while I heal. I know a lot about living in the wilderness, and I'll teach you everything I know if you go with me."

He nodded to Fred and walked over to him. They turned and started walking together, side by side, back to Fred's camp. John sensed from their Chi that they were forming a bond that would last a long time. The boy's Chi troubled him. What had happened to the boy that had left him so troubled?

When they returned to camp, Willie noticed the baseball cap on the tree.

"That's my cap!" he exclaimed.

"Are you sure?" Fred asked, lifting it down and setting it on his own head. "It could be mine."

Seeing the obviously too-small cap just sitting on the top of Fred's large head brought a smile to Willie's face. It was the first time they had seen Willie smile.

"It might be a little small for me," Fred said with a laugh, handing it to Willie. "I guess that maybe it is yours."

"Thank you," said Willie with another timid smile.

Fred then asked, "Marshal, will you stay for lunch?"

"No, I can't. I've got a job to do."

John slipped his pack onto his back, picked up the gun, and walked down the trail with Fred.

"Fred, be gentle with the boy. He's carrying some emotional baggage and needs someone to show him some kindness. It might be a while before he comes out of his protective shell."

"Is that gentleness part of that change you said I needed to make? Maybe we both can learn from this experience."

"I'll look you two up the next time I'm in the village."

3

John continued tracking Jack. There were no prisons anymore—a man this evil mustn't be allowed to roam free to harm the residents of this valley. This was the part of his job that he didn't like.

The rescue of Jill and the fight with Fred had delayed John a couple of hours. One benefit of the creek rescue was that John's clothing was still wet, and he wasn't hot any longer. He hoped the rain would hold off so he could continue to read the trail he followed.

John was surprised Jack left such an easy trail for him to follow. Any human left an easy trail to follow in this valley where few humans walked around, but John knew that Jack could be very good at hiding his trail if he wanted to. John had the additional advantage of knowing the print of Jack's boot. It was easy to see in the earth, softened by the rains. John didn't think Jack knew he was being tracked, so he had no reason to hide his tracks. John was very good at tracking people, even if Jack tried to hide his trail. However, the ease with which he was tracking Jack raised concerns in John's mind.

The Chi always warned John when danger was near as long as he listened to it. It had saved him many times by warning him of someone waiting for him ahead on the trail. In the past, he'd been able to sense danger and arrive in time to prevent innocent people from getting hurt. Was he growing too confident in his skills and senses? He continued tracking, but with a new sense of caution, which slowed his progress.

At the end of a long day, John reached a point where Jack had crossed the creek. Here, the creek was broader and shallower, so the current was less of a problem. It was late afternoon, so he decided to camp and cross the creek in the morning. He carefully selected a campsite that couldn't be approached easily without alerting him. It was far from the noisy creek and satisfied his cautionary mood. There would be no campfire tonight, and dinner would be a combination of dried fruit and nuts from his emergency rations.

Early the following day, John crossed the creek. He needed to pick up Jack's trail on the other side. This could be a difficult task. When a person enters a creek, they may walk in it for some time before leaving it on the other side. This is typically done to lose someone who's tracking you. Sometimes, John would do this to practice his trail skills, so it wouldn't be unusual for Jack to walk in the creek for a while. To pick up Jack's trail, John needed to walk along the bank on the other side and look for signs that indicated where Jack left the creek.

John searched most of the morning, walking about half a mile upstream without finding any indication of where Jack made his exit. He started to worry. Could Jack know that he was being tracked, or was he just being careful not to leave a trail for practice?

John decided to go back across the creek and look on the side where he'd camped the night before. Maybe Jack just walked upstream and then came back to the original bank. John didn't go too far before the creek bank became so overgrown that an exit from the creek would be impossible. He returned to where Jack had entered the creek and sat to think. What was he missing? Where had Jack gone? John asked himself what he'd do if he wanted to hide his trail.

He took the time to closely reexamine the area near where Jack's bootprints entered the creek. And there he found it! A barely visible soft depression in the earth. There was another, and another, leading away from the creek. Moccasin tracks! Jack had removed his hard-soled boots and put on moccasins to walk away from the creek. He'd never crossed the creek. He just used it to hide his trail.

John followed the moccasin tracks for 50 feet. It wasn't difficult once he knew what to look for. He should have known it had been too easy to track Jack earlier and been on the alert for something like this. Somehow, Jack believed someone might be following him.

John found a large tree stump where the moccasin tracks ended and where Jack had switched back to his hiking boots. Where was he going? Jack had reversed his course and now headed back in the direction he'd come. But instead of traveling close to the creek, his path took him about half a mile from it. This made no sense to John. What was Jack's objective?

John tracked Jack until it grew too dark to see. He again spent a dark, cool night without a fire. The moon was almost full, and there was no wind at all. The crickets created the only noise to be heard. Sleep did not come easily for John as he tried to determine Jack's objective. To take this route of retracing his path may have meant he knew John trailed him. He must be cautious and constantly watch for any sign of Jack. He must also warn Jill and Reggie since Jack was now heading back in their direction. John decided to prioritize Jill and Reggie's safety and forget about Jack until he could be sure they were safe. However, a new priority formed in John's mind. He sensed danger to the north, with many people's lives in danger. He must hurry if he was to save them, too.

4

The next morning, John was up at dawn and on the trail without breakfast. He hoped Jill and Reggie's camp was still close to the creek so there would be less chance of Jack stumbling into it if he kept following his current path. John followed a course that would take him back to where he'd met Jill and Reggie. He hurried as fast as he could while remaining alert for any sign of Jack.

After several hours of hiking, John thought he was close to where Jill and Reggie should be. Suddenly, two gunshots rang out in rapid succession just 100 feet ahead of him. He quickly dropped his pack and took his throwing knife from a side pocket. He cupped the knife in his hand and started running as fast as he could toward the place where he'd heard the gunshots. His danger sense, now fully alerted, warned him of trouble ahead. Why had it not triggered him to act sooner? Would he fail to keep Jill and Reggie safe from harm?

He slowed down as he reached the outskirts of their camp. As he quietly entered the camp, John saw Jack holding a rifle, standing with his back to John. On the ground to one side was Reggie's body, with a big red stain on his chest. He obviously was dead. John had failed! He saw Jill lying on the ground on the other side of Jack. She screamed in pain while holding a blood-soaked leg.

Jack must have sensed John's arrival because he slowly turned and faced him. Jack was of average height and weight but had an evil look about him. His dark hair, bushy eyebrows, and deep-set eyes made you feel like you were staring into the eyes of the devil. You could feel the evil radiating from him, and you got an instant impression of danger when you were in his presence.

They were 25 feet apart. John cleared his mind and only focused on the events that were happening at that moment. He started drawing Chi into his body as he knew it would bring calming energy to him. His throwing knife, still cupped in his hand, was ready to throw at any moment. At this distance, John knew he'd have one chance and one chance only. Jack's rifle still pointed downward towards the ground at a 45-degree angle, but his hands were placed on it where he could rapidly bring it up and fire.

Jack smiled at John and said, "Master Smith, I thought you might be tracking me. Did you like my little trick with the moccasins? Evidently, it didn't throw you off my trail. I'm sorry, but I can't let you live and track me down again.

"I see you brought a knife to a gunfight," he said as he looked at John closely. "You know, I always liked you, and I don't enjoy killing kids, but you leave me no choice."

John was focused entirely on Jack's body, watching for any indication of his intentions.

John responded, "Well, Jack, I never liked you, and I'm sorry that I must be the one to end your killing spree."

Jack's face grew angry with that comment, and he started to raise his rifle toward John. John knew his intent before Jack acted, and as Jack's rifle came up, John's knife was already in the air. Before Jack's rifle could target him, John's knife hit Jack's throat, cutting through important veins, just where he'd aimed. Jack quietly dropped to the ground.

John rushed forward to kick Jack's rifle away from his body, but there was no need. Jack was dead. John looked beyond him to Jill. She had a bullet wound in her right leg, not quite in the center. It would be a fatal wound if the bullet had hit her artery. He'd know in minutes.

John looked into her eyes as he knelt in front of her. They were full of shock and fear. "I'm sorry, ma'am. I should have been here sooner."

"I can't believe he shot Reggie! All he did was step between us when this man showed up. It was more of a protective response than an aggressive act. He just shot Reggie without warning, as if he enjoyed doing it. I think he shot me by accident."

John found a blanket to wrap around her leg. It wouldn't help her if the artery were hit, but he was now hopeful the artery was still intact. She would have died already if it had been severed. He got her some water and dragged some camping gear together to give her something to sit up against.

John jumped up, grabbed Jack's body by the legs, and dragged him out of sight to the edge of the camp. He retrieved his knife from Jack's throat, cleaning it on Jack's shirt. He then went back and dragged Reggie's body out of sight as well. Before returning to the camp, he ran back and retrieved his pack. He started thinking about their options. There were no good ones for Jill.

When John returned to Jill, she was still alive and looking a little better. Some of the shock was beginning to wear off. She looked at him and said, "Thank you for saving me a second time. I'm sure he would have killed me if you hadn't come along. So, what happens now?"

John looked at her and replied, "Ma'am, I'm afraid there aren't any good options. It's up to you to decide what happens next. You have a severe wound, and there's only a small chance of survival. I'm sorry, but that's just the fact. I can't stay here and take care of you. Tomorrow morning, I must be at a river crossing 20 miles from here."

"Why?" she asked, with fear building in her eyes.

"I've got a feeling that many people will die if I'm not at the crossing on time. It's hard to explain how I know this, but my job is to save as many people as possible. My choice is clear, even if it means I must leave you so that many others will live," he responded.

Her fear and anger exploded. "You're the most unfeeling person I've ever known. Reggie was right. We have a kid making decisions that only adults are mature enough to make. So, you're just going to leave me here to die?" she said with venom in her voice.

It hurt John to hear her say that, but she was the one who had to be sacrificed for the good of others. She didn't understand that he did have the maturity to make that decision.

Ignoring her barb, he replied, "Ma'am, you have two options.

"Your first option is for me to leave you here with food and water and return in a couple of days after I resolve the situation at the river crossing. I don't know how long I'll be away, so your chances of survival aren't great with this option. It will be like leaving you here alone to die.

"Your second option is for me to sew up your wound, put you on a litter, and take you with me to the river crossing. If you're still alive, I could take you to my camp up north for your recovery. It would be a difficult journey and very risky. The journey would probably rip open your artery if the bullet damaged it in any way. If this happened, I could do nothing, and you'd die quickly. There's also the risk of infection from the wound. Just trying to sew up the bullet hole in your leg could cause the artery to fail. Like I said, you have only a small chance of survival. I'm sorry, but I'm just being honest with you. I can give you 30 minutes to think about your choices before I must leave."

With anger in her voice, she replied, "How did a young boy become so heartless and cruel? Well, I don't need 30 minutes to decide. I've decided I'll go with you. Not because I think I have a better chance of survival, but because that choice is the one that's the biggest pain in the ass for you. That's the only way I can get even with you for being so uncaring to me."

"Yes, ma'am. I'll do my best to keep you alive." He added, "That was the option I hoped you'd choose."

"I don't believe that for a moment, boy. You'd love to be rid of me so you can go rescue those others and be a hero."

He ignored her bitter remark and replied, "My first task is to sew you up. If you survive that, then we will pack for the trip."

He went back to his pack and pulled out his medical kit. It had all that he needed to sew up a wound. As he unwrapped the blanket from her leg, he saw the bleeding had stopped, which was a good sign. The bullet had passed completely through her upper thigh, so he'd have two wounds to sew closed. He noticed a large scar on her lower leg. It appeared to have been a severe injury.

He touched the scar and asked, "What happened here?"

"Before COVID-24, I was a large animal veterinarian. A horse kicked me, and it nearly crippled me."

He handed her two pills and his canteen.

"Here is a pill for pain and one for infection. It will take some time before you begin to feel better."

He looked at her as he prepared the iodine solution to cleanse the wounds. She was still very angry with him. He knew the discomfort she was about to experience would give her another reason to hate him even more.

She looked away from him and said nothing. As he applied the solution to clean the wound on the front of her leg, he saw her flinch, but she made no noise. He scrubbed briskly to clean the wound as completely as he could. She still made no sound. Once the wound was clean, he closed it with several stitches, as he'd done many times before. With the stitching completed, he applied a waterproof bandage from the medical kit over the stitches.

As he helped her roll over onto her stomach, he noticed her eyes were red, and tears were on her cheeks. She'd been crying but had made no sound. She was a tough lady, but that would be necessary to survive in this valley alone.

He completed the closing of the second wound and wrapped gauze around her leg, covering both wounds. That was the best he could do, and now it would be just a matter of time until he knew if she'd live or die. Infection was the most significant danger now.

As he rolled her back into a sitting position, her face told him she was totally exhausted and would sleep most of the journey to the river.

"You closed that wound expertly, boy, like you knew what you were doing. I don't think I could have done it better myself. Do you have medical training?"

"No, ma'am. I just learned by helping other people who needed my help. You're lucky you aren't my first patient," he replied with a smile.

"Where did you get the medical supplies?" she asked. "They must be hard to get nowadays, especially out here in the wilderness."

"My boss provides me with all the necessary supplies to do my job. I don't know where he gets them, and I don't ask."

"So, boy, you have a boss?"

She kept using the 'boy' name to try to belittle him. Little did she know it wouldn't affect him at all.

"Yes, ma'am, his name is Don. He shows up occasionally at my cabin and campsite with supplies just when it seems I need them. We agreed that I'd be the Marshal in this area if he got the supplies I needed. That includes some special food items. And speaking of food, are you allergic to almonds? You need to eat some food before we start our journey."

"You have almonds?" she blurted out excitedly, almost forgetting to be mad at him.

"Yes, I'm pretty resourceful for a kid," he replied with a chuckle as he reached into his pack and came out with a small snack bag of almonds and raisins. "Eat some now and save the rest to eat during the trip. We will leave within an hour after I build a litter to carry you. While I'm doing that, you need to decide on what you want to take with you. You can only take what will fit into your pack. Let me know, and I'll pack it for you so you don't have to move and risk opening your wound."

"OK, boy. And stop being so polite with the ma'am stuff. It makes it hard for me to be mad at you. Just call me Jill."

The building of the litter was an easy task. John had done it many times before and even carried a special harness he could wear to pull it hands-free. He cut branches to build the frame and used blankets for support between the sides of the frame. He made it extra long so it could carry both packs. He also attached a 4-inch wheel to the litter at the point where it touched the ground. Don acquired the wheel from somewhere after John had requested it. With the wheel, he could travel faster and farther with the heavy load he'd carry tonight.

John picked Jill up and set her into the completed litter. Earlier, he had tied their packs to the bottom portion of the litter to keep her from sliding down during the trip. They left about mid-afternoon, and John was thankful it was nearly a full moon. They would have to travel all night to reach the river crossing in time.

5

The first part of the trip was slow and difficult. They were following a trail that was rarely used. At times, John had to stop and lift the litter over obstructions blocking their way. The moon gave him some light, but it was difficult to see when they were under the trees. Finally, around midnight, they reached the paved road.

The road ran along the side of the river. It was still in good shape since the COVID-24 epidemic only occurred about a year ago. This road led them directly to the river crossing where John needed to be. They made better progress with the wheel on the bottom of the litter and a smooth road.

The litter harness John wore steadied the litter and allowed him to walk and run without needing to stabilize it with his hands. He started at a fast walk to make sure everything was balanced and working as designed. He then picked up the pace to a smooth, comfortable jog.

Jill had been sleeping during most of the trip so far, but John sensed she was now awake. He put the litter down flat on the road and touched her forehead, feeling a slight warmth. He hoped she'd fight off any infection from her wounds.

"How are you doing?" he asked.

"Are we stopping for the night?"

"No, we're just taking a break. Now that we have a paved road to travel on, I can make much faster progress."

"Don't you need to rest? You haven't slept in over 18 hours. And it's dark. How can you see to travel?"

"The moon gives me enough light to see, and I don't have time to sleep if we want to arrive at the river crossing by morning. I'll sleep later. Do you need anything? Do you have enough food and water? We probably won't stop again until we reach the river crossing."

"No, I'm fine. I just worry about you. I know you think you're young and, therefore, indestructible, but there are limits to what the body can do."

As John picked up his end of the litter and prepared to continue their journey, he thought to himself, "The Chi will provide me with all of the energy I'll need tonight."

Jill was correct. He'd spent much of his strength and energy over the last 18 hours. He needed more if he was to complete this journey. He cleared his thoughts of past events and future desires and focused only on what was happening at this moment. He was jogging with a litter towards a destination. Nothing more, nothing less.

Focusing on the present moment allowed him to channel life's energy, the Chi, into his body. It was easy now that his mind wasn't cluttered with useless thinking. His tired body became rejuvenated as he felt the Chi flow into him. The weight of the last 18 hours was lifted. The Chi would now give him all the energy needed to pull the litter. He could easily continue at this pace all night and into the morning if needed. He increased his pace to a smooth, graceful run as the Chi was now guiding his journey.

The moon brightly illuminated the road, and the nearby river provided a damp smell to the air. A chorus of frogs serenaded their journey. All of life was in perfect balance at this moment. There were no worries or fears. John was totally surrounded by nature, immersed in the Chi.

Six hours later, John came to the top of a rise and looked down the road ahead of him. The river that they'd been traveling beside all night was now visible. As his eyes followed the road, he saw where it met the river. There was wreckage of an old concrete bridge where the middle span had fallen into the river. The bridge failed many years ago when the soft river bottom had given way. This bridge had been replaced by a newer one 15 miles downstream, where the river bottom was more stable.

The river's water level was high, and storm clouds on the horizon indicated it would rise even higher. On the nearby bank of the river, John could see a collection of tents and people doing their morning chores. He could also see a small herd of goats wandering around. He had a prickly sense of danger as he looked at the camp. He must warn them of the impending danger.

He continued at his running pace down the road toward the broken bridge. Just before reaching the bridge, he turned onto a dirt road that headed toward the camp. As he reached the outskirts of the camp, he sensed two armed men ahead, hidden behind some bushes.

He stopped short of their location and lowered the litter to the ground. He raised his voice and said, "I need to talk to your leader. Your camp is in danger."

They seemed surprised he knew where they were hiding but stepped out into view.

One with a red beard said, "We aren't welcoming any new arrivals into our camp. We have no food to feed you. You should keep moving on."

John sensed Jill was awake now and listening to the conversation. Her fear grew stronger.

"Sir, we will move on, but I just need to speak to your leader for a moment. Will you get him for me?" he replied, using his Chi to project a non-threatening sense of sincerity.

The sentries talked between themselves, and then one of them turned and started walking toward the camp. John turned to Jill and told her not to worry. She'd be safe while she was with him.

The sentry returned minutes later with a woman. She had a German Shepard at her side and a knife strapped to her thigh. She walked toward John without hesitation and stood before him, looking into his eyes.

"I'm Vicki Reese, and this is Rex." She signaled to the dog, and he sat, growling low in his throat. As a gust of wind rose, she pushed back her wavy brown hair. "I'm the leader here; what do you want?"

She was not what John expected. It was unusual for a woman to assume a leadership role in these challenging times. He immediately saw how she'd achieved that role, radiating a calm confidence and control in her demeanor. The fact that she wore a knife strapped to her thigh only accentuated that impression. She also had a dog as her partner in case anyone questioned her command. John immediately liked this woman.

"Wait—a young kid, clean-shaven, tall, and slim. You must be Master Smith. We've heard talk about you. You're the Marshal of this valley."

"Yes, ma'am. I'm Marshal Smith, and I'm here with an urgent warning. Your camp is in danger. There's heavy rain building to the North. Before noon today, the area of your camp will experience a flash flood. You must start moving your people immediately."

Vicki said nothing for a minute, deep in thought.

"How do you know this? Others have told me that your directions should be followed without question, but I find it difficult to believe you would know about a flood before it happens. Where would you want us to move to?"

"Move to the higher ground to the West. The extra 10 feet in height will give you the necessary safety."

"I can see how our camp is in a low spot, so it wouldn't hurt to move to higher ground. I don't know that I am convinced that you can predict the weather, but I'll do as you say."

She immediately turned toward the sentry with the red beard, whom she addressed as "Red," and ordered him to return to the camp and tell them to start breaking camp immediately.

She then turned back to John and asked, "You're welcome to stay with us tonight once we move to the higher ground. Will you join us?"

"No, ma'am. We must cross the river before the flood arrives. I'm taking this injured woman to someone on the other side of the river who can help her. We must leave now if we are going to make the crossing in time."

She stepped forward, and they shook hands. "Thank you for your warning. You may have saved many of us. If there's anything I can do for you, please don't hesitate to ask. Have a safe trip."

She turned and headed back to her camp. John returned to the litter and attached it again to his harness.

"It might be better to stay in their camp. Are you sure we can get across the river?" Jill asked.

"If we don't cross now, it will be days before the river level will be low enough to allow us to cross. I need to take you to a hot spring to help you heal. Don't worry; we will cross the river safely."

6

They headed to an area of the river with the shallowest water, a place John had used many times to cross. As they arrived at the river, John saw the water level was even higher than he thought it would be. It would be challenging, but his intuition told him they could safely make it across. He sensed Jill was scared.

"You must understand that I'll let nothing happen to you. You'll always be safe when you're with me."

"You keep saying I'm safe with you. How can you be so confident? You're just a young kid and know nothing of the dangers in the world."

There was nothing more he could say that she'd understand. He lifted her off the litter and set her on a large rock facing the river. He lashed the packs in the center of the litter, lifted it over his head, and started walking into the river.

The water was cold and the current swift—but not as bad as the creek where Jill had almost drowned. As he walked, the water reached higher and higher on his body. When he reached the center of the river, the water was just below his chin. The current was manageable for him, and the footing was solid. When he reached the other side, he put the litter down and crossed back for Jill.

When he reached her, she said, "I wondered if you'd just keep going and leave me here. I'm such a burden to you. I feel confused. Sometimes, you seem cruel and uncaring, while other times, you risk your life to save me and other people. I'm changing my opinion of you. You seem to be a good, hardworking kid doing more good than bad for your valley. I trust you know what's best, even if I strongly disagree with your actions."

"Thank you for trusting me. I'd never leave you here to die. That's not the kind of person that I am."

He then took her into his arms and turned towards the river. As they entered the water, it started rising higher on their bodies, and he said to her, "You saw me cross earlier. The water will rise to our chins but no farther. Please don't be scared; I won't let anything happen to you. You must trust me, even though I'm just a boy."

They crossed successfully and camped high on a hill overlooking the river. A paved road on this side of the river also ran parallel to the river. At one time, the old bridge connected the two roads. They could see that Vicki's camp on the other side had been mostly moved to higher ground.

They changed to dry clothes and started munching on more almonds and raisins. The sky darkened, and the rain began. The rain forced them into their tents as the downpour continued all afternoon. It rained so hard they couldn't even see the river. They stayed in their tents until late afternoon when the rain finally stopped. As they came out of their tents, the setting sun was peeking through the clouds. As they looked toward the river, it was unrecognizable. The river had breached its banks, and the result looked more like a lake than a river.

The original area of the camp was now deep underwater. To their relief, they could see that the new location of the survivor's camp was safely above the flood level. Jill sat there in stunned silence, and John sensed something troubling her.

After several moments, she turned to him and said, "OK, I've got a few questions, and I want the truth."

"I've never, and would never, lie to you. So, what are your questions?"

She turned to face him, and John felt anger in her Chi. "First, what is it with this 'Master' stuff? The woman in charge of the camp called you Master and followed your commands without questioning them. And now that I think back, Jack called you Master when he first addressed you. I thought I'd misheard him then, and he called you Mister Smith. Now, I believe he called you Master, too. Are all these people in the valley your slaves? Do you own them, and are they required to do your bidding? Are you some sort of Prince?"

John could sense she was angry at the thought of all these people being his subjects, and as he chuckled at her question, her anger increased.

"Whoa, hold on. You have this backwards. I'm their servant. I live to keep them safe, and they aren't obligated to take any orders from me unless they hurt someone," he replied.

"Then why do they call you Master?"

"It's a title they use to show their respect for me. It's no different than someone calling me Marshal Smith. I have two titles that are used in different situations."

"A title? What are you a master of?"

"Besides being the Marshal, I also am a Chi Master," John replied with a wide grin.

She looked at him with a troubled expression and asked, "What's a Chi Master? I've never heard of Chi."

He took a deep breath and explained, "Chi is a form of energy that resides in all living things. It guides us and advises us through what we call intuition. It's always there, guiding us if we're willing to listen. The Chi in animals guides them through what we call instinct. The Chi is always guiding them, too. It isn't uncommon for many animals to move away from the scene of a natural disaster before it happens. This is an example of the Chi guiding them to safety.

"Unfortunately, in humans, our egos often keep us from listening to the Chi. Our egos convince us that we know what the truth is. Sometimes, we get a hunch not based on any facts we know and are surprised when this hunch turns out to be correct. I learned to quiet my ego most of the time and welcome the Chi into my body and life. I listen to it, and it tells me many things about the world around me. I've mastered this skill, hence the title of Chi Master."

"This is all kind of hard to believe. It reminds me of a movie I saw many years before you were born. Disney made some movies about Jedi Masters controlling something called the Force. Is that what this is, and you think you are a Jedi?" she laughed.

"No, I'm not a Jedi. I think the idea of the Force used in those movies may have been based on Chi," he replied. "Chi was first described 2,500 years before the movies came out. If the description of

Chi inspired the Force, then they modified the idea of Chi to create a more exciting movie.

"First, the Jedi seem to describe the Force as existing in all things, including rocks. Chi exists only in living things. While the Jedi in the movies lift rocks with the Force, I can't do that. Another difference is that I can't control the Chi; I can only listen to the intuition it gives me. It guides my actions.

"For example, when I faced Jack's gun, I couldn't use Chi to rip it from his hands. Jack was correct when he thought there was no way the speed of my knife could beat the speed of his bullet. But, by listening to the Chi emanating from his body, I knew when he was going to raise his rifle before he raised it. I increased the Chi in my body to improve my throwing speed and accuracy. The result was my knife got to him before he could fire a shot.

"When Jack referred to me as Master Smith, he meant it sarcastically. He really didn't believe I was a Chi Master, and it cost him his life.

"The third and most important difference is that a person could only become a Jedi if your blood had a high midi-chlorian count, whatever that is. That meant that only certain people could become Jedi Knights. Since Chi is the energy of life, it means that all of us have access to it. Anyone can become a Chi Master. You just need to learn to bring Chi into your body daily. You must also learn to trust and accept the life Chi is guiding you through."

Jill now had an expression of comprehension on her face and said, "I don't know if I believe it or not, but it would explain a lot. It explains how you could cross the river and not be swept away by the current. It explains how you could go so long without sleep and then run for six hours, pulling a heavy litter. You're so accomplished for someone so young. Who was your teacher? Did your boss teach you how to control this Chi? Is he a Chi Master, too?"

"Don is much more skilled in listening to the Chi than I am. I guess that would make him a Grand Master of Chi.

"As for the teaching of Chi control, that's another difference between the Jedi Force and Chi. The Jedi had teachers to teach them how to control the Force. With Chi, there is no teacher because there's no control to learn. Chi is the energy of life itself and the only teacher you'll ever need. All you must do is ask, and the Chi will teach you.

"That's how intuition works. You formulate a question or desire in your mind or sometimes whisper a prayer. You may not realize it, but it's the Chi giving you the answer. I learned to open myself up and encourage Chi, the teacher, to enter my mind and body. The answers to how to use and guide Chi in myself and others came into my mind as an intuitive thought."

"So, you have the ability to know what I'm thinking?"

"Yes and no. The Chi has no words; it only communicates feelings or intuitions. I can feel anger, danger, happiness, and other emotional states you are in. So, I can tell when you're angry with me, but I can't read your thoughts."

"That's a big relief! Some of my earlier thoughts about you weren't so nice."

"I could sense you were angry with me," he laughed, "but none of the details."

"Does the Chi always give you what you ask for?"

"No. It may be easier to think of Chi as the parent of all life forms. Like a parent, sometimes it must refuse a request because it doesn't benefit that life form. Chi has a plan we can't understand, like a parent has for their child. Like a child, we must trust and accept that the parent knows what they're doing. Trust and acceptance are the foundation for learning to be a Chi Master.

"When I pulled your lifeless body from the water, I brought Chi into my body and sent it into yours. Life's Energy, the Chi energy, decides whether you'll live or die. All I did was to express the wish or prayer you'd live. I work with the Chi and don't command it."

"I thank you for your prayers to keep me alive.

"Is there a 'dark' side to the Chi like there is with the Jedi Force?"

"No, not really. Chi is all of life's energy, including our ego. What might be called the 'Dark Side' in our lives is when we live our lives from our ego. When listening to our ego, we do all those bad things. We steal, murder, and rape so we can get things we want. Those things make us feel more powerful or in control. That's all driven by our ego.

"Animals steal food from one another and will kill each other to survive. They do it out of instinct, and it isn't a choice they're aware of making. Humans have a choice in their actions. That sets us apart from the other animals.

"Chi creates the ego to help the human life form evolve. Humans are somewhat unique in that we see ourselves as being separate from one another. We're self-aware. We can look in a mirror and realize that it is ourselves that we're seeing. When most animals see themselves in a mirror, they think they see another different animal. The awareness of ourselves and the world around us drives our creativity and desire to improve our lives. Unfortunately, our ego usually tries to improve our lives by taking something from someone else.

"We can choose to live a life of taking for ourselves or giving to others. Sometimes, we need to take from others to stay alive. When taking from others, we use Chi's energy only for ourselves. That's our ego trying to keep us alive. When giving to others, we pass our Chi's energy to them to improve their life. We sometimes do this at the expense of our own life and happiness. We have a choice of being selfish or selfless.

"A way of summarizing it is to say we're all born with large egos, or born into the Dark Side. Babies and kids need to get things from others to survive. As we grow, we can learn to use Chi to help others and find a better way. But it isn't one side or the other like with the Jedi. The Chi that resides inside of you doesn't have polarity. It's just energy that can be used for good or bad things. You may need your Chi to survive one moment and then use your Chi to help someone else in the next moment. Jack was an example of someone who never learned to use his Chi for good purposes."

"Wow! That's quite a story. I still don't know whether to believe it or not, but you do have some extraordinary talents for someone so young. You have given me a lot to think about. I see why people look up to you," she said, smiling. "Besides the fact you're taller than anyone else."

"So, how should I address you in the future? Master Smith? Marshal Smith?" she said, then added, with embarrassment, "Boy?"

"I really don't care. It's all about you and whether I've earned your respect. If you want to show your respect to me, then you can address me with a title. You can call me John if you feel comfortable using my first name."

"I think I won't be using the Boy name anymore," she said sheepishly. "You seem wise beyond your years, and I want to show you the respect you deserve. I'd also like to apologize. After I was shot,

I was rude to you and treated you badly. I was even thinking those bad things you say you can't hear. As I've gotten to know you, you seem to be a nice person. I'm beginning to like the young man that you are."

"You were shot and facing your possible death. Moments like that make all of us very emotional and especially angry. I understood what you were going through and didn't take it personally. Let's start over and put the past behind us."

He extended his hand, and Jill extended hers into a handshake.

"Hi Jill, my name is John. It's good to meet you."

"My pleasure."

As it started getting darker, John moved over to her and removed the bandages on her leg. "I need to look for any infection," he said. He already knew she was doing OK because he would have sensed it in her Chi if she had an infection.

"Your wounds are healing fine, and I don't think the artery was damaged. Now it's time for you to start using your leg so you don't lose your muscle strength. Besides, I'm getting tired of carrying you around all the time," he said with a grin.

"Is that a snide comment about my weight?" she laughed.

"Never. My mother taught me that all women are perfect the way they are."

John grabbed both of her hands and pulled her to her feet. She winced slightly but smiled, happy to be on her feet again. He put his arm around her waist to stabilize her, and they started walking slowly around the campsite. After several minutes, he could tell she was ready to sit down.

"You did really well. You'll be fully healed in a couple of months and can return to a somewhat normal life. I'll take you to a village I know when you're able. There, you can be safe and be with other survivors."

7

John broke down the camp the next morning and tied their packs to the litter. While he did that, Jill slowly walked around, testing and strengthening her leg. The next portion of the trip would be slower because there were no trails to where they were going. They were heading to John's summer base camp, where he returned after his trips around the valley. The camp was where Don dropped off any supplies that John needed. It also had the unique feature of a hot spring near the camp, providing a warm, soothing bath. It would help Jill's wounds to heal.

Now that Jill felt better, John could sense her mind racing a mile a minute. He knew that she'd created a new list of questions for him. He hoped he could answer them without being purposely vague, which he knew she'd detect.

They stopped for lunch and ate snacks from John's emergency rations. His food supply was getting low since it was supporting two people. Jill could now get in and out of the litter alone but was still too weak to hike very far. As they rested, John suddenly detected a presence nearby. It was a familiar presence that he must prepare Jill for.

"We have a visitor coming our way, but don't be concerned. Don't get up; just stay where you are. She's a friend, and you'll be safe with me," he said.

"Where is she? How far away is she?"

"She's already here. She's cautious since she senses you and doesn't know you. I'm trying to reassure her that it's OK to approach us. She isn't alone."

At that moment, a full-grown wolf emerged from the bushes. She was a beautiful animal to see, even though she was powerful enough to kill a full-grown elk. John heard Jill gasp, but she didn't move. The wolf stopped, looked briefly at Jill, and then limped toward John. They were old friends and had a previous history. He reached out with his hand and stroked the fur behind her ears. She licked his hand and rubbed against it in a demonstration of affection.

John looked into the wolf's eyes and said, "This is Jill. She's a friend of mine and won't hurt you."

The wolf then approached Jill, looked at her, and started sniffing her hair. John could tell that Jill was terrified but excited at the same time. With the introductions made, the wolf turned her head back toward the bushes and issued a quiet bark. Within moments, three little wolf pups emerged from the bushes but stopped apprehensively as they saw Jill and John.

As the mother wolf started licking John's hand again, they realized there was no danger. While the pups initially approached them cautiously, they were soon playing at their feet. One of the pups had a distinctive white patch on its paw. He took a particular liking to Jill and rolled over and let her scratch his belly.

"The mother wolf is hurt," said John.

He reached down and lifted the injured paw to examine it. The wolf pulled the paw out of John's hand and then limped over to Jill.

"What should I do?" Jill asked. "If I hurt her, she may bite me."

"Talk to her. Tell her that you want to help her. Send out feelings of love toward her."

"I just want to help you; don't be afraid," Jill said to the wolf as she reached down and lifted the injured paw.

The wolf didn't pull the paw out of her hand, so Jill started examining the paw closely. The wolf flinched occasionally but didn't pull the paw back.

"A thorn is deeply embedded in the paw between the pads. The wound has festered and is swollen. Do you have a pair of tweezers?" she asked John.

John turned slowly and removed the medical kit from his pack. He took out a pair of tweezers and handed them to Jill.

"This might hurt a little; I'm just trying to help," Jill told the wolf.

Jill used the tweezers to pull out the thorn. When she squeezed around the injury to clear the wound of pus, the wolf whined a little but didn't pull back. When Jill finished, she put the paw back on the ground. The wolf immediately started licking her paw. After a few minutes, she started walking on the paw as she tested it. She wasn't limping as severely.

The wolf then returned to Jill, laid down at her feet, and continued licking her paw. The three pups soon began playing around their mom.

After about ten minutes, the mother wolf stood up. The wolves seemed to be on a journey that couldn't be further delayed. With another soft bark, the mother wolf abruptly turned and headed into the bushes again. The pups looked at John and Jill briefly and then turned and followed their mother.

"Wow!" Jill exclaimed with rapid-fire questions. "That was scary but exciting at the same time. How did you talk with her? Do you speak her language, or did you use Chi? What does Chi feel like? How do you communicate with Chi?"

"So many questions; let me answer the last one first," John laughed.

"Have you ever joined a group of people you didn't know and found that you took an immediate liking to some of them, while others you didn't even want to approach? Later, you found that your initial impressions were correct. You received information about these people without using words. This is how communication using Chi works. You don't communicate with words but with feelings and impressions contained in the Chi.

"I sensed the wolf's fear of you and sent back a sense of calmness. She realized that it was safe to approach me if I wasn't in a state of fear. It's all done without words. Communicating with Chi doesn't require your knowledge of any language, but just listening to the Chi around you. You quiet your mind and let the Chi flow into you, and its meaning becomes clear. Just like a burst of intuition, you know the message.

"Animals have a heightened ability to do this since they have minimal verbal communication abilities. On the other hand, we humans don't use Chi communication as much. We have a highly developed ability to communicate with words, sometimes in multiple languages. We only experience the Chi communication as hunches and intuition. Or, as in my example, to determine who we want to talk to at a party. You were actually communicating using Chi when you played with the wolf pups and were sending feelings of love to them. They picked up on your communication and felt safe with you—all without words.

"Did you notice how the injured wolf knew you were the better person to help her? She didn't know you were a veterinarian. The Chi guided her to the best person to help her. When I told you to talk to her, it wasn't because I knew she'd understand your words. She heard the emotions behind the words. She knew that you weren't trying to hurt her.

"You also asked, 'How does Chi feel?' It has many different feelings because it's a communication of feelings. When danger is close by, I get a feeling of tension or stress, like something isn't right. When someone is expressing loving thoughts toward me, I get a feeling of warmth and caring. I'm sure you have had these feelings before but never realized they were Chi communications.

"Chi also has a different feeling when no communication or emotion is tied to it. You have probably felt it before but never realized it was Chi. Have you ever observed a scene in nature that left you breathless? Not just a pretty view but a breathtaking one. At that moment, you're totally lost in the beauty you are experiencing. You're feeling Chi flow into you. We use words like love, awe, joy, thrill, and excitement to describe how we feel when Chi flows into us.

"Have you noticed how children have so much energy? They run everywhere and are constantly squealing with excitement. They have boundless energy, which we describe as excitement, as the Chi flows into them. Why do they have so much more Chi than adults? Because, as a child, they aren't reliving their past or planning their future. They're experiencing life as it is occurring at that moment.

"You just experienced that Chi flow in yourself when the wolves arrived. Your ego supplied you with fear as it tried to protect you from an encounter with a predator. It did what it was supposed to do. But you also experienced a sense of intense excitement, like a giddy little child. That was the raw energy of Chi flowing into you. Did you feel it?"

"Yes," she gasped. "I felt as if I would explode with excitement from being so close to the wolves. So that was Chi?"

"Yes. Did you notice that you weren't feeling any pain in your leg? You had no thoughts about the past or what might happen tomorrow. You were totally focused on the experience with the wolves happening at that moment. I've found that to immerse yourself in the Chi, you must first leave behind thoughts of the past or future. Chi communicates right now, not in the past or future, but right now.

"Oh, it has existed in the past and will exist in the future, but any communications it has for you, it has right now. You must be in the present moment to receive them. When fighting Jack, I wasn't thinking about what I did yesterday or what I wanted to do tomorrow. I was totally present at that moment in time. I opened up and listened to all the messages the Chi sent me. I let the Chi flow into me so that I could respond to his attack successfully."

"If the Chi allows you to sense danger before it happens, then why couldn't you stop Jack before he killed Reggie and shot me?" she asked suddenly.

Ouch! John knew that this question would come up sooner or later. He'd thought long and hard about it and still had no answer.

"I don't know. I always got enough warning to prevent anyone from dying while doing my job." His throat tightened as he continued. "I've repeatedly replayed that terrible day in my mind, searching for the answer. Was this something that I must accept as the ebb and flow of Chi in this valley? Was I so confident in my tracking skills that I allowed myself to be delayed when he backtracked? If so, it meant my ego had distracted me away from the present moment and the Chi. Maybe I'm not the Master that everyone claims me to be. I failed in my job, and my failure on that day will forever haunt me."

She raised her eyes and looked directly into his.

"I now understand why the first thing that you said to me after I was shot was, 'I'm sorry. I should have been here sooner.' I thought you were just being kind to me, but I now realize your late arrival has deeply affected you. So that you know, I hold nothing against you for not arriving soon enough to save Reggie. I still view you as my savior, the Chi Master who saved my life. Thank you, TeenBoy, for saving my life."

"I thought you were going to drop the 'Boy' nickname," he laughed.

"This is different. TeenBoy was the nickname that I called my high school boyfriend. For me, it's a name that I use with affection. I'm beginning to look at you more like a friend than a Marshal or a Master."

John didn't know what to say. He was so used to having her verbally abuse him when she looked for someone to blame for all her pain and misery. To express affection for him was totally unexpected. He admitted to himself that his feelings for her were also evolving. Initially, he viewed her as a pain-in-the-ass that he was obligated to help. But getting to know her, he found that he was beginning to enjoy her company and would miss her when she moved to the village.

They packed up and continued their journey. They were getting close to the camp, and the terrain had become more rugged. With Don's help, John had picked this spot for his camp to ensure that no one would stumble across it while he was away from the camp.

Finally, he stopped and said, "We can't take the litter any farther, and it's too rugged for you to try walking and risk a fall. I must carry you the rest of the way. I'll leave our packs here and make a second trip to bring them into my camp."

He picked her up into his arms and started following a trail that only he could see. He made sure that he left no trace of their passing this way. After ten minutes of climbing uphill through a field of large rocks, the ground leveled out, and they arrived at the camp. The large rocks kept the camp from being seen from a distance and sheltered it from the occasional strong winds.

As usual, three tents were set up, awaiting his return. One tent was for him, and the second, which had never been used before, was for guests. The third tent kept his supplies out of the weather. There was also an eating area with boards nailed between two stumps serving as a table and some rocks nearby for sitting. Ten feet away, there was a fire pit. He carried Jill to one of the sitting rocks and set her down.

He returned down the hill and retrieved their packs and the litter. Hopefully, they wouldn't have to use the litter again.

"You have a nice setup here," she quipped as he returned. "I see you have two guest tents for all the girls you bring up here to your hideout."

He ignored her comment and moved his pack to his tent, leaving hers outside the guest tent.

"You can use the guest tent since I don't think Don will come while you're here. He's made it clear to me that he doesn't want his presence in the valley known. You're the only one I've told that he exists. I hope you'll keep his secret for me."

"Of course I will. I owe you so much; That's the least I can do."

He hoped that she would stop asking questions about Don. He wasn't ready and didn't have Don's permission to answer any detailed questions.

She seemed happy with his answers about Don, and to his relief, she switched her focus and asked, "So what now?"

He was happy with the new direction in their conversation and asked, "How would you like a hot bath and a hot meal? Get a change of clothes, and I'll show you the location of the hot spring where you can take a bath."

Her face lit up, and she nodded rapidly with a smile. She took a change of clothes from her pack and took John's arm as they slowly walked deeper into the large rock field behind the camp. A plume of steam was visible as they approached a small pool of water. The source of the pool seemed to originate from beneath a rock. It created a small waterfall that ended just above the pool. The water drained from the pool into the ground at the pool's lowest point. The pool itself appeared to be about the size of a hot tub.

They stopped at the pool's edge, and John said, "Your bath, my lady. Make sure that you give that leg a good soak. There are minerals in the water that will help you heal. Give me a shout if you need anything. You should be able to walk back to the camp on your own. I'll be preparing our dinner. You have nothing to fear while you're here at my camp. The Chi will let me know if there's any danger nearby. Here is a bar of soap for you to use. Leave it on the rock by the pool so I can use it tonight. Tomorrow, we'll use the pool to wash our clothes."

He then turned and returned to the camp to start a fire and boil some water for dinner.

8

John always ensured he had dry firewood stored in the supply tent. This was in case he arrived at his camp late at night and wanted a fire. As he grabbed some firewood from the tent, he noticed that Don had replenished his supplies while he was away. Strangely, he noticed that Don had dropped off more supplies than usual. It seemed like he knew that John would need food for two. As for clothing, there was now some clothing in smaller sizes that would never fit him. John took the firewood and started a fire in the fire pit.

He retrieved metal cups, dinner pails, and some utensils from the supply tent and put them on the table. His supplies included many freeze-dried meals that campers used before civilization collapsed. He grabbed one meal labeled "Mac & Cheese" and another labeled "Beef Stroganoff" and placed them on the table. He hoped that Jill would enjoy one of these.

Jill slowly walked back to camp just as the fire took hold. She looked exhausted, as if the hot bath had consumed her energy. John knew that he had to get dinner into her quickly before she collapsed. He ran back to the spring with a kettle, filled it with water, and placed it above the fire. They'd have a hot meal as soon as it boiled.

Jill picked up the meal packages and asked, "Does Don get these for you, too? I sure would like to meet him with the list of items I want."

"Yes. Don gets just about whatever I want. I'm careful not to overstep and ask for things I don't need. Do you prefer Mac & Cheese or Beef Stroganoff?"

"The cheese sounds good. I haven't tasted any in a long while."

When the water boiled, John poured it into the dinner pails and mixed in the freeze-dried food. The aroma was incredible. They both ate quickly, and then Jill got up and headed for her tent.

"There are blankets inside the tent. Sleep as late as you want; you need the rest. I'll do the dishes," John said.

As she disappeared into the tent, John got a change of clothes and headed up to the hot spring. As he slipped into the water and relaxed in its warmth, he reviewed the last five days. He'd constantly been on the move and was tired. He needed time to rest. Jill had been through much more. He was frankly surprised that she'd survived it at all. She had almost drowned, been shot, and carried halfway across the valley on a litter. She did all this with little food or rest and no Chi energy to help her. Her stamina was incredible. She certainly had a strong will to live.

John wondered if it was wrong to bring her here. Honestly, he'd never expected she'd survive the trip. He felt responsible for her situation since he'd arrived too late to keep her from getting shot. Now that she saw how nice his life at camp was, would she ever agree to go and live in the village? What had he gotten himself into? What would Don say? He guessed he'd find out sooner or later and must face the music.

As he relaxed, he looked up at the stars. The view was breathtaking. There was no light pollution from cities to wash out the night sky. He saw a satellite crossing the sky and wondered how long it would keep orbiting the Earth. All the satellites would eventually fall from the sky and burn up, and all that humanity had built would eventually turn to dust.

He was tired and headed for his tent. Tomorrow would be a day for rest and catching up on his chores around camp.

John slept in and didn't leave his tent until well after sunrise. Jill was still not up, but she deserved all the rest she could get. Just to be sure, he reached out, searching for her Chi to verify that she was still alive.

He grabbed a quick breakfast of nuts and dried fruit and started his camp chores. One of those chores was to shave off his beard stubble. He used a rechargeable electric shaver to keep his respectable

"Marshal look." Most of the men in the valley had stopped shaving since the virus epidemic hit. John had a small solar charger in the supply tent that was big enough to keep his shaver charged.

There was also firewood to be gathered, his clothing needed washing at the pool, and he spent some time in deep meditation, replenishing his Chi energy.

Around noon, he heard some motion coming from Jill's tent. He said playfully, "Glad to hear you're finally waking up. I worried that a couple of near-death experiences were too much for you. But seriously, Jill, how are you feeling?"

"I'm hungry and feel like I've been run over by a truck. Is that hot spring available today? I need to soak in it and have a spa day today."

"Well, I've done my laundry, so I don't need it today unless you want me to do your laundry too."

"Right, as a teenage boy, I'm sure you'd love to do my laundry, wouldn't you? Well, there is no chance of that happening. I'll kill two birds with one stone and soak in the pool while washing my clothes. Could you arrange to be off somewhere else?"

He chuckled and could tell that she felt much better today. "I'll make us lunch. Do you have any requests?"

"I'm sure whatever you choose will be fine; just make mine a double. I'm starving."

He started boiling the water, selected four freeze-dried meals, and set them on the table. As she came out of the tent, she moved stiffly. She didn't seem to be in pain, just stiff and sore. It was nice that they weren't rushed and had time to sit and eat in a relaxed setting.

After lunch, he told her she could go into the supply tent and pick out any clothing she wanted. He guessed the smaller clothing sizes Don had dropped off would fit her.

She disappeared into the tent and, moments later, stuck her head out and said with a laugh, "I see that my TeenBoy has his own collection of ladies' underwear. I now see that you don't need to do my laundry to get a thrill."

In an embarrassed tone, John replied, "Jill, I swear, it wasn't there before I left five days ago. Don must have dropped it off while I was gone. That means that he knows that you're here now."

She came out of the tent with a bundle of clothing and then went to her tent and grabbed some more clothes. With her arms full of clothes, she headed up to the hot spring and remarked over her shoulder with a laugh, "You're doing the dishes, TeenBoy."

"That's not fair!" he replied, imitating a whiny teenage voice.

A couple of hours later, she returned from the spring with an armload of wet clothes, which she spread over and on anything that would support them. When she finished, she came over and sat beside him at the table.

"I loved your imitation of a whiny teenager. It sounded a lot like my son," she said, pausing before saying, "I miss him so."

"I'm sorry, Jill. That was insensitive of me."

"That's OK. I know it was meant as a funny response to my teenage dig on you. I wasn't offended by it. I like it when we banter back and forth. It makes life a little easier to bear when we laugh together."

"I'll admit that I try to make you laugh. The Chi coming from you has a feeling of deep sadness. What's troubling you? Is it the loss of your son and husband?"

"Mainly my son. I loved the role of being a mother. I was good at it, I think. My son and I always laughed together, like you and I do. I woke up daily thinking of what my son and I would do that day. I guess meeting you has made me realize that there's a hole in my life now. I feel lost."

"Something that I had to learn in order to understand the Chi is that acceptance is important in life. Yes, disappointments and sadness are part of life, but so are pleasant surprises and happiness. If you can accept the disappointments and put them behind you, then happy memories will be foremost in your life. By remembering the happy times, the sad memories will slowly fade, and you'll only be left with happy memories of your son.

"As for the hole in your life, when you lose someone close to you, part of your life has disappeared. Of course, there will be a hole in your life where that person used to be. Ask the Chi to guide you toward a new chapter in your life that will fill that void. You may be surprised what that turns out to be. Remember to accept what comes into your life as if you had wished for it, and happiness will always be with you. Let's keep laughing together and get through these trying times together."

* * *

"I now have more questions," she continued. "Are you ready? You aren't getting annoyed with my questions, are you?"

"No. I've brought you into my world and the Chi that guides my life. I understand it's strange to you and that you'll have questions. I don't expect you'll believe me without questioning what I tell you."

He smiled, and she continued, "Don seems to be able to get food and clothing that I thought didn't exist anymore. Where's he getting it from? Does he have a factory somewhere still running after the virus epidemic?"

"He doesn't tell me how or where it's made. He said that supplies would be part of our agreement if I became Marshal. He'd supply me with my needs so that I could spend all my time protecting the people of this valley. I honestly was skeptical when he first made that promise. I didn't think these things were still in existence. But he's never failed to deliver on my requests. He even supplies things that he thinks I'll need in the future, like women's clothing. They seem to show up before I know that I need them. I think that his Chi senses are so strong that he sees my needs more clearly than I do. I'm guessing that the clothing was the correct size?"

"Yes, but we won't be discussing my underwear, TeenBoy," she replied with a grin.

"The next question I have is about learning to feel Chi. You said there's no teacher, and the Chi will teach you. So, somehow, you must first learn to feel the Chi so that you can be taught. How did you learn to feel the Chi?"

"There isn't one path to follow. The path that I followed may not work for you.

"An important moment for me occurred when I read the book 'The Power of Now: A Guide to Spiritual Enlightenment' by Eckhart Tolle. He pointed out how we spend most of our time worrying about past events that we can't change, or future events that usually never happen. So, we end up spending most of our lives with useless thinking about things that have no impact on our daily lives. Our life is occurring Now, as he calls it, not in the past or the future. If we constantly focus on the past or future, we're missing out on experiencing our life, which is occurring now. This insight touched a nerve in me as I realized that I rarely experienced my life as it was happening.

"It seemed that I always was in a hurry. As I hurried from one task to the next, I never observed life at that moment. For example, I watched you as you came back from the spring carrying your clothes. Your facial expression was one of intense concentration on what you'd do next. Where would you hang the clothes to dry? Would there be enough places for all your clothes? You didn't notice the things happening around you, like the squirrel on the rock to your left or the bird singing beautifully in the distance.

"I was determined to change when I realized I rushed around missing life. I started by purposely slowing down during everyday activities around my cabin. Common activities were easier to modify since they were frequent and repetitive. Instead of rushing across my kitchen area to retrieve a knife, I moved very, very slowly to get the knife. If normal walking speed is rated as a 10, then I walked across the kitchen at 1. Yes, I really moved that slowly!

"As I slowed down when walking, I noticed a strange thing. While walking that slowly, my attention was drawn to the things around me that I'd never had time to look at before. I observed the grain in the wood flooring and the hinges on the cupboard doors. I saw the shadows projected on the counter from the sun streaming through the window. I had nothing else to do but observe what was occurring at this moment in my life. I was observing the Now.

"If anyone else had been in the cabin, they'd have looked at me like I was crazy since I moved so slowly. How could I ever get anything done moving like that? But I did get everything done; it just took a little longer. I was experiencing life as I was doing the tasks.

"As I moved in slow motion, it reminded me of a YouTube video I'd seen about an exercise called Tai Chi. It was supposed to give you great health benefits. The video guided you through a predetermined exercise pattern, moving your legs and arms extremely slowly. I suddenly realized I was just doing Tai Chi in my kitchen using my tasks as a pattern, and that I could modify any of my daily tasks to do at 'Tai Chi' speed.

"I remembered that breathing was an essential part of the Tai Chi practice. It was taught that you breathed in Chi energy as you moved slowly. So, I tried it. Instead of observing the things around me, I focused on my breathing. I imagined that with each breath, imaginary

Chi energy flowed from the outside world into my body.

"The results startled me. I actually felt that there was energy flowing into me. I felt a feeling of excitement, joy, peace, happiness, and love all at once. I can only describe it as feeling giddy with excitement. Forget the knife and lunch; this was much better than that. That was the first time that I became aware of feeling Chi energy. I liked the feeling of constantly being full of energy.

"So, I started practicing my version of Tai Chi while doing all my daily chores. Brushing my teeth, chopping firewood, and doing laundry were all done in slow motion and were much more enjoyable. Yes, the chores took more time, but I felt that I was more alive when doing them. It was worth the tradeoff.

"Soon, I noticed that my intuition became more active. I seemed to get guidance when making choices. I also noticed how every task I had to do became easier. When chopping wood, all my swings with the axe hit the wood right where it would split the wood cleanly. This was how the Chi began to teach me how to use it daily. Over the years, I've progressed to where I am today.

"Remember that a key requirement to be able to receive the Chi energy is for you to be in the moment, in the Now. You can't worry about things in the past or future if your mind is going to be open to receive Chi's energy. To live your life in the Now requires you also to learn acceptance. Don't worry about what might happen next. Trust that the Chi will lead you to where you need to be. This isn't just fate that you have no control over; it's quite the opposite. With every wish, prayer, hope, or dream, you tell life's energy what you want to happen. You must learn to trust that the Chi will deliver what's best for you, even when you fall into a creek or get shot in the leg. It may not seem like it at that moment, but you must trust in the energy of the Chi."

"That explains why you move so gracefully. You move as if you don't have a care in the world. It's beautiful to watch.

"So, if I pray to live until I'm 100 years old, will Chi make that happen?" she asked with a laugh.

"That's for the Chi to decide. Your life is just one very tiny part of the life energy of the Universe. You may need to die today to feed a wolf and keep it alive. If so, then the Chi will make that happen. You'll die someday, as will I. Until then, living your life filled with Chi is what makes life an adventure. There's always the excitement of not knowing what will happen next but knowing that the Chi is guiding your way. Every moment in your life is part of an adventure. The activity that I enjoy the most is walking in the woods. I'm relaxed, and it's easy to bring a strong flow of peaceful Chi into my body with all the living things around me."

9

"Let's change the subject and talk about your leg," John said. "How is it feeling since you soaked it in the hot spring?"

"It's still stiff and sore but getting better," she replied.

"I think it's time for me to take out the stitches. Do you have some pants to put on that will allow me to look at your wounds without showing me your underwear?" he asked with a snicker.

"You wish," she said with a forced smile. "You get your medical kit, and I'll put on some loose pants."

They returned to the eating area, where she lay on the table and pulled up her pant leg. The wounds were healing nicely, and it was time to remove the stitches.

"Don't look at my spider veins," she said self-consciously.

He smiled warmly and replied, "What spider veins?"

He quickly removed the stitches and wiped the wounds with an antiseptic wipe.

"You're going to have some really cool scars when these heal. At least that's what a guy would say," he joked.

"Right, just what a girl likes to hear: cool scars! That will match the 'cool' scar the horse gave me."

"I have another serious question," Jill said. "Right after I was shot and you sewed up my wounds, couldn't you use your Chi powers to heal me at that point?"

"I have two answers to your question.

"First, my light-hearted answer is: If some young kid, as you like to call me, walked up to you and said, 'Hi, I'm a Chi Master, and if you let me put my hands on your thigh, I can heal you,' would you let him? You seem too smart to fall for that one."

He winked at her and then continued, "The more serious answer is that I've never learned to do any focused healing using Chi. The Chi has trained me to be a warrior, not a healer. I can stitch up a wound and help relieve the pain of a sore muscle, but for any serious wound healing, I'm helpless. I don't know why the Chi hasn't taught me to heal. Probably because I've never asked for or needed that skill."

She laughed, smiled, and said in a sexy voice, "Hey, TeenBoy, would you like to put your hands on my thigh and try to take away some of this soreness? Anything would help."

"I'll try, but let's do it together. I've found self-healing to be more responsive than having an outside person do the healing. I'll bring the Chi into my body and transfer it into your hands. Your job is to use your imagination, take that energy, and use it to heal your injuries. If you just wish for the healing to happen, maybe it will.

"Place your hands on your thigh, one on each wound. Close your eyes and try not to think about anything else except what we're doing at this moment. Bring in the Chi and direct it to do its healing."

He placed his hands on top of hers and closed his eyes. He started bringing Chi into him and directed it into her hands. He could feel her trying to control the energy flow, but she wasn't having much success.

"Relax and become one with the Chi. It isn't a separate thing. It's who you are," he suggested.

He then felt her slowly gaining control and directing the energy into her sore muscles. He sensed the muscles relaxing. After a while, she shifted focus and started directing the energy into the wounds, asking them to heal. As she guided all the energy that he sent her, she wanted more. She began drawing on her own source of Chi. She quickly learned how to bring Chi from outside her and direct it into the wounds. The amount of Chi she commanded was incredible, and he could sense that the wounds were slowly healing.

Then, she seemed to become exhausted from the effort and slowly shut down the flow of Chi into her body as she finished her healing. They both dropped their hands and opened their eyes, looking at one another.

"That was incredible!" she exclaimed and then continued. "I feel tired but exhilarated at the same time. Did I do it right? Is that what I was supposed to do?"

"I don't know; I'm not a healer. The Chi was guiding you, teaching you."

His eyes dropped to the wound on her leg. Where a scar had existed before, now there was just an area of pink skin. He reached out and touched it, which quickly brought her attention to the area. Her eyes widened, and she gasped.

"How is that possible? The scar is gone! My leg feels almost normal again."

"I've never seen this happen before. You were directing a lot of Chi into the wound. When I direct that much energy, I'm usually in a battle, but I focus on overcoming my adversaries. You directed a lot of energy into a small area of your body, and healing resulted. Weren't you just wishing you wouldn't have those cool scars? The Chi seems to have answered your wish. What's more incredible is that you could control that much Chi without any experience. It took me years to be able to do that."

"Stick around, TeenBoy," she smiled, taunting him, "and see what an adult can do with the Chi."

During this time, Fred and Willie made slow but steady progress walking to the village.

After John had left them to continue tracking Jack, they had a quick lunch and started getting ready for the trip to the village. With Fred's broken ribs, it was painful for him to do any lifting. Willie was getting a crash course on taking care of a camp, but he seemed to enjoy learning new skills. Fred had noticed a sadness in Willie that was always present but was pushed to the background as he worked around the camp. Fred had seen this kind of burden carried by soldiers who had experienced a tragedy and knew he would have to wait until Willie was willing to talk about it.

Their first task was to build a litter to carry their belongings. Willie, a young but hard worker, would have to pull it alone until Fred felt better. Willie followed Fred's directions and built the litter. A couple of rope knots needed to be undone and re-tied as Willie learned from his mistakes. Once the litter was completed, they broke down the camp and loaded it onto the litter. Fred gave Willie a pair of his gloves to protect Willie's hands from the work of pulling the litter. The gloves didn't fit Willie's small hands but would still offer some protection.

The first part of the trip was the hardest. They had to follow a narrow trail along the creek to the paved road. Willie struggled at first until he understood how to pull the litter with the least effort. He then settled into a regular rhythm, with Fred making sure they stopped occasionally for rest periods. It was hard for Fred to watch as Willie struggled to pull the litter. It was heavier than a boy of his age should have to manage, but he never complained or admitted defeat.

The trail to the road was only three miles long, but with the frequent rests, it took them all afternoon. When they arrived at the road, Fred saw that Willie could pull the litter no farther. They set up camp, and Fred gave Willie his first fishing lesson so they would have something to eat for dinner. Willie proved to be a fast learner, and within a half hour, he'd caught four fish. As tired as he was, Willie beamed with pride at his success.

Fred then showed Willie how to build and start a fire. After dinner, they were both ready to sleep. Willie had physically exhausted himself while Fred had been trying to manage the pain from his broken ribs. Fred felt like he had a fever and hoped he didn't have more serious injuries from his battle with the Marshal. He decided that they both could use the next day to rest.

The next morning, Fred woke up feeling much better. His fever was gone, but his ribs still hurt every time he moved. Willie had slept through the night without moving. When Willie got up, the first thing he did was to look down the road in each direction as if he were searching for something, but apparently, he didn't find it. He returned to the camp with the heightened sadness Fred had seen before.

"What were you looking for?" said Fred.

"Nothing," Willie said quietly.

Fred knew that Willie was still not ready to talk.

Fred showed Willie how to find and collect quail eggs and scramble them for breakfast. While collecting eggs in the fields, he also showed him some plants that he knew were not poisonous to eat. As Willie was again learning new things, the distraction helped him push his sadness away.

They stayed all day at that campsite. After they went to bed that night, Fred heard Willie crying softly. He was a strong boy, but something had happened that had really shaken him.

The next day, they headed north on the road. Around noontime, they reached the bridge that crossed the river and found a great fishing spot on the river's opposite bank. As they settled down and waited for the fish to bite, Willie suddenly asked a question.

"How did you hurt your ribs?"

"I did something wrong and paid the price for my stupidity."

"What did you do?"

"I accused the Marshal of stealing my food, and without waiting for him to respond, I tried to beat him up."

"But you're bigger and stronger than he is. How did you get hurt?"

"He says that he listens to the energy of life, and it told him what I was going to do even before I moved."

"That sounds crazy."

"I know it's hard to believe, but he fights like no other man I've ever faced. He defeated me as easily as if I was a child. I learned a lesson on that day: the Marshal should never be questioned or underestimated. I would never have been injured if I had done exactly what he said."

Fred's last comment brought a frown to Willie's face. Something was definitely troubling him.

"If I promise to do whatever you say, will you promise not to leave me?"

What a strange question! Had someone just dumped the boy here? Who would do something like that?

"Willie, I'll never leave you. You're my friend now and have helped me. Why would you think I would leave you?"

Willie was silent for a moment, and then his jaw tightened, but he said nothing. John had said that Willie had some sort of emotional scars. Fred could see that now. All he could do was let him see the softer side of this gruff Master Sergeant while at the same time giving him the protection that he needed.

After several days of travel, they arrived at the village and received a hearty welcome from Rob, even though Fred was an Army man.

10

With Jill's leg healing, they started going on longer and longer hikes to help strengthen it. She was getting stronger by the day. They were now both carrying packs to add weight and strengthen her legs. She seemed happy to be living in John's camp. He hated to disappoint her, but the topic of her leaving must be talked about.

"You're getting strong enough that you'll soon be able to hike to that village I talked about. They'll take you in, and you can live with them for the rest of your life."

She turned to him, and her face clouded. "Why can't I stay with you? We get along OK, and I can take on some of the daily burdens around the camp. Are you growing tired of having me around?"

"Quite the opposite," he replied. "I'm really enjoying your company and don't want you to leave, but one of the requirements of the job of Marshal was that I have no wife, no children, and no friends. That's why I seem cold and uncaring to you at times. I can form no relationships.

"You and I have already been together for far too long. It was a rule put in place by Don when I became the Marshal. If there were someone special to me, then someone like Jack would hurt that person to get back at me. He might hold them hostage to get a concession from me. Those entanglements could interfere with my job. I understood the reasoning and agreed to that requirement."

"You must be very lonely, living your life all by yourself. How do you handle it?"

"When you live your life in the Now, full of Chi, there's no boredom. You're experiencing the excitement of life unfolding at every moment. I'm really not alone. With the Chi, I share my life with every living thing around me."

Today's hike took them toward the river that had flooded earlier.

"Where are we headed today?" Jill asked.

"My intuition is leading me toward the river. It feels like I'm needed there today. The feeling is fairly strong, so I expect today to be more exciting than the last couple of days. Are you up for it, or would you rather return to the camp and wait for my return?"

"I feel good, and my leg is strong. I'm with you today, TeenBoy. Where you go, I'll follow."

When they reached the road next to the river, they could see the survivors' camp across the river.

"I feel that we should head north along the road," John said, and they turned in that direction.

The sky was slightly overcast, reducing the heat reflecting off the pavement. They walked along the road for an hour when suddenly they heard a scream coming from the road ahead. They increased their pace to a run. As they rounded a bend in the road, they saw a collection of carts and a tent alongside the road. It appeared to be a family since a man and two young kids stood beside the tent. The man was clearly distressed and came toward them as they approached.

"Do you know anything about delivering babies?" he asked desperately.

"A little," John replied. "What's the problem?"

"We don't know. My wife has been struggling with the delivery. She had no problem with our first two babies, but this one isn't coming out. We don't know what to do."

"Sir," John said to the man. "You and your kids should stay here while we see what the problem is. What is your wife's name?"

"Liz," said the man.

John and Jill dropped their packs and entered the tent. A woman was lying on a blanket. She looked exhausted and was definitely having trouble with the birth.

John said, "Hi, Liz. We are here to help you. I am John, and this is Jill. Is it OK if I examine you?"

Still in the grip of a contraction, Liz murmured, "Yes."

He put his hand on her belly and listened to her Chi. Her baby wasn't properly lined up in the birth canal and wouldn't come out unless they intervened.

"It's a breech birth," he said to Liz. "But your baby's heart sounds strong."

John explained, "The baby has its head up and its knees folded against its chest.

"Jill, I'm going to need your help. Get the medical kit and find us two pairs of gloves and a tube of lubricating gel. Have you ever delivered a breech baby?"

"No. Only breeched colts. Have you?"

"Yes. I will guide you through it. I'll ask the mother's Chi to move the baby up higher into the womb. You'll need to reach up inside of the mother and straighten the baby's legs toward the vaginal opening. Be firm, but be careful. Let your Chi guide your actions. Make sure that you keep the baby's arms alongside its body so they won't interfere with the delivery."

John began connecting with the Chi of the mother. Slowly, the mother's muscles moved the baby higher in the womb. The mother's discomfort was instantly reduced. When John felt that the baby was in the best position for Jill to work, he told her it was time for her to begin. She reached inside and straightened one leg at a time so that both feet were now visible at the opening of the vagina. Then, together, with Liz able to push, they slowly moved the baby through and out of the birth canal. When the baby was born, John cut and tied the umbilical cord and introduced the new baby to her mother.

"You have a beautiful baby girl!" John said.

John stepped outside the tent as Jill helped the mother clean up.

"Thank you so much," said the man. "I thought that they both might die. It's a miracle that you happened to come by when you did. My name is Steve, and my children are Nancy and Freddy. My wife was a pediatric nurse before the virus hit and knows how to care for babies, but unfortunately, that wasn't much help in delivering her own. I didn't know what to do, and I was so scared."

He reached out, and they shook hands.

"I'm John, the Marshal of this valley. My friend is Jill, and I'm glad that we could help.

"What are you doing out here in the middle of nowhere?"

"We heard that there's a village on this road farther north. We found these two carts and were trying to reach the village before the baby was born. Unfortunately, our baby didn't cooperate with our plan. Have you heard about this village? Do you know how much farther it is?"

"Yes, I actually lived in the village for a while. It's about 20 miles from here. It's a good place to live, with many very nice people. Let us help you and your family get there. Jill and I can set up our camp here for tonight. We'll head out tomorrow if Liz is up to it."

John and Jill set up their camp down the road from the family. When the family was out of earshot, Jill lowered her voice and said,

"Wow! That was the most incredible thing that I've ever done. To save a baby's life and hold that life in my hands. I thought that holding my own newborn son was exciting, but saving another baby's life is ... there are no words! Thank you for trusting me enough to help."

"I just trusted the Chi to guide you," John replied.

That evening, they built a big fire, and John shared some of his freeze-dried delicacies with the family. Jill was eager to hold the newborn girl, using the excuse that she was giving Liz time to rest. Liz and Steve would be up most of the night with their newborn daughter. Freddy and Nancy grew tired quickly and retired to the tent.

The light of the fire reflected off Steve's glasses. He wore his hair short and covered it with a blue baseball cap that said, "Gone Fishing." He related that he was an avid fisherman who had fished in both fresh water and the oceans. John learned that Steve and his family were on their way to visit Liz's family when their car had a flat tire. Unfortunately, the spare was also flat. That unfortunate event probably saved their lives by keeping them away from the virus.

Steve, John, and Jill sat around the fire as Liz rested in the tent. They talked about how fast civilization had crumbled. The only survivors were those who were living remotely when the virus struck. Steve asked what would happen next, but John had no answers. Steve took the baby from Jill, said goodnight, and headed for his tent to be with Liz.

The next morning, John and Steve made a bed for Liz in the largest cart. Both carts appeared to have been used for gardening. They had large bicycle wheels that rolled easily and large bins for carrying garden debris.

"These carts are great for moving your family along the road, especially for the kids," John told Steve as they loaded them.

"Yes," he replied. "We passed an abandoned farmhouse along the road and found them in a storage shed. We packed our tent and other supplies in them and then let the kids ride on top. Liz said she'd be fine pulling the smaller one, but I wonder if it caused the baby to come early. I hope that it was OK to take them without permission. You aren't going to arrest us, are you?"

"No. You won't have to worry about me as long as you aren't hurting others. Let me pull the big one, and you can take the smaller one. We should get to the village either late today or early tomorrow."

The cooler weather continued, and they were able to maintain a fast pace. As they got close to the village, the road reached a crest. John could see the village in the valley below him. The term village didn't really apply to what he saw below. There were only four completed cabins, with a fifth being built. Most of the people were staying in tents. He estimated that about 50 people in total were living in the village.

As they entered the village, some inhabitants stared suspiciously at John. Others who recognized him waved a friendly hello. He'd stayed in this village for a month during the winter and had gotten to know many of the people. He saw Rob, the village leader, coming his way with his wife Judy. They were both in their 50s, tall, and had blonde hair.

Rob wore his hair cut short, military-style, and had a mustache. As a young man in the Navy, his job was to be at the controls of a submarine that made it go up, down, or turn. He had a long career in the Navy, eventually commanding a large ship. He was a Navy man and proud of it.

As a Navy wife, Judy was skilled at running a household when her husband was at sea for many months of the year. She also had been part of the close-knit community at the Navy base and was a good organizer. Judy had her hair pulled back into a sleek ponytail and was laughing at one of Rob's jokes when they spotted John. Together, they were the perfect team to lead the village.

"Hi John, it's good to see you. I see that you found some more travelers," said Rob.

"Hi Rob, hi Judy, it's good to see you both again. This is Steve and Liz, and their two kids are Freddy and Nancy. Jill and I found them along the highway and helped them deliver a new little one."

Judy walked around the cart to see the new baby and introduced herself to Liz and the kids.

"I guess that I've not met your friend Jill. Will she also be staying with us in the village?" asked Rob.

John didn't know how to respond. He was planning on eventually bringing Jill here, but his intuition told him it was not the right time yet. He looked at Jill and sensed she also was not ready to stay here permanently.

"Not quite yet," John replied. "She's very helpful with medical issues, so I think that I want to keep her with me for a while."

"How long will you be staying?" asked Judy.

"Just the night. In the morning, we need to head back," John replied. "Have a soldier and a boy shown up here yet? I sent them your way about five days ago."

"Yes. The soldier showed up with broken ribs. You wouldn't happen to know anything about that, would you?" Rob laughed.

John said, "He was a strong man near the end of his rope. He tried to take out his anger and frustration on me. I had no choice but to immobilize him to end the fight. I sensed that behind the anger, there was a good man inside. I think he'll eventually be a good addition to your village."

"If he were a Navy man, it would have been even better," Rob laughed.

Rob continued, "Fred and Willie seem to have formed a bond. They were both alone, and they needed each other. Around the village, they're always together."

"Has Willie talked about what happened to him or how he became lost?"

"Not yet," Rob replied. "We'll just have to give him some time."

"Are Fred and Willie around?"

"You just missed them. They wanted to be useful, so they joined a group that scouts for places where berries are growing. An injured man and a young boy couldn't do much else. I don't think that they'll be back before you leave."

"Tell them I said 'hi,' and I'll catch up with them next time."

"Did you ever find Jack?" Rob asked quietly. "We are still recovering from the trouble he caused."

"Yes, I did. He won't be hurting anyone else."

The next morning, after saying their goodbyes, Jill and John slipped on their packs and headed south on the road. Jill never said anything about not being left in the village as John had initially planned. She was afraid that if the topic came up, John might change his mind and return her to the village.

"You certainly don't have a boring life, Marshal Smith," Jill said. "I see that your interactions with the people of the valley keep you busy, even if you can't form any close relationships with them. I would enjoy this kind of life too, even if it isn't available to me," she said with a bit of sadness. She added cheerfully, "But wherever I end up, I'll continue my effort to learn more about the Chi. You have made a believer out of me."

"You have shown surprising strength when interacting with the Chi, and maybe someday I'll show my respect to you by addressing you as Master."

"I'm worried about that. I felt so powerful directing the Chi while healing my leg. But now, even when I try to focus, I no longer feel that magnitude of power. What am I doing wrong?"

"Have you ever heard stories of people doing extraordinary things during an emergency? People lifting cars to rescue someone underneath? Firemen climbing the outside of a structure without a ladder? Soldiers carrying their wounded comrades for miles over rocky terrain? Miraculous cures from cancer? These are examples of people who had connected with incredible amounts of Chi, and yet, in their everyday lives, they have no such abilities. In emergencies, when you ask for the ability to do an amazing feat, sometimes the Chi energy is delivered to you. Your prayer is answered."

"What you want now is to feel Chi in your everyday life. This takes practice. You must train your body and mind to be in the Now as much as possible. You need to open yourself up to the flow of Chi in everything that you do. Remember how I did Tai Chi in the kitchen? When you train yourself to listen to the Chi in everyday life, you'll feel that power at every moment."

11

They were approaching the river crossing around noon. Something didn't feel right to John, but he couldn't be more specific. He closed his eyes and tried to understand his uneasiness. The Chi was disturbed, but no specific intuitions came into his mind. His only choice was to return to his camp and wait for a clearer understanding of his discomfort.

They stopped for lunch at their old campsite above the river and started a fire to eat a hot meal. This time, it would be freeze-dried scrambled eggs and sausage bits. John's camp was only half a day away, so there was no hurry. They could see smoke from the fires at the survivors' camp across the river. Everyone there was enjoying their lunch, too, but John still felt uneasy.

After lunch, they put on their packs and turned away from the road, heading uphill toward John's camp. Five minutes into their hike, they suddenly heard a gunshot coming from the survivor's camp. John's danger sense was suddenly alert.

"That sounded like a gun," Jill said.

"Vicki needs our help," he replied.

"Leave me and go help her. I'll be all right."

"No. Both of us are needed, but we must hurry. You'll need to draw on the Chi for strength. Remember, be in the Now. Don't think about what we may face at the camp; just focus on listening to and using your Chi energy now."

They turned and started heading back to the river. Because of the terrain, they could only move at a fast walk. When they reached their old campsite on the road, they saw people scurrying around Vicki's campsite across the river. John and Jill moved down the hill to the river as fast as they could and crossed it quickly. Jill kept up the pace, and John could feel her using Chi to support her efforts.

They slowed down as they approached the survivors' camp and saw a large group of people around one of the tents. They approached slowly. The sentry with the red beard that had earlier challenged them when they first met Vicki, turned and recognized them. He had Vicki's dog, Rex, on a leash.

"Hi, Red. We were across the river, and we heard a gunshot. What happened?" asked John.

"Bart shot Chet and kidnapped Vicki," he replied bitterly.

"Was Chet killed, or does he need our medical help? My friend Jill has some medical training."

"He's in the tent. Follow me."

John and Jill dropped their packs. John got his medical kit from his pack and followed.

They entered the tent and found a man with a gunshot wound to his shoulder. John saw Vicki's knife in its sheath lying on the tent's floor. As he examined the shoulder wound, he noticed the bullet had nicked the man's collarbone before passing out his back. He was lucky. He'd eventually recover if he didn't die of infection.

"Jill, do you think that you can sew this man up?"

"I've had a lot more practice with stitches than you. This is something that I'm trained to do."

"At least on horses," she added under her breath.

John raised his voice and said, "For those who don't know me, I'm the Marshal in this valley. Can anyone tell me what happened?"

A man with a small cut on his throat stepped forward. He looked like he could have been a school teacher, but maybe it was his glasses that gave John that impression.

"My name is Bill. Vicki and I were talking with Bart about shirking his duties in camp and being rude to some of our young girls. Chet came in and called him a troublemaker, then asked why he always carried his rifle. It made people feel nervous. Bart became outraged and said it was his right to be armed and that we could do nothing about it. Chet stepped toward him, I think, to calm him down, and Bart brought his rifle up and shot him. It may have been by accident.

"People from outside the tent heard the shot and came rushing in. They were angry and started yelling at Bart. I think he felt cornered. He suddenly grabbed me and put a knife to my throat. He told everyone to back away and get out of the tent. Everyone backed out, leaving the four of us in the tent.

"Bart started walking toward the tent opening while holding a knife to my throat when Vicki stepped forward and asked him if he would take her instead. She said that she would guarantee he could leave the camp unharmed. Bart pushed me away, grabbed Vicki, put the knife to her throat, and started walking out of the camp.

"They left about 20 minutes ago. We thought Vicki would have been released by now, but she hasn't returned. We were just getting a group of us together with some guns to go after them."

"That would be dangerous," said John. "You couldn't approach him quietly with a group, and he might just kill Vicki and run. It's my job in this valley to resolve situations like this. I'll go alone and bring her back to you. You must trust me. And don't let Rex off his leash. He would go after Vicki and just get shot."

The men gathered in the tent talked among themselves for a moment. Bill stepped forward again and said, "Most of us don't even know who you are. Who made you Marshal? You're just a kid, but Vicki trusts you, and so will we. If you don't bring her back alive, many people here will never trust you again. Be quick. The last time we saw Bart, he was heading north along the river."

"What does this Bart look like?" John asked.

"He's a big guy, about 6 feet tall, with a bunch of tattoos on his arms. He has long brown hair that isn't combed, and his beard is long and looks like it has never been trimmed. Be careful; he's given some of us the impression that he's served time in prison for a violent crime."

John turned to Jill.

"How are you doing? Do you need any of my help?"

"No, I don't think so. The collarbone is cracked; he'll have to wear a sling for a while, but I can handle the stitching fine. You get Vicki back, and be careful! This valley needs its Marshal."

John took out the medical supplies that Jill needed and put the medical kit back into his pack. He didn't know if he might have to patch someone else up today. He moved his throwing knife to his belt to be able to reach it quickly if needed.

He easily picked up their trail outside of the camp. Vicki was slightly dragging one boot as if purposely leaving a trail for him to follow. She knew someone would come for her.

"If you keep slowing me down, then I'll just slit your throat and leave you here," said Bart.

"If you'd untie my hands, I could move faster," replied Vicki.

"How stupid do you think that I am? I promise to let you go unharmed once we get to the waterfall. The faster we get there, the sooner you'll go free."

Vicki wasn't too sure that Bart would follow through on his promise. He could kill her and then dump her in the river. If he then disappeared, no one would be the wiser. She hoped that someone from the camp would come after her. Maybe that Marshal kid had heard the gunshot and would help her. Without a rescue, her chances for survival were not good.

John had to be careful. He didn't want to be seen. It was fortunate that Bart didn't have the trail skills that Jack did. Bart's trail, with Vicki's help, was easy to follow. He could focus most of his attention on the woods around him and not the ground. He depended on the Chi of the surrounding life forms to warn him of any danger.

Bart's path took him higher above the river. Up ahead, a waterfall dropped the level of the river about 100 feet. This path alongside the river slowly climbed up to the level of the river above the waterfall. They reached a point where an outcropping of solid rock forced the trail to the edge of a cliff. Here, the path narrowed to only a few feet wide. With the river 50 feet below them, the unobstructed view from this overlook was breathtaking. It was almost a straight drop from the path to the river.

"This is what I've been looking for," he said.

"So, you're going to dump my body from this cliff?" Vicki asked.

"No. I told you I wouldn't hurt you if you cooperated with me. I mean it. I'm more concerned that some of your friends from the camp might be stupid enough to try and rescue you. This is a great place to see if anyone is following us and to deal with them. I want to move farther up the trail and find a place where I can get a clear shot."

Bart found the location he was looking for with a clear view of the ledge. It also offered some trees to give him cover. It was a perfect location. He took some cloth, gagged, and blindfolded Vicki. He knew that he couldn't trust her to be quiet. Now, he just needed to sit and wait for the easy shot.

John was making good progress. The trail was well-worn from being used often. Now that the river was lower than the trail, it was quieter. He could hear the birds singing their songs as they flew among the trees. This also meant that Bart could more easily hear him coming.

He suddenly felt danger ahead. The birds seemed quieter. As he looked ahead, he saw the trail moving closer to the river. A cliff appeared to drop into the river far below, a perfect place for an ambush.

Unfortunately, there was no other path to avoid the cliff. This was one of those times when he had to trust that the Chi would deliver him safely. He took off his pack so that he could move quickly if he had to. He took a couple of deep breaths and focused on the Now, listening to the Chi. As he stepped up to the cliff, he looked ahead for any indication of an ambush. He saw none but felt uneasy.

Bart saw the Marshal step out on the cliff. He had a perfect shot. He slowly pulled the trigger, and the gun fired. Bart saw the Marshal's head snap to the side as the bullet struck his head. The Marshal then dropped to the ground and rolled off the cliff into the river.

"A perfect headshot," exclaimed Bart as he took the gag from Vicki and grinned. "It was that Marshal boy. He wasn't very smart after all."

Vicki's heart sank. He was her only hope, and now he was gone. What a cruel world this had become when teenage boys were murdered in cold blood.

John's head snapped to the side. It was an uncontrolled spasm in his neck muscles. As his head moved to the side, he heard a whistling sound as a bullet passed by his ear. He instinctively fell to the ground and rolled over the trail's edge for cover. Fortunately, the drop to the river was not direct. There was a slight ledge just below the level of the trail. It was narrow, and John had to use all his strength to hang onto the ledge.

He wondered what had happened. He hadn't received an intuition that he should duck. His reaction was instinctual, like that of an animal. The Chi had moved his head to keep him alive.

He remembered a time when he was a child climbing a tree, lost his balance, and started to fall. He was high enough that the fall would have caused severe injury or death. Without thinking, he swung his arm around and caught hold of the only branch within reach. That instinctual reaction had also saved his life. It appeared that in humans, the Chi could operate on both the instinctual and intuitive levels.

He listened intently and heard someone's voice coming from the trail ahead. He waited for several minutes until he felt it was safe again. He climbed back up onto the trail and then walked back to pick up his pack. He'd have an advantage now. If Bart thought he was dead, he'd not be as watchful. As he moved up the trail, the ground flattened out. He must find a way to get ahead of them.

Bart climbed higher on the trail and could hear the waterfall's roar. Vicki seemed deflated. She probably had guessed what his plans were. If he let her go, everyone in the camp would know she was safe and come after him. But, they would hesitate if she just disappeared, not knowing if he still had her. He really didn't want to cut her throat. That was too messy. At the waterfall, he could just give her a little push, and his worries would end.

As they approached the falls, the heavy mist from the waterfall kept blowing across the path. It made the path slippery and obscured his vision, but it felt good. Bart was hot from the long climb up the path, and the cool mist on his face was refreshing, even as it hid the view of the path ahead. Vicki slipped on a rock and just sat on the ground. He could understand. She was defeated and facing her death.

The wind suddenly changed direction, blowing the mist away from the trail. As the mist cleared from the path ahead, Bart saw a man just standing on the path, about 30 feet away. It was that damn Marshal kid. His arms were at his side, and he wasn't carrying a gun. Vicki let out a gasp.

"I thought I put a bullet through your head at the cliff," Bart said. "You're damned lucky, but now your luck has run out. I won't miss this time."

Bart's dismissive attitude toward the young, "unarmed" boy caused him to hesitate for a second. That was all the time John needed to launch his knife at Bart's heart.

As Bart raised his rifle, he noticed how slowly his arms moved. It took an extreme effort to bring up the gun and point it at the Marshal. It was then he noticed the knife sticking out of his chest where his heart was located. How did that get there, he thought. His vision started fading, and he collapsed to the ground.

John walked down the path to Vicki. Her body was shaking, and she was crying as her pent-up emotions were being released. She was now safe. John knelt, cut the rope tying her wrists, and put his arms around her.

"Are you OK? Are you hurt at all?" John asked.

"I'm OK, I think; I'm just numb. I thought for sure that you were dead, and I'd be dead soon, too. He was so sure that he'd killed you, and I believed him."

"Sometimes things aren't what they look like. The Chi saved me so that I could save you."

"Your belief in this Chi energy is hard to understand. But I'll not question it since you think it saved both our lives."

John continued, "It's getting late, and you look exhausted. I'll set up a camp near here, and we can spend the night. You'll have to share a tent with me. I hope that will be OK."

John set up camp and built a fire. The roar of the waterfall sometimes drowned out the roar of the fire. With either sound, the background noise was peaceful. Vicki needed some time to relax after what she'd been through. He made two meals of freeze-dried food. When she saw the food packets, Vicki raised her eyebrows but didn't speak. He liked Vicki. She was a good person.

"What can you tell me about yourself?" Vicki asked. "I know so very little about you; most of it is from rumors. How did you become a Marshal at such a young age?"

"They needed someone to do the job. With my connection to the Chi, I had the ability to do the job better than anyone else."

"You certainly have proven that to me! I can't believe that I'm still alive. How is Chet? Is he alive?"

"Yes. It was a shoulder wound, and Jill was stitching him up as I left to come and find you."

"Who's Jill? Does she live with you?"

"Only temporarily. She was shot in the leg, and while she was recovering, I took care of her. She has some medical training, so I like it when she travels with me."

"So, how did you end up in this valley?" John asked.

"I was in Search and Rescue in Crescent City. Rex is my partner. Some of us from work were camping in a remote area when COVID-24 hit. Our group included Chet, a dispatcher, and Betty, a file clerk. Betty also brought along her two boys. Red is a good friend of mine who supplied the truck for our camping adventure. When we heard about the virus killing everyone in the city, we moved farther into the hills.

"As we kept moving, we picked up additional stragglers along the way, and our group kept getting larger. One day, we met a man from the village in your valley. He told us that the valley was just over the next ridge and was protected by a Marshal. That was how we heard about you and decided to head into this valley.

"Bart joined our group about two weeks ago, and Rex immediately disliked him. He looked like a wild man with his long, dirty hair and beard. Bart was a troublemaker, causing fights, and I think he was stealing, but we never turned away anyone who wanted to join us. After all, we were all just trying to survive.

"We decided to rest for a few days when we got to the river. We would have lost many in our group if you hadn't warned us. After the flood, we decided to stay by the river.

"It just occurred to me that I never thanked you for saving me. I was caught up in the emotional turmoil of the event at that moment. I know I wouldn't be alive if it weren't for you. Thank you."

"I was just doing my job," John replied.

"Is there anything that I could do for you in return?"

"The only way you can help me is to accept the occasional people I might send your way. I'll only send people who I believe will help your group."

"That won't be a problem. We don't see many new people coming into the valley anymore. It's like everyone that survived the COVID-24 epidemic is here now."

"I'm seeing the same thing, too. At first, I saw people every week, but now I hardly see anyone at all. It does make my job easier, but it worries me at the same time."

The next morning, they packed up camp and headed down the trail. Vicki seemed to be fully recovered from her ordeal. She was a strong person. As they passed the ledge where John had almost died, he showed her how he'd escaped death. By noon, they were almost at the survivors' camp when John sensed a group of people coming their way.

He said to Vicki, "Some of your friends are coming to meet us. I think they thought that you needed rescuing."

"How do you know this before you can see them?"

"I can sense their presence in the Chi. This skill helps me do my job as Marshal."

"It doesn't seem fair to the 'bad' guys."

"It isn't. Just don't tell them."

At that moment, five men with rifles and a German Shepard came around a bend in the trail. Rex barked excitedly and ran up to Vicki. He licked her face as she hugged him. Rex then turned toward John and licked an offered hand as if to thank him. Rex knew instinctively through the Chi that John and Vicki were now friends.

"You're OK," one of the men stated.

"Yes, this fine young man rescued me and dispatched Bart."

She then continued more seriously, "Guys, I want to make one thing perfectly clear. You can trust your life to the Marshal. Don't misjudge him because he's young. Bart made that mistake. John has skills beyond those that you or I have. He should be respected as our Marshal."

John saw Jill sitting by a fire as the group entered the survivors' camp. When she saw him, she smiled and started walking toward him.

"How is your patient?" he asked.

"He's doing fine," she laughed. "The only problem is that he whinnies like a horse when he's hungry."

"Did you tell him you were a horse doctor before treating him?"

"No, I was too busy and didn't think he'd care."

"So, how did the rescue go? Any problems?"

"No, but Vicki and I've become good friends."

"Saving someone's life will do that. I know that for a fact," Jill replied with a look of affection in her eyes.

They spent the rest of the day in Vicki's camp, getting to know more of her group. Vicki had told her friends the details of her rescue and how John had appeared out of the mist to save her. Many people stopped John to thank him for saving Vicki. He could tell that she was well-liked and respected in her camp. John also gained the respect of many on that day.

12

They left the survivors' camp the next morning and crossed the river. A heavy layer of clouds obscured the sun, making the hike much more pleasant. On a hot sunny day, the rugged hike through the rocky terrain to his camp could make it uncomfortable. John suddenly felt a familiar presence when they were about a mile away from his camp.

"We have company waiting for us at the camp," he said apprehensively. "Don is there, and he may not be happy with me because I've shared my camp with you. But don't worry, this is between Don and me. It shouldn't concern you if you see Don and me having tense private discussions. His presence here probably means that I'll be taking you to the village as soon as tomorrow. I'll admit, I've enjoyed your company and will miss you."

"I'm sorry if I've gotten you into trouble with Don. Thank you for all that you have done for me and taught me. You'll always have a warm place in my heart."

As they entered the camp, Don was sitting at the table. John could never read Don's emotions, as Don had much better control of his Chi energy than John did.

When Jill first saw Don, she was surprised. She expected a high-power executive who could control a vast manufacturing empire. Instead, he appeared to be a harmless older man with a disarming smile. He wasn't too tall, short, fat, or thin. He was just your average man, except he seemed to radiate incredible kindness with every look from his eyes and that fabulous smile. Yes, it was apparent that this man was indeed a Grand Master of Chi. Even she could feel this man's presence in the Chi.

Don smiled warmly, greeted them, and said to John, "You appeared to have picked up a straggler." He then faced Jill and said, "My name is Don, and I'm glad to make your acquaintance."

Her reply was quiet and short, "I'm Jill. It's nice to meet you, too."

Don then turned back to John and said, "John, why don't you start a fire and make us all a cup of tea? We all need to have a serious talk."

John had only heard Don use this tone of voice when he'd first met him. At that time, Don asked him to become the Marshal. John was worried. Certainly, Don wouldn't harm Jill, but John hated to think that he had disappointed Don. This situation was totally John's fault.

As John built a fire and made the tea, Don and Jill conversed politely. Don asked about her history, about which John knew very little. Jill told Don about how her husband and son had died and that she was now alone. She also told Don how John had saved her life twice.

When John joined them at the table, she suddenly blurted out what seemed to be a carefully prepared speech:

"You're probably here to talk about me and my future. I want first to ask both of you if there's any way that I could stay here at this camp. I'd promise never to leave and would gladly play the role of a Camp Mother, helping with the chores around the camp. I realize that if someone wanted to get to John, my life might be in danger. I'm willing to give up my life if necessary to help the people in this valley."

She stopped as if to catch her breath but didn't continue.

"Is that it?" Don asked. "Are you done stating your proposal?"

"Yes," she whispered.

"Well," he responded, "that's an interesting proposal. John, why don't you tell her about how we met?"

He looked at Don and didn't quite know what Don wanted him to say or how much detail to include. So, he thought that he'd be truthful up to a point and started the story.

"Well, it was about seven months ago, and I was living in a cabin built by Max Everitt. Max had correctly predicted that civilization would collapse and built this cabin to escape the coming troubles. It was very self-sufficient, with solar panels and a reliable water supply. When I moved in, it had everything I needed to escape the world so I could continue learning about the Chi.

"I'd only lived there about a month when the news channels started reporting on the growing COVID-24 epidemic. I watched as the situation grew more and more dire. Finally, the news channels went off the air, and I knew society was breaking down. I knew I could be happy alone, so I just started a new life of trying to survive as long as possible.

"One day, about a month later, I put on my day pack and headed out for a long hike through the woods. It was one of my favorite activities. I hadn't gone far when I saw an older man sitting on a log, rubbing his calf. It was unusual that I'd meet anyone on my hikes. He looked like he was in his sixties and wore a wide-brim hiking hat with his gray hair showing beneath. He wore hiking shorts and boots and almost looked like a model from an L.L. Bean catalog. He had no backpack and looked out of place in this valley because his clothes looked clean and new.

"I approached him and asked if he needed some help. He said his calf had a muscle cramp that wouldn't go away. I offered to massage his calf to see if I could get it to relax, and he extended his leg toward me.

"As I knelt in front of him and grasped his calf with my hands, I felt that, indeed, his calf was cramped and hard as a rock. I closed my eyes to focus on the Now, started bringing the Chi into me, and directed it into his calf. Nothing happened. The energy I directed into his calf seemed to have no effect. I focused more intently on drawing more Chi into my body, hoping to break through the resistance that I was meeting. When I thought I could do no more, his calf suddenly relaxed as the Chi brought relief to his muscles. I gave his calf a good massage and let go.

"I suggested that he drink more fluids to avoid getting a cramp and handed him the water bottle from my pack. He drank deeply and offered it back to me, but I told him to keep it to ensure he would get safely home. When I asked how far away his home was, he replied with a vague, 'Not far.'

"I was concerned that he needed more time to recover and shouldn't be left alone. I told him I didn't live far and would love to share some lunch with him. He could recuperate in a more comfortable setting if I could get him back to my cabin.

"He pointed out that we were strangers and asked if I was sure I wanted to do this. I told him I was trying to live my life by just enjoying each day as it unfolded and would enjoy his company for lunch just as long as he didn't kill me.

"We both laughed and headed back toward my cabin. When we arrived, I offered him a comfortable chair and a glass of water, which he gladly accepted. Since the cabin was supplied with electricity from the solar panels, I was able to make us a nice hot meal. After the meal, we moved out to the front porch to enjoy the cool breeze.

"I asked him if he was feeling better and suggested he could spend the night in my guest bedroom if he wanted. He pointed out my kindness and said he wanted to repay me. He then offered me the Marshal job, and I accepted it."

John stopped his narrative and looked at Don.

Jill spoke up, asking, "I kind of thought the story was something like that. Why did you think it was important for me to get the details? It doesn't affect my proposal at all."

Don prompted, "John, you're a good man and have kept my secret well. Now tell her your secret. Tell her who you really are."

John looked at Don, who nodded, so he continued. "I go by John Smith these days, but my real name is Max Everitt. I built the cabin that I lived in when I met Don. Jill, you asked how old I was when I first met you. I evaded the question and let you believe that I was a teenager. My real age is 78 years old."

Jill's face turned red, and she didn't try to hide her anger. "Are you guys pulling a joke on me? If so, I don't like it. This is kind of creepy. I know that you aren't 78 years old. My God, you have pimples!"

Don shifted in his chair and looked directly at Jill. She could feel sincerity radiating from his Chi. He said, "Now it's my turn to tell you who I really am. John didn't enjoy that he couldn't be fully open with you about who he was and who I am. That's my fault because I asked John to keep our secrets private."

He paused for a second and then continued.

"This may be difficult to believe, but the truth is that I'm not a being from this planet. My home is on a planet that orbits a star very far away. I'm here to help for a short time and am responsible for John's youthful appearance. When I first met John, he was a good man with an old body. I needed a Marshal to protect this valley who would be strong enough to keep the peace. He also had to deal with the very violent men that might come this way. I also needed a man who understood the Chi energy well.

"My species has the advanced technology that can create a human body and transfer the memories from the old John into this new human body. With John's permission, we did just that. While we can't create or teach the use of the Chi, we can find those people with a natural ability to feel it. That's why we chose John. He's unusually strong in his ability to use the Chi to help him keep the peace in this valley. We gave him a new body to reinforce and support his job as Marshal."

He paused here to give Jill time to think.

"This is unbelievable and yet believable," Jill offered. "John looks young and yet seems very wise for his age. I'd believe I was talking to an adult about my age if I wasn't looking at his face. This is a shock. I now understand why you needed to tell me this. I need to understand what's in the mind behind those TeenBoy eyes if I'm going to stay here. It still seems a little creepy to think about. I'll need some time to think about this before deciding whether to stay in the camp, but if I decide to leave, I promise to keep your secret."

There was a long silence, and then Don looked at John. "Well, there's more to my story than even TeenBoy here knows." Don chuckled with amusement at his TeenBoy reference.

He then continued, "John, I know that you carry a Bible with you in case you must read from it at a burial service. Would you get it out of your pack? I want you to turn to Genesis 9:29 and read it to us."

After a minute, John returned with the Bible and read, "Genesis 9:29, And all the days of Noah were nine hundred and fifty years: and he died."

Don continued, "Now, non-believers find some Bible stories difficult to believe, but this fact is true. Noah lived to be 950 years old."

"How can you know this?" Jill countered. "It happened thousands of years ago."

"I know because my species made the body that allowed him to live so long. It's written in our history. Let me explain.

"Your species is somewhat unique in the galaxy. We've been observing your species develop for thousands of years as a matter of scientific curiosity. Our guidelines don't allow us to interfere with your development unless we decide to save it from extinction. This is much like your species when it tries to save a particular bird or fish from extinction. Your species will make a great effort to save the animal species that are in danger. We do much the same.

"When the great flood threatened to eliminate your species, we stepped in to keep that from happening. To be honest, we did it more for our benefit than yours. We didn't want to lose the opportunity to study your unique species.

"There's a problem when a massive extinction event like this happens. The surviving population is so small that it takes tens of thousands of years to recover. So, to encourage a faster recovery, we modify the lifespan of a few remaining members so that they live longer. That gives them more time to reproduce. We program the DNA coding so that the lifespan improvement slowly decreases over time. Each future generation lives a slightly shorter life. Eventually, the lifespan modification disappears, and future generations will live a normal lifespan for your species. While Noah lived for 950 years, by the time of Moses, the human lifespan was back to a more normal 120 years."

"So, was the great flood described in the Bible true?" John asked. "What caused the entire Earth to be flooded?"

"The Earth's surface wasn't entirely underwater," Don replied. "The water covered all the areas where human development was occurring, making it almost certain that no human life would survive. The flooding was caused by another star making a brief pass near your solar system. While the additional heat from this star wasn't much, it was enough to melt all the ice at the Earth's poles. The melted ice caused the sea levels to rise significantly. This flooded the low areas where humans were living. We saved Noah and his people from the first human extinction event in human history.

"Currently, a second human extinction event is occurring. When we determined that your species had no natural defense against this artificial virus, we took action to neutralize it. Unfortunately, by the time we could travel here and neutralize the virus, your human species was almost entirely infected and dying. There are very few humans left alive on your planet. Your group in this valley is one of the few we could save."

"So, how did you choose to save the people living in this valley rather than another group somewhere else?" John asked.

"We didn't choose the people in this valley. We just listened to the Chi. It always ensures that life's energy will continue in the Universe. The survivors migrated to this valley following their intuition, guided by the Chi itself. John's unusual strength in the Chi attracted them to this valley. Life forms are attracted to other life forms that have a strong Chi influence. We saw that the Chi collected a group of survivors around John. We decided that with John's strength in the Chi, he was a likely candidate for our lifespan enhancement."

"So, are the people of this valley the only survivors left of humanity?" Jill asked.

"No. Some people in remote areas around the world have survived. Most will die before ever creating a society that can become self-sufficient. The Chi has brought the people in this valley together and also in other places around the world. You can think of each location as if the Chi is planting a seed to help humanity survive. As in gardening, not every seed will sprout, and there is no certainty that this group in your valley will survive. We use our life-extension technology to help those seeds survive and grow. There are similar places around your planet where we are trying to help other groups with strong Chi.

"Our species has decided once again to enhance the lifespan of a few couples around the planet so that the population has time to recover a thousand years from now. Max, or John as he goes by now, was our first enhancement in this area of your planet. I'm sorry, John, but while I could give you a younger body, I couldn't tell you how long you'd live at that time. We knew that with your connection to the Chi, you wouldn't have a problem adjusting to a longer lifetime."

John looked down as he thought about the implications of living for a thousand years.

"Wow, a thousand years," John said in a low voice. "That's hard to imagine." He paused and then added, "No, I don't think I'll have a problem with a long lifetime. Living daily with the Chi has given me a new perspective on what life is all about. Now I'm curious to see where the Chi will guide me during the next thousand-year adventure."

"So now, Jill," Don continued, "I want to make you a counteroffer to your offer to be 'Camp Mom.' My species would like to offer you the opportunity to have your lifespan extended to match John's. In a way, you could become not just the mother of this camp but the mother of the future of humanity in this area of your planet. We watched as you drew on the Chi to heal your wound and were surprised at how well you manipulated the Chi with so little experience. The Chi seems to have brought you to our attention. This resolves the issue of finding someone to be John's mate to help the re-population of the human species. If you accept our counteroffer, you and John will be the only people in this valley with extended lifespans.

"You must understand that the purpose of this extension would be for you to be John's mate for the next one thousand years or so. There's something else that you both need to realize. When John's mate is selected, his role in this valley changes. The virus epidemic has taken its toll, and very few new people have recently entered this valley. John has ensured that the valley is at peace, so his role will transition to one focusing on rebuilding your species. He'll be allowed to build friendships and have a family. Someone will still need to protect and maintain order in your group of survivors, so you must also keep your Marshal role, too."

"So how does this lifespan extension work?" Jill asked. "Do our children have to mate with one another to keep the extended lifespan going? Wouldn't that cause genetic issues in their offspring?"

"Just as you do today," Don replied, "your children shouldn't mate with one another. You're correct in assuming that it would cause weaknesses in the genes to occur. This means that your children must choose mates from the other survivors. This won't, however, interfere with the extended lifespan that we've enabled.

"When your children mate with the other survivors, the extended lifespan gene will also be passed on to their children. The children from you and John will live long lives, as will your grandchildren from the survivors. With each generation, the length of the extended lifespan will slowly decrease.

"Your children develop as normal human children until they're 18 years old. At that point, the genetic modifications that extend their lifespan become active. We set John's age at that point in his lifespan when we created his body. From now on, John's lifespan extension will be active. We will do the same for you if you accept our offer. You and John would be the same age.

"Our role as an outside influence will end once we have two of your species with extended lifespans. There will be no more supplies given to you. We will have given you a strong start, but you must continue the rest of the journey on your own without our help. The extended lifespan will cause issues between those with long lives and the survivors with normal lifespans. These are issues that you must deal with on your own.

"Jill, you need to take your time and think about this offer. Please don't feel pressured to accept our proposal. The Chi will direct us to someone else if you choose not to accept our offer. You don't need to make the decision now. You and John should talk this over between the two of you. He's gone through the experience of getting a new body and should be able to answer most of your questions. If you decide not to accept our offer, John will take you to a village where you can live the rest of your life in peace.

"I must leave now. I'll know through the Chi when you decide and will contact you again."

With that last statement, Don got up and started walking out of the camp. As he left, he said with a chuckle over his shoulder. "I'll let TeenBoy do my dishes." When he reached the edge of the camp, there was a blue flash, and he was gone.

"Well, that didn't go how I thought it would," John said, "and I'm guessing you're even more surprised than I am. As we talk about this in the coming days, we must be 100% truthful with each other. This is a big responsibility, and one thousand years is a very, very long time. I struggle to understand what it would be like to live for a thousand years. Just think about how large a birthday cake would be to fit a thousand candles on it."

His attempt to laugh at their situation through humor didn't go over well. She was in shock like he'd been when Don first told him he was an alien. It was hard to believe they were talking to an alien from a highly advanced civilization. For Don, they must be like ants, something inferior to study. Jill remained quiet.

John got up and started to take the cups to the spring to wash when suddenly she said, "I'm sorry. I don't mean to chase you away; I just can't believe this is happening. How does someone make a decision that will affect all of humanity? I don't know where to start."

"Let the Chi be your guide. Maybe you aren't prepared to take on this responsibility. That's OK. Ultimately, your Chi will guide you to where you need to be. It will guide you to your answer."

Suddenly, she said, "Would you take me to your cabin if it still exists? That's where this whole thing started when you first met Don."

"That's a great idea," he answered. "It was still there a month ago when I last was there. The power was still working, and it had hot and cold water and a real kitchen and bathroom."

"A toilet?" she asked.

"Yes, a real toilet that flushes, too."

"Let's go!" she said excitedly. "How far away is it? Can we get there before dark?"

"No. It's in a higher valley over the ridge behind this camp, and the trail is rugged. It will take most of a day to get there. We should wait and leave in the morning."

13

When morning came, Jill was up early. Some of the shock seemed to have gone from her expression. They stowed their loose gear and prepared the camp for an extended absence, not knowing how long they'd be gone.

As they slipped on their packs, she asked, "Which way?"

"We must go higher first to get to the top of the ridge behind this camp. Follow me and tell me if I'm going too fast for you. It's a steep climb."

They followed a path that John had taken many times over the last year. They stopped at the top of the ridge for a break. The sky was clear, with a gentle breeze blowing across the valley. The view was breathtaking. They could see the whole valley and the river running through it. A pair of eagles circled the valley, looking for their lunch, as John and Jill munched on nuts and dried fruit.

Jill asked, "What went through your mind when Don told you that you could have a new body and life? You must have thought that your life was winding down and had accepted that your death was near. And then to be offered a 'do over,' with a new body and another set of years to live your life again. How did you handle it?"

"Well, when Don first offered me the job, he hadn't told me it came with a new body. I turned him down, saying I was too old to do that job. I could be happy living my last years in peace in my cabin. Then he told me he could give me a new, younger body if I accepted the job.

It was surreal. It gave me a chance to relive my life and not make all the mistakes I'd made before. It was a new life with a new future and new mistakes to be made. It was an easy decision for me. In my later years, I learned to enjoy helping other people rather than just thinking of myself. When you're young, you just seem to focus on yourself. Even when you're volunteering, you still have thoughts in the back of your mind about how this will look to your friends.

"Don assured me I'd retain all my memories of what I'd learned over the years. I saw it as an opportunity to have a new life fully dedicated to helping others without the baggage of a big ego from being a young person again. For me, the job of Marshal was exactly what I wanted."

"Didn't the idea of being alone without friends or family bother you?"

"No, not at all. I'd been married and had a full life. My first life was a great time that I'll never forget. But when my wife died, and I was alone, I adjusted to a life alone and found I could be happy. That was when I first started listening to the Chi. My new focus for the rest of my life was learning about the Chi and how to listen to it daily. I'd made great progress when Don found me."

They continued toward the cabin and arrived in mid-afternoon. The cabin was in a small valley that sat high above the broader valley below. Most of the valley was flat, had an excellent area for growing crops, and had its own small creek running through it. That was why he'd selected it: It was secluded but offered a good place to survive if the world collapsed.

The cabin was on the valley's north side and had great southern exposure. A line of solar panels was near the cabin, and an outbuilding and garage were located between the cabin and the solar arrays. The solar panel area was enclosed with a tall fence to keep animals out. Next to that was another larger enclosed area extending into the trees. That fencing surrounded a chicken coup. The enclosure had screening across its top to keep out any eagles looking for a chicken dinner. It also contained a vegetable garden. Several chickens could be seen wandering around, looking for bugs to eat. The outbuilding contained the batteries for the solar system and was also a place to store extra food and equipment. A generous front porch on the cabin looked out over the valley.

"When you said cabin," Jill commented, "I was thinking something with two rooms and a fireplace. This is a house. How many bedrooms does it have?"

"It has two bedrooms, one bathroom, a laundry room, a living room, a dining area, and a kitchen."

"A laundry room with a washing machine?"

"Yes," he said with a smile, "but no dryer. A dryer uses too much electricity for the solar system to handle."

They entered the cabin and set their packs down on the floor. John pointed toward one door and said, "That will be your room. Feel free to explore the cabin while I go out and make sure that everything is still working."

He checked the solar system, which was in perfect shape. He switched on the circuit breakers for the water heater and baseboard heaters. Since it didn't freeze this time of year, the water pipes were charged, and the water system was fully functional. He returned to the cabin and found Jill sitting in a comfortable chair in the living room. She was smiling.

"I can't believe you don't live here full-time," she said incredulously. "Why do you live in that dirty camp and sleep on the ground?"

"This cabin is too far from the people I've chosen to protect," he replied. "And I'd become too soft staying here. Someday, the electricity and water will fail, and this will become just a shelter instead of a home. But for now, you deserve to be pampered, even if it's just for a few days. We'll have hot water in an hour, and you can shower and wash any clothes that need washing. I'll start preparing dinner. Does baked macaroni and cheese with a salad sound good to you?"

"Do you really have fresh cheese?" she asked excitedly.

"It's not fresh; it's in the refrigerator, and the package says it's good for a year. I'll have to check out the garden to see what choices we have for a salad."

14

After dinner, Jill jumped into the shower, and when she was done, John followed. By the time they finished their showers, it was approaching dusk, so they moved out to the front porch to relax. Four deer were at the bottom of the valley, munching on the tall grass as John and Jill watched. The deer looked up and seemed to notice them, but they didn't seem concerned and returned to their meal. It was a peaceful time.

Jill broke the silence, asking, "Will you tell me about your life before Don?"

"Sure, I don't mind. I graduated from college with two degrees, one in electrical engineering and the other in economics. I thought the economics degree would help me get into engineering management, but my career never developed in that direction. When I was 35, I met a woman who became my wife one year later. We had a happy life, and since neither of us wanted children, we enjoyed our life together to the fullest.

"The biggest problem we faced was that we loved each other dearly and only wanted to make the other person happy. This resulted in difficulties when we were trying to make decisions together. We never communicated what each of us truly wanted. We only spoke of what we thought the other person wanted. Sometimes, we came to a joint decision that neither of us wanted, only because we each thought the other person wanted it. When we eventually discovered our mistake, we'd laugh and promise to be more truthful next time, but we never were.

"We were madly in love; that was all I needed to be happy. I was able to retire early because that economics degree had taught me about money and investing. I was good at the investing part.

"After I retired, my wife and I traveled all around the country. We visited many of the national parks and saw all of the wonders of nature. I learned to enjoy being outside, surrounded by nature, and that's why I eventually ended up here.

"Just as we were settling into life in our seventies, my wife was diagnosed with cancer. We were told at the outset that it was terminal, but she lived an additional two years. That was a tough time for me, but I tried not to show it so I could be strong for her in her final years.

"She also showed her love for me in those final two years. Instead of dwelling on her approaching death, she set about preparing me for the time after her death when I'd be living alone. She taught me to do the tasks she'd been doing around the house. I learned to cook, do the laundry, and even clean the toilets. That was one task that I never enjoyed.

"After she died, I was living alone without any children. I buried myself in investing activities to take my mind off her death. It was fun for me to understand where the economy was going and how to make money from my knowledge.

"So now you know my life story."

"I know something about how you felt," she replied with sympathy. "Losing my husband and son simultaneously was tough for me too. The COVID-24 epidemic was terrible. I was camping up in the mountains with some girlfriends when it struck. I've always enjoyed camping and felt at home with nature. My husband called to say that he and my son were both sick and that I shouldn't come home. I ignored his wish and was heading home when my car broke down. I was stranded in the forest and, eventually, ended up here in this valley.

"My next question may be difficult to answer, but you need to be honest with me. In your first life, you said that you didn't want kids. Now, Don wants you to be the father of humanity. Are you really sure you want to do this?"

"A very insightful question. In my first life, I had a strong ego and thought that children would hold me back from doing all of the fun things I wanted to do. I'll admit it; I was selfish. As I grew older, I learned more about how children develop into adults, and I found it fascinating. I learned how they needed toys to help their brain develop and how eating dirt actually improved their immune system. While I never regretted not having children, I am excited about being involved in helping my future children grow into adulthood. I think I will be a much better parent now than I would have been with my big ego. Their growth will now be my focus."

"Well, that's good to know before I make my decision.

"So how did you end up here in this remote home, or cabin as you like to call it?"

"Things got strange after the COVID-19 crisis when the economy recovered. Governments lowered interest rates to zero in the U.S. and to negative numbers in Europe. Usually, when anyone borrows money from a bank, the bank charges them interest on that loan. You had to pay back the loan plus a certain amount of interest.

"Negative interest rates meant the bank paid you to borrow money from them. That made no sense! Never in the entire history of banking had any bank paid people to borrow from them. When I say the entire history, I'm even talking about ancient Babylonia. Something was definitely broken in the worldwide monetary system.

"So, what did everyone do? They started borrowing this free money as fast as they could and investing it. Businesses borrowed the free money and bought back their own stock. The stock market streaked higher. The rich got richer because they could borrow and invest, while the poor couldn't benefit because they couldn't qualify for a loan. The gap between the rich and not-so-rich widened.

"Debts in countries around the world rose much faster than their income. Every country was getting further into debt, more than they could ever repay. It was like a family using their credit cards to finance a luxurious lifestyle and getting deeper into debt every year. Almost every country did this. I knew this situation couldn't continue forever, but I didn't know how long things would remain stable.

"Then good fortune came my way. I won the lotto! I won five million dollars in the state lottery. I decided to escape from the coming financial collapse and build a cabin in a remote area. So, 18 months ago, I bought this land and started building this wonderful cabin using my lotto winnings. It was finished last August, and I moved in to wait for the financial world to collapse.

"I figured that there was a very good chance that I'd die before the collapse. The financial leaders were very good at delaying the consequences of their mistakes. They kept creating new agencies to cover up the debt crisis they were creating.

"I enjoyed living with nature and was somewhat self-sufficient. No matter what happened, I could live the rest of my life in peace and focus on learning more about the Chi. I never realized that the collapse would happen so soon. I also never realized that the COVID-24 epidemic would be the cause of the collapse."

"Right now, I'm certainly glad that the lottery paid for your water heater and washing machine. Oh, did I mention the toilet, too?" Jill said with a laugh.

"I'm glad that you're enjoying it. It won't be here a thousand years from now, so enjoy it while you can."

"So, what's it like to get a new body?" Jill asked.

"Well, it isn't as shocking as you might think," he answered. "If you look at yourself today, you realize that your mind and body are separate. Your memories aren't in your hand or leg but in your brain. Your collected memories and intelligence aren't altered if you lose an arm or a leg. While the doctors can give you a new hand, heart, leg, or liver, the person that you are isn't changed. Getting a new body is like getting a new heart, except you're getting a whole new body, too.

"Don's scientists will transfer all your memories from your old brain to your new brain. You wake up with a new body, and all your old memories remain. It reminds me of a movie that I saw called 'Avatar.' The hero was paralyzed and in a wheelchair. Using technology, they were able to transfer his memories into an alien's body. In that way, he could interact with and study the alien species, which is almost precisely what Don is doing. In the movie, the hero's awareness is transferred into his new alien body, which isn't paralyzed. He's so excited to be able to move his legs and jump around that he ends up causing a commotion. I've always had an issue with that movie and the wheelchair. Why was he moving around in a wheelchair from the 1970s if they had the technology to transfer his mind into an alien body that they built?

"But regardless, the body transfer was like that experience for me. At my advanced age, my hearing was failing, my eyesight was blurry, and when I woke up in the morning, I hurt all over. I now have the body of a teenager, and I feel great. Don made sure that this new body functions perfectly. It's taller and a lot stronger than my old body. Overall, I'm thrilled with it, and it's even immune to COVID-24. I must warn you about something. Your new face won't look anything like you do now or when you were young. They're giving you a new body with new and improved DNA. The physical characteristics from your old DNA are lost."

"Was there any pain?"

"None at all. Don and I walked down into the valley in front of my cabin, and there was a blue flash of light. That was the last thing I remembered until I appeared in a new body, standing beside Don in that same valley. I was unaware of any time passing during the body transfer, but when I returned, my vegetables had grown, and I had the same number of chickens. I think it took about a week, but I have no memories of what happened during that week."

"That blue light that you saw. Do you think that was the transporter that Don used back at your camp?"

"I don't know. I had no memory of going anywhere; there was just a blue flash, and I was gone and then back. If it is a transportation device, I don't think that Don lets anyone see it in operation unless you have been chosen to have a body transfer. I guess he's proving to you that he truly is an alien with advanced technology, just in case you don't believe him. He could have just been an old man pranking you with the body transfer offer.

"I guess we need to talk about us. It's truth time now, so please don't worry about hurting my feelings. This is far too important. Could you be happily married to me ... for a thousand years?"

"It's strange to think about you in that way. Until now, I've thought of you more like a boy I once met in high school. I've come to really enjoy your more mature company while being around you this last week. I wasn't looking forward to going to a strange village without you. At this point in my life, I feel that you're my best friend. It's like being able to be with my high school crush after he's become a man. It's just strange to think about."

"It's strange for me, too, although I've been enjoying your company through the mind of an older adult. In that context, the older man in me really likes the woman you are today. Your strength of character has really impressed me. I've enjoyed your company and would have enjoyed living with you as two older adults.

"I'll make you this promise. If you decide to take this giant leap and become my wife, I'll do everything in my power to make you happy and take care of you. We would share one life together as equals. I know this because that was the kind of husband I was for my first wife. The longer we were together, the stronger our love grew. I know no other way than to make a total commitment to you and our future life together. Living with you for a thousand years would just be a blessing."

A big smile spread across her face. "That's what I wanted to hear. And I promise you that I'll always try to be the one who makes you happy, too. I know that we'll have a wonderful life together raising our family. You're the engineer; how many kids will we have in a thousand years?"

"That will be your decision. I don't want you to feel that you're just a breeding machine. We'll have babies when you feel like having them and when we can provide them with food and shelter. Have you decided, or do you need more time to think about it?"

"I've decided, and I'm excited about our future together. So how do we contact Don to let him know?"

"We don't have to tell him. He'll know of your decision and its sincerity through the Chi. Now it's time to get some rest. Tomorrow will be a big day."

15

John and Jill had scrambled eggs and some dried fruit for breakfast the next morning. The chickens were still producing eggs from their diet of chicken feed provided by Don. John didn't know where he got the feed, but as part of their agreement, he also provided food for his chickens.

It was a beautiful morning, and it had rained during the night. The air was crisp, and the smell of pine trees was in the air. A hummingbird was already busy collecting nectar from the wildflowers near the porch. It was mesmerizing to watch them fly so quickly from flower to flower.

After breakfast, they enjoyed the luxury of hot showers and moved onto the porch to enjoy the beautiful morning.

"Are you still firm with your decision after sleeping on it?" John asked.

"More than ever. I could hardly sleep last night in anticipation."

At that moment, there was a blue flash of light in the valley, and Don appeared. He started walking toward them with a big smile on his face.

"How does he do that?" she asked. "Is he always listening to our conversations?"

"I think he does it through his connection with the Chi. As you learn more about it, you'll find that you know when things are happening around you. Living things are all around us, and Chi is the energy of all life forms. It knows what's happening if you learn to listen to it, and it will tell you of an impending ambush or when a friend is near."

As Don arrived at the porch, he said, "So you have arrived at a decision. I can give you more time if you wish. This isn't a decision to be made lightly."

She reached over and grabbed John's hand. "I've made my decision. So, what happens now?"

Don climbed onto the porch and took a seat. "This may be the final time that we talk. If you have any questions, now is the time to ask them. I can't talk about my species or other galaxy species in detail. I also can't offer my opinions on what you should do. This will be your journey, and we can't interfere. I'll only answer questions that might help you in your task of restoring the human population."

John asked a question that had been on his mind for a long time. "What went wrong? How did we fail as a species, or was the virus epidemic just a random event?"

"You remember I said that your species was special, and we wanted to study you? What makes you special is that your species reproduces with only two sexes. Most other species in the Universe need more than two beings to create new life."

"That sounds like it could be fun!" John quipped and received a glare from Jill.

Don chuckled and continued. "Because most other races need more individuals to reproduce, their societies develop a communal aspect of working together on every decision. It's built into their culture that one individual doesn't decide things alone. The negative aspect of this is that their society and technology evolve much more slowly. A consensus must be reached on every decision. The benefit is that there are fewer wars or wrong decisions made. They avoid bad decisions that could negatively affect their society and cause an extinction event.

"Your species with only two sexes progresses differently. Traditionally, the woman has taken on the task of raising the young ones, while the man offers the family food and security. In this role, the man is often put into the position of independently making decisions for the family. This encourages the development of a powerful ego. He must believe that his decisions are the correct ones for his family, as he alone is responsible for their lives."

"So that's why men have such big egos," Jill added, giving John a wink.

Smiling, Don continued. "Your society develops with one person as a leader vs. a group in another society. With an enlarged ego, that leader believes only he can make the correct decisions. He alone feels responsible for the lives of his people. Because of this, he'll do whatever it takes to remain the leader. This includes starting wars or making poor financial decisions with the country's finances. Your society was already heading toward financial collapse before the virus epidemic struck."

"So, it was just a random virus that caused this latest failure," John suggested.

"Well, not really," Don replied. "The virus didn't come into existence naturally. It was created by one country during its research on biological warfare. Their intention wasn't to wipe out all humans; that part was an accident. They created a strain of virus transmitted between humans, much like the COVID-19 virus. The new virus contained a two-stage infection process when they engineered it. At first, the virus would only initiate a mild immune response like a common cold. It would then go dormant while hiding in its host.

"This allowed the virus to spread among the population without anyone becoming alarmed. After a certain number of reproductive cycles, the virus was programmed to self-mutate and become instantly lethal to its host. People started dying by the millions. There was no way to stop it with your technology. The virus had spread silently and infected everyone on the planet.

"We sensed the massive death through the Chi and made the trip to your planet to neutralize the virus. Unfortunately, most of the human population had been infected and died by the time we could arrive. The first people who were infected died first. People like yourselves who lived outside of the cities were infected last. These were the only ones that we were able to save."

"Yes!" John exclaimed. "I remember feeling sick at the epidemic's end after the news channels quit broadcasting. I thought that I'd gotten COVID-24 and was going to die like everyone else. But I recovered and figured that I'd just caught a cold. That must have been when I got infected.

"It seems like we humans never learn. So, either way, your species would have swooped in to save us from ourselves, either financial collapse or COVID-24?"

"No. The financial collapse might have set your species back for 500 years, but it would have survived in the end. The virus epidemic was an extinction event. We can only step in to prevent the extinction of your species."

"So, you helped Noah, and now you're helping us because if you didn't, then humanity might go extinct."

"That's correct. We've watched your civilizations rise and fall. The Egyptians, the Greeks, and the Romans all let their egos destroy their civilizations. They followed a very similar path. A civilization grows and gets rich from its growth. When their population ages or shrinks and isn't growing anymore, it fails to cut back on their spending. The leader's strong ego refuses to deliver the news to the people that they'll have to reduce their standard of living. The leader refuses to take this appropriate step because they fear they might not stay in power."

"To be fair," Jill added, "in this country, the people will only elect leaders who promise them more benefits. With this system, we were doomed to fail eventually."

"Yes, and that's why we study you. Group leaders seek solutions to problems so everyone shares equally, in good times or bad. However, with a society built around strong egos, there's this continuing cycle of boom and bust. Each cycle may take thousands of years to complete. We're interested in seeing if there ever can be a different result. Or, if a species with only two sexes is doomed never to become highly developed."

"You're putting a lot of responsibility on our shoulders," John said. "Somehow, unless we change how we govern ourselves, we'll never develop beyond a certain stage before we collapse. We must create a new society where the consensus of a group is used to make decisions. We mustn't let a single person make decisions for everyone. It must start with us. People will want us to be the leaders because we're different and are close to the Chi. We mustn't let that happen and make sure our children believe that too."

"Do you have any other questions?" Don asked.

"I have one," Jill replied. "Is there any way we can use the Chi energy to force people to not listen to their ego?"

"You have a misunderstanding about Chi. It's controlled by no one, including my species, with our advanced technologies. It's a natural energy that resides within us and directs all life throughout the galaxy. It's like the wind; we can't see it, but we can feel its effects. We can use it to guide us through life but not to control life around us. It's in control of what happens in life, not us."

"But doesn't the ego come from Chi?" Jill asked. "If so, then the Chi itself is destroying humanity."

"And that's why we're studying your species so closely. You're asking a question that we have no answer to yet. Maybe the Chi will guide the two of you in answering that question for us. We will be watching."

"Is there anything good about our ego-strong species?" Jill asked.

"Yes, something that I'm glad to be able to share with you while I'm in this body. Your strong egos seem to help you develop an uncommon sense of humor. Other species have something similar, but in your species, your laughter is richer. It has a unique mixture of emotions that go with it. It's like the Chi energy is laughing with you. To experience laughter in your human body is truly unique and very appealing. I'll miss it when I leave."

Don then asked Jill, "Are you ready? It's a painless process and will be over instantly in your memory. We will just walk down into the valley, and it will happen."

John gave Jill a long hug. "I'll see you in a few minutes ... in your time. I've come to love the person that you are and will miss you while you're gone." That was the first time he'd said that to her, and he meant it. Something about her Chi made him happy and hopeful.

"So long, TeenBoy."

"See you later, Jill."

John watched as Don and Jill walked down into the valley. They both waved to him, and then, with a blue flash, they were gone.

16

After Jill left, John sat down to plan what he should do next. He had a week before Jill would return and a lot to do. The highest priority was to organize the survivors before winter set in. Last winter was unusually mild, and the survivors could survive in tents. He had a feeling that this winter would be much worse.

He had to find a safe place to gather and form a community. The best place would be a town with existing houses. He'd been in a town about 80 miles to the south before the COVID-24 epidemic. The town sat on a large freshwater lake. It was a nice community of about one thousand people. Being on a lake provided them with fish and fresh water. Unfortunately, there would be no electricity in the town, but it seemed like a good solution to check out.

All the survivors he'd encountered feared any city or town. They'd heard stories of towns where every inhabitant had died from the virus. They'd escaped the virus and believed that if they went back into any town, they would die. John now knew from Don that the towns would be safe, and there would be no trace of COVID-24 left to infect anyone.

The next morning, John headed out toward his camp. The town was far away, and it would be easier if he could use the litter to carry his supplies, both of which were at his camp.

He didn't stay long at the camp, just eating lunch and packing up his supplies. He had to carry the supplies by hand through the rock field that was too rugged to drag the litter. He headed toward the river once he'd packed his supplies on the litter. He wanted to make it to the paved road along the river before dark.

There were two paved roads, one on each side of the river. The west road was the one he'd traveled with Jill. They'd used it to reach the camp of people in danger from the flood. The east road went north to the village where he'd once lived but, in the southerly direction, led away from the town. He'd need to cross a bridge from east to west to get to the road that ran directly into the town.

He camped beside the road that night. He'd only gone ten miles today. The trail from his camp was rugged, and travel was slow. Now, he could follow the roads the rest of the way to the town. He had to travel about 70 miles from here to reach the town and hoped to make it in two days.

He could see the fires from the survivors' camp across the river. There was no wind this evening, and the smoke settled in the low areas near the river. He wondered if he could convince Vicki's group to move to the town. He'd have to convince them that the COVID-24 virus was dead.

The next morning, he was off and running, literally. The wheel on his litter worked well, and he maintained a good pace. He was carrying a week's worth of supplies on the litter, which was heavy but easily managed. He focused on the Now and absorbed Chi to fuel his steady pace.

It was strange traveling on the roads. There were no cars anywhere. When COVID-24 started killing people, everyone headed home and locked themselves inside, but it was too late. The virus had already spread too far and wide, and they couldn't escape it.

The land grew flatter as he headed toward the lake. He saw more open fields overgrown with grass. Occasionally, he saw cows and horses grazing on the grass. It was fortunate that Jill knew how to take care of livestock. Having cattle for food would make the winter more easily managed.

Just after lunch, he crossed the creek that had swallowed Jill, but this time, he used a bridge provided by the road builders. There was a sign designating it as Sloan's Creek. He was only about three miles downstream from where he'd rescued Jill. It seemed so long ago.

As the sun set, he stopped beside the road to camp for the night. He made a fire and cooked some freeze-dried chicken and rice. As he rested, waiting for sleep, he thought of Jill. What would her new body look like? Would she be happy with it? He hoped so. He could hear the river in the distance. It wasn't as loud as before, now that the flood waters had receded. The sound of crickets and frogs helped him drift off to sleep.

The following morning, he was up and traveling on the road again. If he'd planned correctly, he'd arrive in the town before dark. He was thankful that the weather had been good. He encountered several light showers, which felt good and helped to keep him cool.

Late in the afternoon, he saw the town as he reached a crest in the road. He worried that some natural disaster, other than the virus, might have occurred there. Fortunately, it seemed untouched, nestled up against the large lake, which appeared to be about five miles across.

The town was creatively called Lakeside, probably because it was on the side of a lake. It was a summer resort town on Indian Lake with about one thousand permanent residents, but its size swelled during the summer months. Many summer cabins were spread around the shore of the lake, but this town was where everyone came for food and fuel during their vacation. Some permanent residents had long ago built beautiful Victorian-style homes west of town overlooking the lake. It was your typical quiet, peaceful summer resort town.

He decided to camp on the outskirts of the town and wait until morning to enter. Some survivors might have been brave enough to move back in, and he didn't want to surprise anyone living there after dark. He wanted to arrive in bright, sunny conditions.

As he sat by the fire that night, formulating a plan to explore the town, he sensed a presence outside his camp. He sent a calming, friendly emotion into the Chi, and slowly, a horse walked out of the dark toward his campfire. He could see the fire reflecting in the eyes of other horses that remained beyond the camp. He got up, approached his visitor, and stroked its neck. It seemed to enjoy his touch like it was something enjoyed from a previous time. John was glad that there were horses still living near the town. He was sure that Jill would be happy, too. To survive, they would need all the help they could get.

The next morning, he loaded his day pack with food, water, and medical supplies. He headed straight for the lake and the docks. The streets were empty, and he only occasionally encountered a human skeleton. Human bodies decompose rapidly when they aren't embalmed, and after almost a year, no soft tissues are left, only bones. There was a musty smell in the town, and he didn't know if it was from the skeletons or whether he was just used to the fresh air of the valley.

When he got to the docks, he found boats still tied to their moorings. Many were dirty after a year of no maintenance. A few had sunk into the water, but most looked like they could be used again. Of course, there might not be any fuel to run their engines. Eventually, the survivors would run out of the limited fuel, and the boats would become useless. As he looked around, he saw a few rowboats and sailboats that would be useful for a longer time.

He found an empty fuel drum and started banging loudly on it with a piece of steel, hoping that the noise might attract anyone alive in the town. He sat down to eat his lunch and waited to see if he received any response. After an hour, he concluded that he was alone in the town.

He started walking through a residential area. All the houses looked habitable. He tried to enter several of them, but their doors were locked. Finally, he tried a door, and it opened. He yelled inside, but no one responded. As he entered, he immediately saw why. In a chair in the front room was a skeleton with clothes hanging on it. It was depressing to realize that this person had sat down, knowing they'd never get up again. He looked around the house and found some canned goods in the pantry. Most of them should still be edible.

He next headed into the downtown area. There were a few broken windows; most storefronts appeared dirty but intact. He found a store with an unlocked door and went in. It looked like it had been ransacked, and most shelves were bare. He tried the light switch and found that there was no electricity.

As he continued down the street, he came to the main square, the center of the town. There, he found what he'd been looking for: a library. It was a big building, and when he tried to open the front door, it was locked. He walked around to the back and found a closed window, which was not locked. He climbed inside.

From his pack, he brought out a hand-cranked flashlight. He cranked it for 30 seconds and switched it on, and a bright beam of light cut through the gloom. The library was extensive, and the rows of books were dusty but appeared to be in good order. This was a great find. The survivors could learn any skill from these books they didn't already have.

At the end of the day, he figured that he'd seen enough. This would be an excellent place for the survivors to live since there was a lot of food and houses. His next task was to see if he could convince the survivors to move here.

He returned to his camp and settled in for another night. He built a big fire and stayed up late, hoping that someone would be around to see it, but no one ever arrived.

He had trouble falling asleep. His mind was racing with all the actions that would need to be done if the survivors moved into the town.

There were close to a thousand houses and buildings. Each structure probably held items that the survivors could use. The private homes had still-edible canned food and tools. Some of the businesses had been looted, but others still might have items that they would need.

The natural instinct of the survivors would be to become looters. They'd gone without so many basic things for so long. Now, all those things were free to take. They belonged to no one. Would fighting over the spoils break out? Would it become a town of mob rule? He was determined that, as Marshal, he would not let that happen.

The survivors' leaders needed to prepare them for the bounty they'd find as they entered the town. They could only ask them to stay civilized and act together to help the group survive. John didn't know if that approach would work, but they could only try.

The next morning, John started retracing his route back to the north. It would take two days to reach the survivors' camp. Rain showers increased as the day wore on, and the building clouds looked heavy with rain. When he reached the place where he'd camped during his trip to the town, he stopped and reused the campsite.

After dinner, heavy rain started, forcing him to retreat to his tent. As he lay there, listening to the drumbeat of the rain on his tent, his thoughts returned to something Don had said. "There will be issues that arise between those of you with long lives and the survivors with a normal lifespan." John started thinking about those issues.

As one of his sons married a "normal" survivor, that son would watch as his wife aged, and he didn't. The son's longer-living children would also have to watch as their "normal" mother died. This would be an issue until all the "normal" survivors had died. But there would be "normal" couples having "normal" babies for a while. It might take a hundred years or longer before everyone left alive would be living with an extended lifespan.

This would create two classes of people in the community. There was a danger of "normal" individuals being shunned as inferior. However, life-extended people depended on the "normal" people to preserve humanity. They couldn't mate with anyone else. Both groups were equally crucial for the future, but how could the differences be managed?

Even after all the "normal" people had died, there was another issue arising from the fact that the extended lifespan was shorter for each generation. John realized that his children's lives would be shorter than his. He'd probably live to see his firstborn children die of old age. This would be true for all new parents of life-extended children.

Don was right. There were complicated issues with this extended lifespan. Those with extended lifespans would become obvious as "normal" people grew old and died. The "normal" people would feel betrayed by the people with extended lifespans if they tried to hide this fact from them.

John thought the best solution would be to tell the truth at the beginning. Tell everyone about Don and his involvement in preserving humanity from extinction. Tell everyone why John and Jill were chosen, and explain in detail all the issues resulting from the life extension process. Make sure that the "normal" people understood how important their role was in preserving human life on this planet.

Honesty was the best way to approach the problem. The "normal" people might not believe John and Jill at first, but as they aged more slowly, they would understand why. It would then be evident that John and Jill had been honest with them from the beginning. But John had promised Don not to discuss Don's involvement in this valley. Would Don allow them to talk about him once he was gone?

John was growing tired and needed some sleep. Tomorrow would be another long day of hiking.

17

John arrived at the survivors' campsite at the end of the next day. As he approached the sentries, there was no challenge. They gave him a wave and passed him through to the camp. He stopped in the center of the camp and set the litter on the ground.

Almost immediately, Vicki approached him. "Is there a problem?"

"No, ma'am, nothing immediate. You can relax. I'm just here to talk. I'd like to have a meeting with you if that's possible."

"Sure. Let's go to my tent. Please stop with the ma'am. We spent a night together in a tent. Vicki is fine."

She pointed to a large tent nearby. As they entered the tent, John noticed a small folding table and a couple of lightweight lawn chairs. They each took one of the chairs and sat down to face one another.

"Do you have an idea of your future plans?" he asked.

Her face clouded, and she looked down at the ground and said, "The people in this group have drifted in from the surrounding countryside to the west. We've survived so far, but I'm concerned that this coming winter might be difficult. We have some goats, but not enough to feed our entire group. Some of us want to stay here and start chopping down trees to build cabins. The ground is flat and fertile, so we might be able to grow some crops next spring. It seems like a good place to start over if we survive the winter. Do you know of any alternatives?"

"Actually, that's why I'm here. I've been talking to many people coming into this valley. They reported seeing many dead people in the towns that they passed by. They were too scared to enter the towns for fear of catching the virus."

Vicki added, "Yeah, we noticed the same thing. That's why we don't go near any of the towns or cabins in the area."

Don told John that his species had neutralized the virus, but he couldn't tell her. He had to create a plausible story. He had to lie. He didn't like lying, but it had to be done, so he said, "From what I heard about viruses, they don't last forever. They need to have a live host to keep replicating. I traveled to a town about 70 miles south of here to test my theory. I went into the town's library and found a book on viruses. It confirmed my theory that viruses only live three months at a maximum without a living host. I stayed in that town all day, going into houses and finding the bodies of people who had died. They're mostly skeletons at this point."

"And you're not showing any symptoms of the virus?"

"No. This is the fifth day," he lied, "and by now, I should be showing some symptoms. If I'd felt any symptoms, however minor, I would have never entered your camp. I believe the virus has either died out or has changed to a form that isn't harmful to humans anymore."

"That's incredible news. Tell me about the town."

"It's on a large lake with a dock area and fishing boats. It has about a thousand houses that mostly seem to be in good shape. There are canned goods and tools that should be useful. Its library has books to teach you skills you don't already know. It might be a good place to move your people for the winter."

"70 miles is a long distance to move my group. We have women with babies and some older people."

"I've got an idea that may help. The population of the town seemed to have died quickly. Many cars and trucks could be used if we can get them running and find fuel for them. You won't need much fuel to travel 70 miles. I'm sure you'll find enough in the town from the many automobile fuel tanks and gas stations. Do you have people in your group who have automotive skills? If so, you could first send them to the town on foot. They could get some trucks running and return to transport the rest of your group to the town. I've traveled the road between here and the town, and it's in good shape."

"That sounds like a good plan. Are you sure that the virus is dead?"

"I'm sure. But there may be another problem. How would your people react when entering a town full of items they thought they'd never have again? Would it cause looting and fighting among the survivors?"

"There shouldn't be a problem if you're there as the Marshal to enforce order. After my rescue, you have built a reputation and respect, at least in my camp. I don't think anyone would dispute your orders.

"Overall, it sounds like a good plan. Not bad for a kid," she said with a smile. "I noticed that you never seemed to include yourself in our plans. Are you going somewhere?"

"I'll help, but not initially. It seems that the only people to have survived the COVID-24 epidemic have formed into two groups. You're one group, and there's another group across the river to the north. That group has established a sort of village and started building log cabins. These two groups, totaling about 100 people, could be the only survivors of humanity left in existence in this area."

"That's hard to believe - most of humanity killed by the virus epidemic. So, what are you proposing?"

"I think the best chance of survival for all of us is if we join the two groups and move to the town for the winter. With two groups, we have a better chance of having someone with the skills we need to survive. We need people who know boating, fishing, farming, and livestock management. We need people with medical skills and engineering skills. The more skills we bring together, the better our chance of survival."

"I agree with you. But can it happen?"

"I think it can. The most difficult part of merging the two groups will be creating the right leadership. Each group will want their leader to lead the new combined group."

"Well, I'm certainly willing to step down. These last months have really been stressful. How about you? You're young, but everyone seems to respect you. You already are a leader by default because you're the Marshal in this area."

"No, I don't want to be your leader. I want to propose another solution. Throughout history, solitary leaders have let their egos take us into war after war. Now, we have an opportunity to change things since we're starting over. What if we select four leaders from each group to form a sort of council when we merge the two groups? This council will debate any decisions before they're put into effect. You could be one of those council members. We don't want to lose the wisdom you have gained from helping your group survive. This would also relieve a lot of the stress that you're under. I could be a ninth council member as a tie-breaking vote if needed."

"You seem to have so much more maturity than your years. I need to present this idea to my group of survivors. If we approve of it, what are the next steps?"

"You should select your council members and start planning as a group. The sooner you use group decisions to guide you, the better it will be. Then, form your first exploratory team to go to the town and try to get some vehicles running. Follow the plan and get your people moved to the town.

"Your people need to understand that we're joining together two groups to form just one. We will settle in the town as the last surviving humans. The people from the village should be welcomed as equals. They'll be implementing the same plan for relocating their people but may be on a different schedule. Each group must work with the other, regardless of who arrives first. We must learn to work together as one group if we are going to survive."

"It's late. Will you stay for a meal? I want my people to get used to having you around."

"Yes, I'd like to meet as many as I can. I'll cross the river and head to the village tomorrow morning. The people from the village won't come this way when they travel to the town. They'll use the road on the other side of the river and cross 20 miles downstream, where there's a bridge. The only place where your paths may cross will be south of the bridge or in the town."

Word had spread quickly about John's presence in the camp. Vicki met with her survivors, who voted to go to the town. Four council members were also selected at that meeting, and she introduced them to him. The meal turned out to be more of a celebration. This group of survivors felt that, for once, there was a future that they were excited about. They had something to look forward to.

The next morning, as John was ready to leave, Vicki approached him. "So, will I see you next in the town?"

"Yes, but it won't be right away. After meeting with the village group, I must pick up my new wife before we go to the town."

"I didn't know that you were married. You're so young, and with the virus killing so many, I assumed that you were single. You traveled with Jill before. Will she be coming with you?"

"No, not at this time. It will be just my wife and me."

"I'm looking forward to meeting her, so I guess I'll see you in the town. As we discussed earlier, it's important that you arrive in the town as soon as possible. We need our Marshal to keep things orderly. I feel bad asking that you shorten your time with your new wife. Will she agree?"

"I'll have to discuss that with her."

She laughed and said, "You're very smart for such a young man."

18

The next morning, John crossed the river once again. Wading through the river was happening more often than he liked. He hoped this would be the last time for a long while.

He reviewed the previous day. He thought that convincing Vicki's collection of survivors would be easy. They'd just arrived and started settling down near the river. The village, with the other survivors, might be more difficult. They'd already started building cabins and had accepted their location as their future home. It might be too much to ask them to pick up and move again.

Vicki had exposed a wrinkle in his original plans. When Jill returned, he hoped to get to know her as his wife—a honeymoon. But as Vicki had pointed out, he needed to be in the town before the survivors arrived in larger numbers. His presence as Marshal would ensure that everyone worked together … or else. The survival of humanity was at stake.

Hopefully, he wouldn't be doing much law enforcement work. His presence and reputation should be enough. He just had to convince Jill to postpone their honeymoon.

After crossing the river, he headed to the higher ground where he and Jill had camped before. When he reached the road, he set up his litter and headed toward the village at a fast pace. He had about 20 miles to go and hoped to get there by noon.

* * *

When he arrived at the village, he immediately sought out Rob, the village leader.

As they shook hands, Rob said, "Hi, John. This is the second time in 5 days. What brings you to our little village this time?"

"I've been scouting around the valley the last couple of days. I thought that you might want to know what the situation is."

"Great. Let's go into my cabin, and I'll get you something to drink."

The cabin had only two areas: one functioned as a living area and the other as a sleeping area. A blanket hanging from a wire separated the two areas. Rob's wife, Judy, greeted John as they all sat at the table.

"John, I've missed you. We didn't get to visit last week when you were here. Where's your friend Jill?" asked Judy.

"She's not with me today."

"So, where have you traveled recently?"

"Oh, all over the valley. I found another group of survivors camped on the other side of the river south of here. That group has about 50 people who just arrived in the valley. They arrived from the west and are still living in tents. I've talked to many people across the valley, and it appears that this new group and the people in your village are all that have survived the COVID-24 epidemic. I've heard of no other people surviving outside of this valley."

"Have you traveled outside of the valley?" Rob asked.

"Not myself, but I've talked to many people entering the valley from outside. They all tell the same tale. There appear to be no survivors in the cities or surrounding countryside. The virus hit fast and hard. The only people who seemed to have survived were those living outside the civilized world. I don't know why we were spared," John was lying again. They'd survived because they were the last to get infected by the virus before Don's species neutralized it.

"So, have you come to stay with us for a while?" asked Judy.

"No, ma'am, I can only spend the night here. I must head back to my camp in the morning and collect my wife."

"Your wife! Judy exclaimed. "You have been busy since the last time we saw you."

"Yes, ma'am," John smiled with a big grin. "I've met a wonderful woman and will marry her the next time we meet."

Judy, always eager for the details, asked, "You said woman like she's older than you. How old is she?"

John had slipped up. Today, in his mind, she was an older woman. He had to recover quickly.

"I know better than to talk about a woman's age," he laughed, and Rob laughed too. "You'll have to meet her for yourself. Let's just say I think she's close to my age."

"So, how did you meet?" Judy continued, looking for more details.

"She came into the valley from outside and happened to fall into a creek. I pulled her out, gave her CPR, and we've been together ever since. She's special, and I've grown to love her."

"So, she fell for you first, even if it was into a creek," said Rob, laughing at his own bad joke.

Judy and John laughed politely, rolled their eyes, and both groaned.

"His jokes haven't improved over the last couple of months," John said.

"Well, enough of the small talk." Rob continued, "If you're only here for one night, there must be an important reason for your visit."

"There is. I've come to believe the viral infection is over, and it's safe to enter the cities and towns again. As a matter of fact, I've been to a town 90 miles to the south and felt no ill effects. I've told this to the group of survivors on the other side of the river, and they've decided to move their camp into the town. Both groups need to join and become one if we want to survive. I'm here to ask your group to join us and move into the town."

John then gave him the details of his trip into the town and made a case for why it would be easier to survive in the town by the lake. He also reviewed the plan to try to get vehicles running and make the move easier.

John continued, "I know that you're getting settled in this village, and some people may want to stay. That's OK. They'll be welcomed if they change their minds and show up in the town later. This isn't an all-or-nothing proposition. Those who don't have cabins yet and would like to move into an existing home by the lake are welcome to head toward the town.

"There's one stipulation, though. Those in your village must join those in the other group. People living separately won't be tolerated. I know this may sound harsh, but we must learn to live together as one group to survive."

"I don't know how everyone will react," Rob said. "Your offer of a home with furniture on a lake will convince many immediately. Our life here is difficult, but I can't decide for everyone."

"Take your time to decide. If you decide to head to the town, first send a small group that knows how to get some trucks working. Then they can come back for the rest. They'll probably meet the other group in the town who are already working on this same plan. It's important to encourage the joining of the two groups to work together on one plan."

"You have convinced me, at least. So, will I meet your new wife in the town?"

"Yes, you will. I hope that you'll like her as much as I do. She has some medical experience; we'll need those skills in the new town.

"Changing the subject, I'd like to go and see Fred and Willie, the soldier and the boy I sent your way. Are they still collecting berries, or can I find them around the village?"

"Fred is working with the group building the new cabin. You'll find him there, and as I said, Willie won't be far away. I'll get busy organizing a group meal tonight. Those who don't know you should meet you before you leave tomorrow."

As John approached the new cabin being built, he easily recognized Fred, the tallest man in the group. Fred seemed to be offering advice to others rather than doing any lifting himself. John guessed that he was still hurting from his broken ribs. When Fred saw John, a big smile spread across his face.

"Master Smith," he greeted him with respect. "How are you?"

"Please, Fred, just call me John. I'm not here on official business.

"You seemed to have settled in here nicely, according to the reports I've received. I'm only here for the day and will head out in the morning, so I wanted to stop by and see how you were doing."

"I'm doing fine, and I wanted to thank you for allowing me to prove myself. I'm glad that I'm able to help people now. And you were right; I do like Rob. He's not bad for a Navy man."

"You're a good man and can make a good life with these people," John replied. "I think that there may be some kind of feast tonight. I hope to see you there."

At that moment, Willie came running up. The change in his appearance was surprising and pleased John. Someone had cut his hair, he had newer clothes and had gained some weight. He definitely had taken a bath since John last saw him. He looked good and now had a smile on his face, but deep down, John could still feel the guilt and sadness.

"Marshal Smith, I got Fred here safely," he said. "Fred and I built a litter, and I pulled it here by myself."

"That was a big job, and I'm proud of you. Are you happy here?"

"Yes. There are a lot of guys my age, and we have a lot of fun exploring the woods."

"Well, make sure you obey Fred and stay out of trouble. I'll come after you if you get into trouble, and you don't want that."

"No more stealing for me. I promise."

There was a feast that night. John saw many people he'd known and talked to many new people. He hoped that most of them would choose to move to town. If they could get some trucks running, the move would be easy. Without trucks, it would be a long hike that could easily be made before winter set in. John had done all that he could do. It was time for him to leave.

19

John was taking a different route to his cabin this time. The builders of his cabin had bulldozed a dirt driveway to his cabin. The driveway started from an existing unimproved county road near his cabin. That county road connected to the paved road he'd followed to get to the village. Taking the existing roads was the most direct route when arriving at his cabin from the village. It was also the most accessible route by far. The trip was about 15 miles long, and his litter traveled well, even on the dirt roads, ... until the rain started. The weather, which had been unusually pleasant during the last week, turned nasty, with frequent showers and wind. The resulting mud slowed him down.

He focused on the Now and drew in Chi to support his efforts as he hiked in the rain and mud. It was difficult for John to stay focused on the Now because his mind kept drifting to the future. He'd meet the new Jill soon. What would she look like? Would he still have the feelings for her that he experienced when she was in her old body? Would the new Jill love him? He had all these questions, but when he reached out to the Chi, he only felt warm, happy feelings in his future. He'd trust the Chi to guide him to his future happiness.

He finally reached the cabin late in the afternoon. The rain had increased and was now a downpour. He unloaded his gear from the litter and placed it on the front porch. He stored the litter on the side of the cabin and then walked around the property, checking all the systems. He turned on the electrical breakers for the water heater and space heaters in case he needed heat later.

By the time he finished, he was soaked. Before entering the cabin, he stripped off his clothes on the porch and wrapped a blanket around himself. As he entered the cabin, he turned on the lights since the gloomy day wasn't illuminating the inside of the cabin. It seemed like nothing had been disturbed since he left almost a week ago. For a moment, he thought that he'd caught a scent of Jill remaining in the cabin, but that was probably his imagination.

He decided to grab a snack and sit on the front porch while waiting for the water heater to heat up. It felt good to sit and relax as he watched it rain. It had been a hectic week. He felt that progress had been made in getting everyone together in one place. The town would protect them from the coming winter. John would learn in the coming weeks if the two groups would work together. Actually, it would be his job to make it happen.

His thoughts again went to Jill as he listened to the rain. Would the new Jill look like him? After Don gave him this new body, his ego wanted to see what he looked like in the mirror. He looked different from his old body, even when he was a teenager. This body was tall and lean like the Scandinavians. He saw an Asian influence in his brown eyes. His skin color wasn't white or black, but more olive in tone like that seen in the Mediterranean area. His hair was brown and had a slight natural curl to it. His body seemed to be a blend of all the different races on Earth. That would make sense if Don's species were trying to preserve the best of all that was humanity.

John wondered what it would be like to live for a thousand years with the same woman. Would he ever grow tired of her company? With his first wife so many years ago, life had only improved the longer they were together. They each adjusted their lives to complement one another and ended up living just one life together. A thousand years together? No problem.

The hot shower was wonderful and well worth the wait. It was followed by a hot meal. TeenBoy did his dishes and went to bed.

John slept a solid eight hours without moving. When he woke, the sun was already up, and he could hear the birds singing their beautiful songs. He lay in bed for a while, enjoying the feeling of not having to rush somewhere today. He'd just have to wait for Jill's return. If his estimate of his own body transfer time was correct, she should return today or tomorrow. He hoped for today.

It suddenly occurred to him that he should clean the cabin to prepare for her in case she returned today. It wouldn't do to bring his new wife into a dirty cabin. That meant that he had to clean the toilet, too! Yuck! He jumped out of bed and decided to start his cleaning chores after breakfast.

It took him all morning to clean the house. He wanted to impress her, so he was meticulous with his efforts. Every surface was wiped down, and the floor was vacuumed. He really loved electricity! He hung fresh towels in the bathroom and cleaned the shower. The sheets were washed and hung up on the front porch to dry. They dried quickly, and he remade the bed.

Making the bed brought up something that he hadn't thought about yet. Would they have some sort of marriage ceremony? Would she require it? Who'd officiate it? Or would just a kiss be sufficient? He knew enough about women to know he had to offer her a ceremony rather than assume a kiss would be OK. Women liked those kinds of things. John wouldn't want to start their life together with a serious social miscue.

John found a vase that, of course, he'd never used before. He then set off to collect some wildflowers. He created a beautiful arrangement from the many choices outside the cabin. He included a rose from a rose bush beside his cabin. The rose was blooming, and the smell was intoxicating. He set the vase in the center of the eating table. John thought that he was all ready for Jill to come home.

He made lunch and carried it out to the porch. The air smelled clean and fresh, and the pine trees added their own background scent. The rains had refreshed everything; even nature itself felt energized. The birds were singing, and everything about the day was perfect.

He fell asleep after eating. He didn't know how long he'd been sleeping, but suddenly, he became wide awake with a feeling of expectation. The Chi energy was surging into him. As he looked down into the valley, he saw a sudden flash of blue light, and two figures appeared. One he recognized as Don. The other was a woman. John couldn't see her clearly from this distance but sensed her Chi. It was Jill.

Don steadied her for a moment to give her time to adjust to her surroundings. She then looked toward John and smiled. John waved to her, and she waved back. Don and Jill were having a discussion as they slowly walked toward the cabin. As she got closer, John saw that this new Jill was a tall, beautiful woman. She looked to be about six feet tall, slightly shorter than himself. Her hair was shoulder length, the length most of the surviving women wore. John's heart raced when he looked at her. With her olive-toned skin, she looked like him. Well, she did have some obvious differences that immediately appealed to him.

She saw John admiring her and gave him a big grin.

As Don and Jill arrived at the porch, she came to John and fell into his arms. He enjoyed holding her. He asked her, "How do you feel? Are you OK?"

"I feel great!" she replied emphatically. "Just a little dizzy."

Don spoke for the first time. "That will pass in a few minutes. Your body is waking up and needs time to adjust."

"Maybe we should go inside and sit down," John suggested. "Will you stay for a while, Don?"

"Just a little bit. It seems I have one more duty to perform before I go," he replied.

"Duty? What duty is that?"

"Jill asked me to marry you two. To make it official."

John gave her a big smile. "That's perfect. Now I know what you two were talking about while walking up to the cabin. When you feel rested, Jill, we can move out to the porch again. I'd like to have the ceremony outside, surrounded by all the natural Chi energy."

"I'm OK and ready now. I want to marry you before you change your mind," she grinned.

"I'll never change my mind. My heart is so happy that it hurts. But I have a question for you."

"You want to know how I became so beautiful?" she laughed.

"Yes, that too," he replied with a grin. "But more seriously, what name do you want me to have? I was called Max Everitt in my old life and then became John Smith for my job as Marshal. You only knew me as John Smith, so I could understand that you might want me to continue using that name. I don't care either way, but it might be embarrassing if you called your new husband by the wrong name."

Don laughed and suddenly asked, "Is this your first fight?"

They all laughed together, and then Jill said, "The person I've come to know is that 78-year-old kind and loving person inside the TeenBoy body. That's who I'm marrying. If it's OK with you, I'd like to take your last name as mine and become Jill Everitt. I'm old-fashioned when it comes to marriage names. Besides, John Smith sounds so made-up to me. I mean, really. Couldn't you have come up with something more original than John Smith?"

She looked first at Don and then at John.

"So, you won't be Marshal Smith anymore?" she asked.

"Nope. Marshal Smith has served his purpose. He was someone who lived alone and couldn't have friends. Now, there will be a new Marshal in the valley: Marshal Everitt. But remember, my first priority for the next thousand years is to make you happy and keep you safe."

"I like this new you!" she exclaimed. "You're making me happy already. But now I must have a new name, too. I can't be Jill anymore, or people would find that to be a strange coincidence. What if I use my legal name, Jillian, instead of my nickname, Jill?"

"That works for me," Max replied. "I can't get into too much trouble if I slip up and call you Jill."

With their new names determined, they all moved out to the porch, and Don performed a simple ceremony, which ended with their first kiss. Max was excited to kiss this wonderful woman he'd fallen in love with. There would be so many more kisses in their future. Well, this wasn't actually their first kiss. Their lips had met that first day when John (not Max) had given her CPR. But since she was technically dead, that kiss didn't count. But he'd never forget their first meeting.

With the wedding over, Don indicated that he had to leave. "This will be the last time we meet," he said with some sadness in his voice. "I've truly enjoyed meeting both of you, but now you must continue this new life without me or any help from my species. Let the Chi be your guide, and you'll be OK. Oh, and TeenBoy," he said with a chuckle, "take good care of your new TeenGirl."

"Don," Max said, "I have one last question. I've been thinking about how we communicate to the survivors about our extended lifetimes. They'll notice we aren't growing old, so we can't avoid discussing it. Am I able to tell them about your species' involvement in this? I'd rather tell the truth than make up a lie."

"Yes. You have kept my secret while I've been working in this valley to preserve your species. But now that I'm leaving, I'll release you from that promise. I was careful never to reveal anything about our species or give you information that might compromise our work. You can tell anyone anything you want, and it won't cause any damage to us. Your history is full of stories and myths about aliens visiting your planet. Any story you tell will be watered down and embellished over the coming centuries."

Don walked down into the valley and turned to wave once more. There was a flash of blue light, and he was gone.

"Don called you TeenGirl and not Jill," Max laughed.

She grabbed his hand, smiled, and led him toward the bedroom. "Come with me, and I'll show you why TeenGirl is a much more appropriate name."

PART TWO

A NEW BEGINNING

20

Max and Jillian sat on the cabin porch, basking in the warm morning sun. The deer were back in the valley below, grazing on the grass, and the hummingbirds were drinking nectar from the wildflowers. Max and Jillian's happiness was amplified by the peace existing in the valley at this moment. They'd been married only a few days, but worries from the outside world were already creeping into their lives.

Max explained to Jillian why he had to hurry to the town to keep the peace. As Marshal, it was his job. As the two groups of survivors moved into the town, fights and issues would arise between them. It would be Max's job to ensure the two groups merged peacefully into one. His reputation was such that he wouldn't have to do anything. His presence would keep the peace. She understood but requested a few days to relax and be newlyweds. That time was now over.

The delay was an easy request for Max to agree to because out in his garage was an all-electric SUV. Max had covered it with a tarp when the virus epidemic struck, thinking he'd never need it again. If he could get the car running, their trip to the town would take only hours rather than days. Earlier, he plugged it into the solar array to start charging the battery, and it should be fully charged by now. They should be able to drive 300 to 400 miles before it would need recharging, and the town was only around 100 miles away. Their task today was to pack up the car and drive to the town.

Max had built this cabin as a refuge for when society would

collapse. He'd included solar power, knowing that the electricity would eventually fail. In case some of his solar components failed, he ordered ten extra solar panels and two extra inverters as replacements for his system. The backup components were now going to help them. He could stack the extra panels on the top rack of the car and bring along the inverters. When the battery in the car needed charging, he could set up his own recharging station powered by solar energy.

They'd made a list of what they should take from the cabin to the town. The town should be full of canned food items, so food wasn't necessary. Of course, they included their camping gear and enough food and water for several days. If the car broke down before they reached the town, they'd be on their own. The stack of solar panels on top of the car was rather precarious because of its height. They could travel only at slow speeds and had to watch for low branches so the panels wouldn't be damaged. Max filled the leftover room in the car with various canned goods from his supply building.

They showered one last time and enjoyed a hot meal before setting off toward town. The first part of the trip was the slowest since Max's dirt driveway hadn't been maintained for almost a year. Some ruts needed to be avoided, and one branch had to be cut down. The drive got easier when they reached the county road, but obstacles still needed to be avoided. Because it was a county road, it was constructed with better materials and had held up to the past year of neglect. They traveled only about 25 miles per hour until they reached the paved road.

"Now remember, when we meet anyone else, they'll only know me as John," Max said. "But I'll introduce you as Jillian. It will be confusing for both of us until we reveal our past history."

The paved road allowed faster travel, but because of the solar panels on top of the car, they kept their speed at 30 miles per hour. There was no hurry; safety was the biggest priority. After 25 minutes, they reached the village, and Rob walked over to the car and greeted them with a surprised grin.

"Hi John, that's Max's car; I'd recognize it anywhere."

"Yes," John answered. "When I bought his cabin last year, I also bought his car. This is Jillian, my bride!"

"I'm glad to meet you finally," Rob replied, reaching through the open window to shake her hand. "Are you guys in a hurry, or can you stay? I'm sure Judy would like to meet Jillian."

"No, we can't stay. We don't know how long the car's battery will last, so we'll keep going until we reach the town. Have you selected your advance team to go to the town? We can take them if they're still here."

"They left this morning. You'll probably catch up with them within an hour."

John got out of the car, opened the back door, and said, "Help me unload this canned food from the back seats so there will be room for them. How many are there?"

"There are only three, and Fred is one of them. It will be tight, but they'll all fit in your back seat. Wow! Where did you get these canned peaches?"

John laughed. "They were part of Max's emergency stash in his storage shed. I bought everything from Max, including his peaches. Why don't you spread them around the village and give everyone a taste? There should be enough here to give everyone at least one slice. You can use all this food if you want because there should be more in the town when we arrive."

They said their goodbyes and continued down the road. He hated to rush away like this, but the car hadn't been driven in almost a year, and he didn't fully trust it yet.

"That was strange," Jillian said. "It's like we both have dual personalities. We have to be careful until we can get it all sorted out. How are we going tell the survivors about us, and when?"

"It needs to be done as soon as possible. We must get everyone together at one meeting and tell them the truth, the whole story."

"Will they believe us? It's a pretty crazy story."

"I don't think most of them will. Would you believe our story? We have no proof. We might convince the people who knew us when we were old by relating our experiences with them. It's important to tell everyone, even if they think we're crazy. If we don't tell them and they find out later, they will think we are hiding something from them."

Ahead of them, they saw three people walking. Fred was quickly identified by his height. John honked the horn, pulled up beside them, and stopped.

"Would you like a ride?" John asked.

"Hi John, where did you get the ride?" asked Fred.

"Jump in, and I'll tell you all about it. There's not a lot of room, but it's better than walking. Once you get in, you'll have to put your packs on your laps."

The three hikers climbed in. It was a tight fit, but none of them complained. John introduced Jillian and told the same story about buying the cabin and the car. John knew Fred, of course, but not the other two. Ray was introduced as a former auto mechanic, while the woman, Lola, was a former truck driver. She also had driven school buses in her town. Moving the survivors to town would be easy if they could get a couple of trucks and buses running.

A couple of hours later, they entered the town. They honked the horn to see if anyone from Vicki's camp was already there. Within minutes, two men appeared out of a side street. John knew Red, of course, and the other looked familiar to John. He was a middle-aged Asian man, clean-shaven, with black hair. John thought that maybe he'd seen him in a Hallmark movie.

Red smiled when he saw John, saying, "You have been holding out on us. Is this one of the perks of being the Marshal, or is it your wife's car? We could have used a ride two days ago."

"Sorry," John replied. "I just got it running today. As we drove here, we ran into these hitchhikers. They're from the village up north."

When the introductions were made, the new man was introduced as Kenny. When asked about his skills, he was described as a "Jack of All Trades." He seemed to be able to take on any role as needed.

John asked Red, "What have you discovered? Why don't you give us an update?"

"We just arrived here about four hours ago. Our first job was to find a place to live, and we found some nice homes on the lake to the west of town. We had to remove a couple of skeletons, but the house was in good shape. There was a lot of canned food in the pantry, which was a plus. There's another house right next door that might be a good place for you guys. Our council sent us and two other people, Sam and Mary, who are back at the house cleaning up a year's worth of dust."

John returned to the car and followed Red and the others as they walked down the street to the house. It was a big gray Victorian-style house with an inviting front porch that looked out over the lake. As the car pulled up out front, two people emerged to stand on the porch. Nine survivors now comprised the advance group.

After introductions, Red grabbed some tools and said, "Let's see if we can get inside the house next door. It looks big enough for the five of you."

Red easily defeated the door lock with his tools. John wanted to remember to ask Vicki about Red's past and which side of the law he'd learned that skill from. They went inside to discover the house was empty of skeletons but had a generous coating of dust inside. It had four bedrooms, which gave everyone their own room except John and Jillian. They weren't disappointed with the arrangement.

They all went back outside. It was almost noon, so it was decided that the entire group would get together at Red's house for lunch. Red had said there was a large open kitchen and dining area that could accommodate them all.

Lunch consisted of a variety of canned goods. Everyone shared the bounty so they could taste foods they hadn't eaten in months. After the meal was cleared away, they had their first meeting.

"Well," Fred said to John, "what should we do first?"

"I first want to clarify that this isn't a law enforcement problem, so I'm not in charge. We're equals on this team and must work together to prepare the town for the rest of our group. I'll suggest some actions, but if any of you have a better idea, please speak up. We'll debate all ideas and then come up with a plan."

"OK, I'll start," said Fred. "My Army training says that we must first agree on our goals. We already have our immediate housing and food problems solved. What's next?"

"Well," said Mary, laughing, "using your Army terminology, our 'orders' were to 'secure' transportation for the rest of our group. How do we go about finding the vehicles that we need?"

Red responded, "Maybe the first thing we need to do is split up and get a feel for what's in the town. We must find car and truck repair buildings, gas stations, and schools where buses might be located."

Mary suddenly got up, went to a drawer in the kitchen, and returned with a piece of paper. "I found this town map while searching for a can opener. We can each take a section and see what's there. There are also some pads to record our discoveries."

"There are nine of us," John said. "For safety, we should break up into four teams of two and search in the four directions on the map. I need to unload the solar panels from the car and set up a charging station for the car. Keep your eyes out for any tools and other items that run on batteries. We'll be able to recharge them, too.

"When you form your teams, try to team up with someone you may not know. We need to get to know one another well. Our lives may depend on it."

John unloaded everyone's packs and set them on the front porch. He then got into the car and started driving around the town. He wanted to find a location with good southern exposure and sheltered from the wind since the solar panels would initially not be bolted down.

He finally found the location he wanted; a two-story motel had been built with an enclosed courtyard. The courtyard was sheltered from the wind and big enough for the panels to receive the sun all day. He found an entrance to the courtyard on one side of the motel and started unloading the solar panels. Until he could build a solid frame to hold them, he had to find some way to keep them at the proper angle to receive the most sunlight. He used some lawn chairs and chaise lounges stored in the courtyard and secured the panels to them. It would have to do for now.

His education in electrical engineering allowed him to wire the panels into the inverter. The inverter converted the DC electricity produced by the solar panels to AC electricity that would charge the car. After an hour of work, he was ready to try it. He turned on the inverter and watched it go through its power-up cycle. If anything was wrong, the inverter would detect it. The inverter's status light turned green! They now had solar power to charge the car and any other device with rechargeable batteries.

He plugged the car into the inverter to start charging its battery. He wanted a fully charged battery at all times in case there was an emergency that needed a vehicle.

His walk back to the houses took him through the center of town. As he looked around, he noticed a complex of buildings with a flagpole in front. He walked over to them, and a sign indicated they were the town's office buildings. The buildings included the mayor's office and a clerk's office. He tried the main entrance to the office complex and found that it was not locked.

He walked into the lobby, which had a plaque on the wall listing all the town officials. Under that plaque was a bookshelf where he found what he was looking for: a stack of town maps. He also found a couple of pamphlets listing contractors and businesses in the town. He picked up about a dozen maps and headed back out to the street.

When he arrived at Red's house, he saw that two teams had returned from their scouting trip. Lola and Mary were sitting on the porch along with Jillian and Red. John hoped that Jillian wouldn't slip up when using her new identity. She'd met Red when she was a middle-aged Jill.

Jillian asked Lola how she had ended up at the village. Lola, 30, petite with short dark hair, replied that she drove tour buses during school breaks. It was a way to make extra money and go on great trips. She was driving a group through the mountains when they heard on the radio about the pandemic. Most wanted to return to Crescent City to check on their families, but Lola and a few others left the bus and headed south. When they arrived at the village, they were invited to stay.

When the last two teams arrived, they all entered the house and sat in the kitchen/dining area to disclose what they had found. When everyone sat down, Jillian turned to Ray and said, "Lola told me she can drive anything you can fix. You must be some mechanic."

Ray, who was in his early 40s, was of medium height with wiry hair in dreadlocks. He responded, "I worked in a repair shop with my father and brothers. I can fix anything I can get the parts for. Lola and I make a good team."

Jillian then asked Ray if he had a family. He laughed and said, "Yes, three teenage girls and a wife eager to get here to go shopping."

John then distributed his maps and pamphlets, and the meeting turned more serious.

Each team revealed what they'd seen in their section of town. They'd found a medical clinic, auto repair shops, and hardware stores. Lola had found some large trucks and school buses she could drive. Red had found hand-operated fuel pumps that he knew how to operate. John again had questions about his background. The town had everything they needed.

Now came the hard work. The team needed to prepare about 100 homes for the rest of the survivors. This meant defeating any locks, removing the skeletons, cleaning out the garbage, and stocking them with some food items. There needed to be enough food to get the new residents through their first couple of days until they were settled. The dust removal from the homes would be left up to the new arrivals. One person from each of the two camps would assign a house for each person in their camp. They'd know how big the family was and how big a house was needed.

John started the conversation. "Getting a bus running is high on the priority list. Ray, why don't you start by estimating how long it will take you to get one running?"

"Well, Lola and I found four buses in a servicing depot. One of them looks very new. I must charge its battery, pump up the tires, change the oil, and check the filters to get it running. The biggest problem is that we have no electricity to charge the battery. Once the first vehicle is running, we can use its battery to jump-start the other vehicles to get them started. I also don't look forward to pumping up truck tires by hand. If we had electricity, we could use compressors to pump up tires. We'll also need gas."

"With a full tank, the bus will go over 400 miles", Lola said.

"I think that by the time the maintenance on the bus is complete, I can have the tank full of gas," Red added.

"It appears we need some of your electricity," Jillian told John. "Can they carry the battery to your solar panels at the motel to get it charged?"

"That would work, but truck and bus batteries are very heavy," John replied. "I have a better idea. We need to have our power source on wheels to move it to where we need it. I know how we can do that, but I'd need battery-operated power tools and some lumber. Did anyone see a hardware store in town?"

"Yes," said Red. "Go north on 3rd street, and there's a hardware store with a small lumber yard behind it."

"Great," said John. "I think I can assemble a mobile power source in two or three hours."

"How does such a young kid know how to do all this electrical stuff?" Red asked suspiciously.

John had to be careful with his answer. At this point, his actual age hadn't been revealed. He had over 50 years of engineering knowledge and experience, but this couldn't be disclosed quite yet.

"My father was an electrical engineer and taught me all about electrical systems," he lied and then quickly changed the subject. "So it appears that we'll have the bus to transport people before we have any place ready for them to live. Our limiting factor is how quickly we can get 100 houses cleaned and ready for the survivors. Does anyone have an estimate of how quickly we can have the houses ready?"

Mary said, "There are three tasks to getting a house ready, assuming we won't do the actual cleaning. First, we must remove any remains and put them into a truck for burial later. Second, we need to ensure there's enough food in the house. We need someone to collect canned goods from around town and drop them off at each house. The third task is the awful one. Without electricity, a lot of food will have spoiled, and dead pets may be in the house. We'll need a truck to pick up all the garbage we collect from the homes and transport it somewhere else."

"I'll volunteer to collect and transport the skeletons and garbage," Fred offered. "But I'll need two trucks and another driver."

"I'll volunteer to drive," said Lola.

"I'll help to load the trucks," Red said.

"So, how long will it be before we're ready to transport survivors from the camps?" John asked.

"With the people we have here, I think we could be ready in a week to ten days," Mary said. "Does anyone think it should take longer?"

Everyone agreed with the estimate.

"The survivors in the camps are probably wondering how things are going here," John said. "What if I take the car and visit both camps? I could give everyone a timetable so they'll be ready, and I could bring back four more helpers to add to our team here. The additional help would take some of the burden off your shoulders."

"That's a great idea!" said Red. "To be fair, you should bring two people from each camp. Knowing the tasks, I can give you the names of people that would best fit our needs."

"Why not decide as a team?" John asked. "Currently, we have two teams here, one from each camp. Each team should write a letter to their camp leader indicating whom they want me to bring back. You can also tell them in your own words how things are progressing here. I'll deliver the letters to each of your leaders."

It was decided that John would leave the next morning if the car was fully charged and he had finished building the mobile power station. The other eight discussed how the tasks would be divided among them.

After the meeting, John got into the car and visited the local hardware store. It had a wide selection of battery-operated power tools, so he loaded what he needed into the car. He drove the car behind the store and loaded the lumber he'd need.

When he arrived back at the motel charging site, he first plugged in several battery chargers for his tools. The batteries had all discharged over the last year, so they needed recharging. He next collected four luggage carts from the motel lobby. The carts were built from steel to handle the heavy luggage that travelers always carried. Most importantly, they had large caster-type wheels that would roll in any direction. He used a metal cutting saw to cut off the upper metal bars from the carts. These bars are what people used to hang their garment bags on. He only needed four strong platforms with wheels.

John planned to build two mobile power units, each with five solar panels and an inverter to produce AC electricity. He built two wooden frames to hold the solar panels, angled to collect the maximum sun for this latitude. Since the solar panels were three feet wide, five of them placed together needed a frame at least 15 feet long. A frame this long required two luggage carts to support its weight.

To combine two carts into a single platform, he next built a rectangular frame from 2x4s that was 16 feet long and four feet wide. After nailing a piece of plywood on top of the frame, he now had a platform big enough to hold one of the solar panel frames.

That platform was then placed on top of two of the carts, one at each end of the platform. His platform was now on wheels. After nailing the platform to the carts underneath, he nailed one of the solar panel frames to the platform. All that was needed now was to attach the solar panels to the frame and connect the wiring.

John built another identical rolling platform for the other five solar panels. The platforms were ugly and somewhat unstable, with two separate sets of wheels underneath. As long as they weren't moved quickly, they'd work fine to transport power where needed.

Each platform was wired to work independently of the other, or they could be joined together if more power was needed, such as when charging the car. Behind the panels, on the plywood platform floor, John mounted the inverters and electrical outlets for both 120-volt and 240-volt power. He tested his design by hooking both power units together and plugging them into the car. Everything worked as expected. He also tried rolling one of the units around the parking lot and found that while it worked, two people controlling it would be better. With the caster wheels, the power unit platform tended to want to roll in a direction of its own choosing.

It was getting late, so he moved the power units to collect most of the late afternoon sun and plugged them into the car.

21

That evening was delightful. The sun was almost gone, lighting the sky with red and pink clouds. John, Jillian, and Fred sat on their front porch, enjoying the beautiful sunset over the lake. Ray and Lola had decided to walk down to the docks to check out the boats. The rest of their advance team, staying in Red's house next door, were also on their front porch. John could hear them laughing at someone's story. Fred used this time to clean his rifle as the Army had taught him. John was relaxed, enjoying the evening and thinking about the trip back to the survivors' camps the next day.

Ray and Lola were having fun. They explored the buildings around the dock area and shared ideas on how to get some of the boats working again. They'd walked out on the dock to look at a boat but turned toward the shore when they suddenly heard a growl. A pack of six dogs was running through the boatyard. They saw Ray and Lola and ran onto the dock, growling and barking as they attacked. Ray motioned for Lola to climb onto one of the boats, and he followed. They climbed up a ladder to the Bridge Deck just as the dogs arrived on the boat. The dogs seemed confused by the ladder but were determined not to leave. Ray and Lola were trapped.

Suddenly, John felt fear in the Chi. Ray and Lola were afraid, and they needed help. John jumped up and ran into the house to grab his knife. As he came out, Fred was standing with a concerned look.

"What's wrong?" he asked.

"Ray and Lola are in trouble; bring your gun."

John sprinted down the street toward the dock area with Fred behind him. As John ran past Red's house, he yelled at them, "Trouble at the docks."

The docks were about a half mile from the houses. John quickly covered that distance, leaving Fred behind, and arrived at the docks to find Ray and Lola standing on the bridge of a boat. He raced onto the dock toward them before he realized that a pack of dogs, out of his sight, was already on the boat. When the dogs saw John, they jumped off the boat and came after him.

John had nowhere to go. There was water to his left and right, and he couldn't outrun the dogs. He'd have to fight his way out of this. A moment later, the lead dog leaped into the air, trying to take John down. John's knife struck quickly as he sidestepped the dog's body. He heard the dog's cry of pain and felt blood spurting onto his shirt. The second dog came from the side so quickly that John only had time to avoid its bite. The dog's mass slammed into him, sending him off the dock and into the water. In the water, John had the advantage and quickly dispatched the dog.

Four shots rang out in rapid succession. Fred had arrived with his gun. As John swam back to the dock, Fred was there to give him a helping hand out of the water. Jillian arrived as John lay on the dock, trying to catch his breath. She saw the blood on his shirt.

"Are you hurt?" she cried out.

"No," he replied. "It's dog blood, not mine. Thanks, Fred. You arrived just in time. It seems like you are an expert marksman with that gun."

"Just one of the things they teach you in the Army," he replied with a laugh.

When everyone got back to the house, they had a group meeting.

"We should have expected something like this," John said. "There probably were a lot of dogs in this town that had to survive on their own after their owners died. Everyone needs to be more careful until we can eliminate this problem. Especially while I'm gone, anyone comfortable carrying a gun should carry one. There should be a gun store in town where you can find what you need. Fred can help you select a firearm and teach you how to use it if necessary. If you aren't comfortable carrying a gun, then you should always be with someone who has one. These attacks can be unpredictable, and you should always be prepared, even if it's just an evening walk to the dock."

John then looked at Fred and said, "Even if you think you can take care of yourself, you should never travel alone. Even with my skills, their surprise attack almost got the better of me. I needed Fred's help to fight off the pack."

22

The next morning, Jillian walked with John to load the car. John was taking his full pack and enough food for three to four days. If the car broke down, he'd need to hike back. The rest of the car would be empty so he could bring back another four people.

Ray, Red, and Lola also came to see the newly built power units. John demonstrated how to align them with the sun and turn the units on. He also cautioned them about rolling the platforms too quickly through the town streets. The three of them grabbed one unit and started rolling it toward the garage where the bus was parked. John heard their laughter as they fought with it, trying to gain some control. The power unit seemed to be winning the battle.

As Jillian embraced John, she kissed him lightly on the neck and whispered in his ear. "Come back to me, TeenBoy."

"I will, TeenGirl. I should be back tomorrow if everything goes as planned."

"Right, just like a quiet walk on a boat dock," she laughed.

"Don't get too worried if I'm a couple of days late. I may have to walk back if the car breaks down. You have my promise that I'll come back to you ... always."

John got into the car and headed toward the village. He could drive faster now since he didn't have solar panels on his roof. He planned to stop at the village and then go to his cabin to recharge the car. If the car kept running, this should be a quick trip. He drove without the air conditioner to preserve the battery. Driving on the empty road was strange but relaxing. Without traffic, he was free to enjoy the summer views of the valley.

John arrived at the village in under two hours. The car was a lot better than hiking. As he pulled into the village, he noticed something was wrong. People were racing around, and many were armed. He reached out into the Chi and sensed worry, but no danger. Everything seemed to be as it should be.

Rob saw him arrive and ran over to the car, closely followed by Steve, the father of the baby he and Jillian had delivered.

"You always seem to show up when we need you."

"What's the problem?" John asked.

"The little boy, Freddy, from Steve's family is missing. We searched all morning, and we couldn't find him. Can you use your Chi sensing abilities to tell us where to look?"

John got out of the car and took a deep breath. He welcomed the Chi energy from the surrounding area into his body. He tried to feel where little Freddy was in the energy. He sensed nothing.

"It's strange; I can't feel him at all."

"Does that mean he's dead?" Steve cried out.

"Easy, Steve. There can be many reasons why I can't feel him. While I may not be able to help you, I know someone who can."

John turned to Rob and said, "You remember that I told you about the group of survivors south of here? Their leader, Vicki, was a Search and Rescue member, and she still has her rescue dog with her. Our best chance is to get Vicki and Rex here to help. With my car, I can have them here in an hour."

"Please go," Steve said.

John jumped back into the car. This time, he'll be breaking the posted speed limit. He drove hard and reached the river crossing in 15 minutes. He could see Vicki's camp across the river. He'd thought he wouldn't be using this crossing for a while, which was proving to be wrong. He rushed down the hill and waded through the knee-deep river.

He ran into the camp and received worried looks from many. He saw Vicki and Rex across the camp and ran toward her. When he approached her, she said, "What's the matter? Is someone from my advance team hurt?"

"No. A child from the village is lost. They need you and Rex to help find him. Can you come?"

"Sure. Let me get my camping pack and food for Rex and me."

"That's not necessary. I've got a car on the other side of the river. I can drive you both there in 20 minutes. Just get your day pack."

Vicki looked at John and slowly shook her head. "You never cease to amaze me. I'll be ready in five minutes."

Once Vicki returned, they left the camp and headed toward the river.

John asked, "Can Rex swim the river, or will you carry him?"

Vicki responded, somewhat offended, "Rex is a rescue dog. Of course, he can swim. But I'll carry him because I don't want to live with the 'wet dog' smell for the rest of the day."

They crossed the river and headed up the hill to the roadway above. When they got to the car, Vicki whistled and said, "Nice ride. You wouldn't happen to have a safety harness for Rex, would you?"

"Sorry. I know I'm just a teenage driver, but he'll be safe with me."

"I've learned not to question your abilities."

Rex was given the back seat to himself, and John accelerated down the road to the village. As promised, John had made the round trip in under an hour. As they got out of the car, Rob, Steve, and a group of others carrying guns ran toward the car.

Vicki saw the guns and said, "I thought this was a rescue operation, not a manhunt. One rifle is sufficient, but if anyone shoots my dog, there will be hell to pay."

She had her knife strapped to her thigh and a large German Shepherd on a leash, so no one argued with her instructions. She was now in command of the operation.

"I need an article of clothing recently worn by the child," Vicki commanded.

Steve disappeared briefly and reappeared with a shirt.

"Do you have any idea as to where we should start?" asked Vicki.

"He was always fascinated with the river," Steve replied, his voice choking with the implications of that statement.

They headed toward the river, and once outside the camp, Vicki asked Steve for the shirt. She let Rex smell the shirt and said something to him in a lowered voice.

"I want you all to stay behind Rex and me. Stay quiet, don't distract us, and let me know if you see the boy."

Vicki first led Rex back and forth parallel to the river, trying to pick up the boy's scent. They were having no success. She widened the pattern beyond the direct path between the village and the river. Finally, Rex let out a loud bark and started pulling Vicki not toward the river but parallel to it. Rex had the scent!

The boy seemed to be following a game trail. He must have mistaken it for the trail to the river. Instead of leading him to the river, it led him away from any place the searchers would have looked for him. Rex followed the trail for about a mile, where it turned to go around an outcropping of large boulders. At that point, Rex stopped, turned around, and returned to the boulders. He looked toward the boulders, sat down, and barked.

John had finally sensed the boy's Chi. It was very weak but close. John jumped onto the nearest boulder and started climbing. It wasn't steep, and a child could have easily climbed it. As he came to the top of the boulder, there was a crevice between the boulder he was standing on and the next one. As John looked down into the crevice, he saw the boy. He lay at the bottom of the crevice, unconscious, with blood on the side of his head.

Steve had come up behind John and cried out when he saw his son's motionless form. John slowly eased himself into the crevice until he could reach the boy. He leaned against the crevice wall and held the boy in his arms against his chest. He remembered how Jillian had directed so much Chi into healing and wondered if he could do the same. He closed his eyes and whispered a quiet prayer that the boy would live.

John brought his focus into the Now. He felt the Chi energy flowing into him and directed it into all parts of the boy's body. John felt the body warming as the energy worked its magic. After a few minutes, the boy opened his eyes. From above the crevice, Steve gasped and began crying. John passed the boy up into his father's arms and climbed out of the crevice.

"It looks like the boy was climbing in the rocks and fell into the crevice," said John. "He was wedged in and couldn't get out. He's suffering from dehydration but should recover. Somebody give him some water and let me bandage the cut on his head."

The search group gathered around the boy at the base of the boulder while John attended to the head wound. The boy was still dazed but looked better as he drank more water. Steve walked over and gave Vicki a big hug, and he thanked Rex by patting him. Rob had sent one of their group running back to camp to let everyone know the boy had been found.

As they started walking back to the camp, Vicki, Rex, and John were at the back of the group. John stopped, knelt, looked into Rex's eyes, and thanked him. Rex responded with a muted bark and a lick to John's face. Vicki looked at John and smiled.

"I know I said this just an hour ago, but you never cease to amaze me. You're young but more of a man than most men I know."

"Thank you. I was just doing my job. By the way, I need to take my car up to my cabin in the hills to recharge its battery before I can drive you home. Are you OK with spending the night here in the village? I'm sure Rob can fix you up with whatever you need. I also need to update you and Rob on what's happening in the town. We can do that when I return tomorrow after my battery is charged."

"I have a more delicate question. I've noticed that Red has the skills to open any locks we have encountered in the town. I really like Red, but I'm just curious; which side of the law did he learn that skill from?"

Vicki laughed so hard that it caused Rex to look up at her.

"He's a good guy. He told me that he worked in a store selling locks and safes as a teen. The owner, a locksmith, started teaching him all about locks and how to pick them. He got good enough that the owner would send him out on simple service calls. After college, he returned to Crescent City and stopped in the lock store to visit the owner, who had become his friend. When the owner asked him if he had future plans, he said he had none.

"At that point, the owner indicated that he would retire in about five years and wondered if Red wanted to take over the business. He would need training to become a professional locksmith, but it shouldn't take too long. The owner told him he would teach him how to run the business, but that wasn't too hard either.

"So, five years later, Red was a locksmith with his own business, so his skills were obtained through a totally legal process. He helps the police by opening safes and lock boxes. Rex and I have worked with him on some cases."

"I was hoping his story was something like that, but as the Marshal, I had to ask. I like him, and the advance team depends on his skills."

When they got back into the village, Liz was waiting for them. She carried her newborn in her arms. She thanked John as he walked over to peek at the baby. Vicki respectfully kept Rex at a distance from the baby.

"We've decided to name her Jill to honor your friend. I was hoping to have the opportunity to thank her again. She saved both me and my baby's life. Naming our new little one after her only seemed fitting."

"Thank you. Jill will be honored. I'm glad we could help you when you needed it.

"This is Vicki and Rex. They were able to find Freddy and save his life, so he should recover quickly. It won't be long, and we'll all live together in the town."

He found Rob before he left and gave him the letter from his advance team. He told him that he could take two people with him and to have them ready in the morning.

John got back into the car and headed toward his cabin. When he arrived, everything was in good shape, so he started charging the car and turned on the water heater. The car battery was only discharged halfway, so hopefully, it would be charged by morning. He didn't want to risk running the battery down too far. He never knew when an emergency like a lost child might require him to drive farther.

While he waited for the water heater, he made a hot meal and took it to the porch. The deer were nowhere to be seen, but the hummingbirds were active.

He brought more healing Chi energy into the boy than he'd ever directed before. Jillian had shown him what was possible. The Chi, through Jillian, had been his teacher. It was interesting how the Chi worked, as it taught you what you needed to know when you needed it. You just had to learn to trust it.

Before his shower, he walked out to check on the chickens. There were more in the pen than the last time he counted. Once he settled in the town, he would come up with a truck and take them to town. He collected several dozen eggs and planned on dropping them off with Rob when he picked up Vicki and Rex.

Someday, he'd also take down the solar panels and take them to town. He could disassemble the panel support frames and reuse them, too. Soon, this cabin would become just an empty shelter.

The next morning, John checked the car and found it fully charged. He scrambled eggs for breakfast and loaded his stuff into the car. He was careful with Rob's eggs, as he didn't want them broken before he could deliver them. He turned off the water heater and made sure all of the windows were closed. He never locked anything because if someone stopped by and needed shelter, they'd break in anyway.

When he arrived at the village, everything seemed normal for once. He saw Rob, Judy, and Vicki sitting on a log near the road and pulled up near them. Nearby were two other individuals waiting with packs. These must be the two people he'd be driving to town. John went over and sat on the ground near Rex and Vicki. He scratched Rex behind his ears. Rex loved the attention.

He updated them on what was happening in the town, including the wild dog problem, and asked them to prepare their people for the move.

"I'm sending Craig and Pam back with you," Rob said. "They're a married couple and were requested by Fred and the team."

John handed a letter to Vicki. "This is from your team. I can also take two of your people to the town today. I can give them time to prepare since we'll be driving. With these four people helping, we should be able to come and pick everyone up in a week or so."

As they loaded the car with Craig and Pam's packs, John asked Vicki, "Where should we put Rex? Can he ride in the cargo area or the back seat between Craig and Pam?"

"I treat him special. Is it OK with you guys if I sit with him in one of the back seats? One of you can sit in the front seat."

Craig nodded enthusiastically. "I'll sit in the back with him. I'm a dog lover."

"You two sound like you're going to fight over who gets to sit with the dog," John said. "And you call me a kid?"

The trip to the river crossing was short. When they got there, Vicki and Rex got out. John and Vicki said their goodbyes, and Vicki and Rex headed downhill toward the river. She promised her two people would return to the car within an hour.

"Well, Craig and Pam, as you already know, I'm John. So why did your advance team pick you to help them?"

"I think that it was because of my good looks," Craig said and immediately received a punch in the arm from Pam.

"I'm not quite sure," Craig said. "I was a backhoe operator, and something was said about burying bodies."

John explained. "Not quite that gruesome. The bodies have decomposed. We'll be burying the skeletons in a mass grave."

"And Pam, what about you?"

"They needed someone to keep Craig in line," she laughed. "I also am good at organizing things. I think that they want me to help organize the housing assignments. I know most people in the village and even care for some of their children when needed."

True to Vicki's promise, less than an hour later, two people with packs came up the hill from the river. They introduced themselves as Zack and Evelyn. Their belongings were loaded into the car, and John drove toward the town.

23

The moon hadn't risen yet, so the night was dark. Across the lake from the town, Jason had walked away from his camp toward the water. He needed to think. He'd collected seven men who'd escaped the virus epidemic. They'd survived for nine months by breaking into empty summer cabins and stealing whatever food they could find. He'd always sent the young kid into the cabins in case the virus was still contagious. Jimmy wasn't too bright. He appeared to have some mental difficulties but always followed Jason's orders.

Jason and Gary were escaped convicts hiding out in a cabin when the virus struck. Jason was serving two life sentences for murder. Gary was younger and smooth. He was sentenced for running con games on senior citizens. Jason liked him a lot. They'd picked up the other six from an illegal drug operation carried out in the woods. None of the others were upstanding citizens, so Jason got along with all of them. There were two guys with tattoos, an old man who was a driver, a young, stupid kid, and two guys named Tim and Mike. They all did whatever Jason asked as long as he kept them fed.

Now, there was pressure on Jason. He rubbed the scar on his face as he thought about their future. They couldn't stay out here in the woods for another winter. He had to find a place for them to hang out when it got cold. Since the kid never seemed sick from going into the cabins, Jason thought maybe the towns and houses would be safe now. As a boy, he remembered his family coming to a town on this lake to vacation during the summer months. That town should be somewhere on the other side of the lake from here.

As he looked across the lake, he saw a tiny pinpoint of light in the black of the night. It had to be a fire. Without electricity, nothing else could make a light that bright. He could see it flicker as wood was added to the fire. Someone was alive in the town.

As he walked back to their camp, he formulated a plan. It would require deceit and clever planning, but he was good at that.

"Gather round, guys," he said. "How would you like to have all of the food you can eat and be able to stay inside homes during the winter? Since Jimmy has never gotten sick from the virus, I think we can accept that the virus is dead and won't bother us anymore. There's a small town across the lake. Tonight, I saw someone light a fire in the town. Let's hike around the lake and check out the town. We can send Gary into the town first to do some spying for us. Once we know what we're up against, we can create a plan to settle in the town for winter."

A paved road ran around the lake, allowing the summer tourists to access their cabins. They followed the road, and by the end of the following day, they were camped about two miles west of the town. They made sure their campsite was hidden from the town and settled down to wait for Gary to come back with some information.

Ray and Lola were working on a bus in a garage on the outskirts of town. They were having trouble getting it to run smoothly. Ray thought that the problem might be with the spark plugs. He was currently installing a new set he'd found in the garage.

They noticed a man walking down the street toward them. He was a slender man without a backpack with blond hair and a big smile. They stopped their work and walked out into the street to meet him.

"Hi," he said. "My name is Gary. I saw you from a distance and figured it was safe to come into the town. Is the virus dead, or should I run away screaming?"

They all laughed together. Gary was one of those people that you instantly liked.

"You're safe," Ray said. "The virus is dead, and you have nothing to run away from. My name is Ray, and this is Lola."

"I see that you're trying to get this bus running. What do you need with a bus? Lola looks too young to have had enough kids that you would need a bus," Gary said smoothly, causing Lola to blush.

"It isn't for us," Lola responded. "There are a bunch of survivors living up higher in the valley. We need a bus to transport all of them into the town before winter sets in."

"I've been hiking in the wilderness for the last several months. I'm tired of hiking. Is there any chance your group would accept another person willing to work for his food? I don't know if you have room for one more."

"There are only nine of us in town now, and we could certainly use another pair of hands to help prepare the rest of the houses for our group."

Bingo! Gary had the information that he needed. Only nine of them. He was often amazed at how people would so easily tell you anything. You just had to appear to care for them.

"Is it safe here in town? Are there any groups that would bully a gentleman like me?" Gary asked, searching for more information.

"Not a problem," Ray responded proudly. "We have our own Marshal. He's only about 18 years old, but he keeps us safe."

"He must be a good hand with a gun," Gary suggested.

"He doesn't even carry a gun, only a knife," Ray said. Turning to Lola, he asked, "Have you ever seen him with a gun?"

"Nope, never."

"Can I meet your Marshal? I want to form my own judgment if I'll be safe here."

"You just missed him. He headed up the valley to update the rest of our group on our progress. He should be back tomorrow, sometime. I don't think he'll be later than that because he's a newlywed and will be in a hurry to get home."

They all laughed again. Gary thought he had all the information he needed. If they moved quickly, they could take the town and stop the migration from the valley. If the bus was disabled, they'd have no way of getting here. The town would be all theirs.

"As you can see," Gary said, "I didn't break my camp this morning. I didn't expect to be sleeping anywhere new. I need to go back to my camp and pack up. Where can I find your group when I return to town?"

They gave him directions to the two houses where they were staying. It was like they were handing him the keys to the town. This was going to be easy.

Red's dining room was packed again for the evening meal. The advance teams had gotten into a regular habit of eating together at Red's. Ray and Lola had just finished telling everyone about the nice man who'd be joining them. Everyone asked if he could join their team because they could all use an extra hand. Lola said she was surprised that he hadn't arrived yet, but it was still mid-summer, so it would be light for another couple of hours.

Suddenly, four armed men burst through the front door and four more through the back door. Fred started moving toward his rifle but stopped when one of the men shoved a gun in his face. No one else ever came armed to the meals at Red's house. The taller invader with a scar on his face told everyone to stay still. He obviously was the leader as he scanned those seated at the table. He pointed to Fred and told one of his guys to watch him closely. Fred had the bearing of a military guy, and the leader knew it.

The leader then directed his men to search everyone for weapons and to tie their hands.

"It's you," Lola growled, nodding at Gary. "You suckered us into telling you everything."

"Yes, and thank you," he replied. "You made it so easy for us."

"What do you want?" Fred asked.

"Your town," the leader answered. "We need a place to stay for the winter and have decided this is the place."

"But we were here first," Mary objected naively.

The leader laughed, saying, "But only if you can hold onto it, which you didn't. It's ours now, and all we have to do now is reel in the boy you call your Marshal."

He turned and looked at Jillian. "I take it that you're the bride. I'm sure that he'll bring his little knife and try to rescue you. There are eight of us with guns against one boy with a knife. I like those odds. We're going to move all of you to the elementary school. It has a big playground and is more defensible. He won't be able to sneak up on us."

The leader then addressed the group of survivors. "You have a choice, including the Marine here," he said, pointing to Fred. "You can come quietly to the school with us and put your faith in the boy scout coming to your rescue, or resist us, and we'll kill you right now. Your choice."

"I put my faith in our Marshal," Fred said.

The invading group all laughed together.

The leader said to Jillian, "Write a letter to your lover. Tell him what happened and where to find us. Tell him to come unarmed, and we'll let the rest of you go."

The invading group again laughed at that last comment. They knew that the prisoners in this room would never be left alive once they had the boy.

Jillian wrote the note and left it on the table. She signed it with eight love and kiss symbols, knowing John would understand. The prisoners were then led away to the school.

The drive with Craig, Pam, Zack, and Evelyn had been pleasant. It turned out that Zack had some experience with diesel engines, so when both Zack and Craig came to town, they had the skills to get some diesel vehicles running. The four new additions to the advance team were excited about being able to join the effort. The fact that they'd now be sleeping indoors didn't hurt.

As they approached the town, the Chi alerted John of the danger ahead. Something was wrong in the town, so he pulled into an unused parking lot.

"What's wrong?" Zack asked.

"I don't know. The other members of the advance team are in danger."

"Do you have any guns in the car? We can help," Craig replied.

"No. It's better if I go alone. You guys stay here. If I'm not back by dark, turn the car around, drive back to the village, and tell them what happened. Don't come after me. You'll just be in the way."

John left the car and started running toward Red's house. At this time of day, everyone should be there.

He approached Red's house with caution. He didn't sense any

presence there, but he wanted to be safe. The back door was wide open. He quietly slipped in to find the house empty. A letter on the table had Jillian's handwriting and gave the details of what had happened the previous evening. This gang made a wise decision to choose a location that was difficult to approach. She'd signed it with eight love and kisses symbols. She never used those symbols in her notes to him. It could only mean one thing. He had eight adversaries to overcome.

Jillian had been separated from the others in the advance team. She was kept in one of the classrooms and always under guard. The person guarding her varied as they took shifts. There were two men with tattoos who never talked at all. They had dark skin, looked like brothers, and seemed like hard men who may have killed before. They scared her.

A young boy guarded her sometimes. He had a maniacal laugh and seemed like he could be dangerous because he didn't care about anything. He just did things for the fun of it, which she thought probably included killing her.

Her fourth guard was an older man. He talked to her often as if he needed to unburden his conscience. He poured out his life story to her when no one was around. Before the virus, he'd been involved in the manufacturing of illegal drugs. He was a driver who'd deliver the final product. He first got involved in the drug trade because of his addiction. The haze brought on by the daily drugs helped him get through life without facing any of the realities of his actions.

When the virus hit, they quit making the drugs because they couldn't buy the ingredients they needed. He was forced into stopping his drug habit "cold turkey." It was a difficult time. He considered killing himself, but Jason helped him to survive until he was over his addiction. He owed everything to Jason, the leader of the people holding her.

He talked about his life and all of the bad things he'd done while under the influence of drugs. He seemed sad now that he could see all the pain he'd caused others. Jillian didn't think he'd stay with this group of men if he had any other choice. But there was no other choice. She wondered if maybe he was thinking about suicide again.

They had her sitting in a chair with her hands tied behind her back. The old man would let her get up to stretch her legs, but none of the other guards did.

Jillian drew in more Chi to help her endure her captivity. She tried to sense if John was near, but he was not. She was alone for now but knew he'd come for her. He always did.

She knew she had to become a warrior like him if she was going to survive. She had a taste of what it felt like to use the Chi to heal, but she had no idea how to use it to defend herself. John described how the Chi communicated the moves of his adversaries before they made them. He was able to act before they did. She sent a silent prayer into the Chi, asking to be taught that skill. She didn't know how it would help her while being tied to a chair, but it was the only thing she could do.

She focused on the Now and increasing the level of Chi in her body.

It was lunchtime. They hadn't fed the prisoners and had given them very little water. It didn't matter since they would be dead soon. Jason had placed Jillian alone in one classroom while the other prisoners and most of his men were in a room next door. He wanted to make sure that the kid wouldn't try anything, knowing that any disturbance would cause his wife to be executed immediately. He had the old driver standing guard with the girl since he needed his younger men to help subdue the Marshal. The guard had instructions that she should be killed if he heard any disturbance.

About noon, one of his men came running into the room where the prisoners were being kept.

"A boy is walking across the playground with his hands up."

Jason replied, "Search him and tie his hands. Then bring him here with his friends."

John was met at the school door by two well-armed men. They each carried a rifle and had a semi-automatic handgun tucked in their belt. He put his wrists together and extended them in front of his body. He sent out energy into the Chi that he was not a threat and they had nothing to worry about. They tied his hands in front of him and searched him. They found his knife tucked in his waistband under his shirt, as he'd expected. It made them even more confident and relaxed as they led him into the school with one man in front and one behind.

As they entered the room, John saw seven advance team members tied up and sitting on the floor. They were all crowded into one corner. Two men were guarding them; one was very young and had a wild look of excitement in his eyes. Two other men with tattoos stood on the other side of the room. They also had guns pointed toward John. One man with a scar was standing alone and holding a revolver. That was seven. One man was missing.

One of John's guards threw John's knife onto a nearby table. "He didn't come unarmed like we told him to."

"That's OK," the leader laughed. "I didn't expect him to."

"So, your name is John Smith," the leader said with a chuckle. "I knew a lot of John Smiths in prison. They usually were trying to hide something. Are you hiding something? I want to let you know that your pretty bride is being held in the next room. One of my men has a gun on her. If you cause any trouble, she'll die instantly."

John increased the flow of Chi into his body. He now knew his eight targets. He reached out and could feel Jillian in the next room, strongly radiating Chi's energy. He could also feel the other person in the room with her. His Chi was weak and radiating fear and dread. He knew this leader was enjoying his power and control over everyone in the room. He also knew that once the leader grew tired of this game, he'd give the command to have all of the prisoners killed. John had to act before that happened.

John's hands were tied in front of him, but he could still hold a handgun. He first stepped back to knock the rifle in his back to one side and spun around to face the man. He reached forward and grabbed the semi-automatic handgun from the man's waistband. His first two shots hit the men in front and behind him. He spun and fired two more shots, taking out the men guarding his friends. The two shooters with tattoos both fired at John, but he spun again to avoid those bullets. Two more shots from John, and the two shooters with tattoos went down. One more spin to avoid a bullet fired by the leader, and then John fired one shot and hit the leader between his eyes. It was then that John heard a shot fired from a gun in the room next door. Without hesitation, John faced the wall between Jillian and himself and fired one more bullet. That bullet passed through the two layers of sheetrock that made up the wall, exited the wall, and entered the ear of the man on the other side. The man died instantly, but was John too late? Had Jillian been shot?

Jillian could feel John now. He was close. The old man was guarding her now. He seemed conflicted. She focused on the Now and kept filling herself with Chi. John had taught her to relax and trust that the Chi would guide her actions. Jillian heard the shooting begin in the room next door. She focused all of her attention on the man holding the gun on her. Her intuition told her he was going to shoot her. He hesitated for a moment and then raised the gun and fired. Jillian was already moving when the gun fired. She threw herself and the chair to one side, falling to the floor. The bullet hit the wall behind her with a thud. It was all that she could do. His next shot would kill her quickly.

John grabbed his knife from the table and cut his hands free. He then raced to the room next door. As he opened the door, his heart sank. He saw an older man lying on the floor with blood on his head. Jillian, still tied to a chair, was lying motionless on the floor. He was glad that he couldn't see her lifeless face. He didn't want that to be his last memory of her. He cried out in anguish as tears rolled down his cheeks. His heart hurt.

"Don't cry, TeenBoy, I'm OK," came the words from the floor.

She was alive! He raced over, cut her free, and pulled her up into his arms. They kissed passionately and held each other close.

"Finally, you got here on time to save me, TeenBoy."

"Third time is a charm, TeenGirl. Come with me. There are seven people tied up in the next room. They may want me to cut them loose instead of standing here kissing you."

They moved into the next room. It wasn't pretty. There were seven bodies spread around the room, and blood was everywhere.

John walked over to his friends and used his knife to cut them free.

"I didn't know you knew how to use a gun," Fred said. "You shot that gun like an expert marksman."

"I never said I couldn't shoot," John said. "I just don't like guns. They are too noisy."

"As a military man, I have to ask. How did you know to take the shot to save Jillian as your last shot? Weren't you afraid that at the sound of your first shot, the man in the other room would kill Jillian?"

"I let the Chi guide me. I had to trust it would guide me to a successful ending."

"I may have helped a little," Jillian said with a smile. "I was tied up. The only thing I could do was to ask the Chi to help me. I projected a feeling of 'no need to hurry' toward the man holding the gun. When the shooting started, he hesitated for a second before he shot. It could also have been that he was old and didn't like the idea of killing a teenage girl. The Chi told me when to hit the floor, and John's shot saved me."

They all left the school and started walking to their homes. Everyone was moving slowly; they were still recovering from being tied up for so long.

"I left four people in my car at the edge of town," John said. "They must be wondering what happened. I'll go back to the car and drive them to the houses. Do we have a place for them to stay?"

Yes," Mary said. "Their house is next door to ours."

24

John walked back to the car. He found everyone sitting outside wherever they could find a place to sit. He filled them in on the events at the school and told them that a house was waiting for them in town.

"Is this type of event going to be common?" asked Craig.

"I don't think so," John answered. "There just aren't that many people left alive. Once our whole group is moved into town, it will be much more difficult for a small group like this to take over the town. We'll have safety in numbers."

"But it looks like I'll have some bodies to bury right away," said Craig.

"I'm afraid so," John replied.

They all got into the car, and John drove them to the houses. Along the way, they saw several houses with bags of trash placed at the curb. John saw that the advance team had made good progress while he'd been gone. The entire advance team was in Red's house eating and drinking. They hadn't had much to eat in almost a day. They talked among themselves, trying to decompress from the last 24 hours. When John entered the front door, the exchanged greetings appeared more sincere. They were all happy to be alive and to greet old friends again. More food was provided for the newcomers. Red's dining area had become crowded, but no one complained.

After eating, Mary took the new people to their house. She'd found time to quickly clean it to make it more welcoming. Everyone decided to meet in the morning for breakfast for a status update on the preparations for the survivors.

The next morning, the planning began. Ten houses had been prepared while John was gone. The houses for families with kids were chosen to be near the school and playground. Ray and Lola had two of the buses running, along with one large open-bed landscaping truck that would be used to collect the trash. Everyone decided that the first priority would be to clean up the mess at the school. Fred and Craig volunteered. Fred said that he'd seen death up close before and could handle it. No one asked for any details. Ray told Fred where he'd find the truck and that it was full of gas, thanks to Red.

"What are we going to do about water?" asked Jillian. "Does my electrical wizard of a husband have any ideas on moving water for 100 people from the lake to the homes?"

"I don't know," John answered. "I need to go check out the town's water system. With some solar panels, I might be able to get some water pumps running. If I shut off some of the underground water valves to the unused streets in town, I might be able to get some limited water flowing into the homes."

"You'd be our hero if we didn't have to use buckets of water to flush the toilets," Mary said. "Will the sewers continue to work without electricity?"

"Sewers usually work by gravity," John replied. "I'll try to figure out the sewer system for the town after I get us some water. Has anyone determined where we can take the skeletons? We must bury them respectfully."

"I found a farmer's field about two miles north of town," Red replied. "We can place them there today, and when we get a backhoe working, we can bury them later. It would also be a good place for the bodies from the school."

"Zack and I will work on getting a backhoe," Craig said.

"I want you all to know that the car is available for anyone to use if needed," John said. "Everyone must remember to keep the battery charged after we use it. But please, let's avoid using it to pick up garbage."

Everyone laughed and got up to start working on their part of the plan. John got into the car. He needed to understand better where the town got its water. He headed uphill, away from the lake, to find the source of the town's water. He reached a point where no more houses were built, but a paved driveway continued heading higher into the hills. Electric utility lines followed the driveway. At the end of the driveway, he found a city-size water tank secluded behind a hill with an accompanying pump house.

John found a wrench in the pump house and banged it against the metal water tank. The ringing echo indicated that the tank was empty. Next to the pump house was a well. It appeared that the town had drilled a well for their water and pumped it into the tank. Since the tank was higher than any place in the town, the water from the tank used gravity to supply the town with water. This was great news. If he could get the pump running, he could refill the water tank and supply water to the town.

He first needed a diagram of the water mains for the water system. That would be located in the water department, housed in the complex with the mayor's office. Something had caused the water tank to run dry after the electricity failed. Someone might have left a water tap or a bathtub faucet open. Whatever the cause, John had to find shutoff valves under the streets to isolate the problem.

The water department didn't get a prime location like the mayor's office. It was located at the back of the town offices. When John entered the water department office, he found a skeleton in an office. Someone had decided to keep the office open to the very end. He went straight to the flat file cabinets where the large drawings were kept. It didn't take him long to find what he needed. There were drawings of every section of the town showing where the water main shutoff valves under the streets were located. He rolled up one chart that showed the area around the water tank.

He walked out the back door and found three water department trucks sitting in the parking lot. He located what he needed in the back of one of the trucks. It was a special tool that was needed to operate the water valves under the streets. It had a handle about eight feet long and a special fitting on the end to grasp the head of the underground water valve. He took the tool and the map and returned to the town's water tank. The drawing showed that one main valve would shut off the water to the whole city. He turned off that valve.

John returned to the hardware store and collected some heavy-duty electrical wire, a switch, and the tools necessary to wire the solar panels to the pump. The pump was hard-wired to the town's electrical grid, which wasn't working. John needed to break open that circuit and hook in a regular plug with a switch so he could plug the town's water pump into the solar power units.

It was nearly noon when he completed the wiring modifications, so John returned to Red's house. The food was now served in dishes rather than out of the cans—a lovely woman's touch. None of the men would ever understand why it was necessary, but they appreciated it. As everyone sat down to eat, John gave them an update.

"I think I can fully restore the water system if we have solar power. To test my idea, I'll need the help of four volunteers. I've got to get both power units moved to a pump station high on the hill behind the town. I can use the car and some rope to slowly pull the units up the hill. I'll need two people walking with each unit to help guide them. Had anyone planned on using either of the power units this afternoon?"

"I don't think so," Red said. "Those units roll fairly well, but you're right that you need someone to keep them from going off on their own. Are they big enough to power a big water pump?"

"They can, by using the full sun at this time of day. It will be just long enough for me to test my idea. If it works, we'll need to get the solar installation at my cabin and move it down here. It's big enough to power the pump throughout the day. We could dedicate that solar system just for providing water to the town."

The idea of pulling two 16-foot-long luggage cart contraptions up a hill on a rope was humorous enough that everyone wanted to watch or help. Some wanted to go for the laughs, while others wanted to see the cool water tank. Everyone decided to meet at the bottom of 4th Street in one hour. Two teams would roll the power units from their existing locations to 4th Street while John found some rope.

The group gathered at the appointed time. John tied the power units to the car and slowly started up the hill. Not to be disappointed, there were a few hilarious moments when the power units decided to go their own way. The crowd laughed at the men as they chased the power units. One of the bystanders commented on how it was like chasing chickens. After 30 minutes, they finally made it to the water tank.

It took John about five minutes to orient the power units and turn on the inverters. The inverter lights turned green, and they were ready for the test. John tentatively flipped the switch to send power to the water pump inside the pump house. Without hesitation, the pump started humming. Craig put his ear to the side of the tank and reported the sound of water splashing. Everyone cheered!

"How soon until the tank is full?" asked Craig.

"About 40 hours if the pump ran continuously, which it doesn't," John replied. "If the pump ran seven hours a day when the sun is up, it would take five or six days."

"How about a useful answer?" Lola said. "I don't care if or when the tank is full. How long until we can flush toilets?"

Everyone laughed.

"Here is the answer," John replied. "These two power units aren't powerful enough to run the pump for more than a few hours daily, and we can't dedicate them to this location. We need these power units around town to help us prepare for the survivors' arrival. The only solution is for me to go to my cabin, disassemble my solar system there, and transport it here."

"Can that be done in time?" Mary asked. "We only have five days left until our deadline."

"It will be tight," John replied. "If our transportation team can get a box truck running for me, I'll drive to the village. There, I can pick up three helpers to take to my cabin. The four of us should be able to disassemble my solar system in one day, and then we'd all drive back to town. With the help of these new workers, we should be able to reassemble the solar system and start pumping water. The tank won't be anywhere near full when the survivors arrive, but there should be enough water pressure to flush toilets."

"I think we should do it," Fred said. "The worst-case scenario is that we have to delay the survivor transfer a couple more days until we have water for them. I'm sure they'd understand. Let's just do the steps in order and not set a deadline. First, we get a truck, however long it takes. When that's done, John goes to get the panels and installs them here. We transport the other survivors only when the panels are installed and we have enough water in the tank."

There was a short discussion, and everyone agreed to the plan.

"While I'm waiting for the truck, I'll be trying to turn off the water mains going to the areas of the town we aren't using. I need someone who likes that kind of work to help me. If I have to leave before the job is completed, that person must complete it before I return. But first, we must figure out how to get these power units back down the hill without destroying them."

Everyone laughed. It was decided that they'd divide into two groups. Each group would determine the best way to get their power unit down the hill. It became a contest, which is an excellent way to build team spirit. John was happy to see that the two advance teams had bonded into one.

John returned to the hardware store and filled a toolbox with every tool he thought he might need to disassemble his solar system. He also collected battery-powered tools and chargers. He'd watched when the system had been installed, so he knew how to disassemble it. He took his tools to the house to wait for the truck.

Just as the sun was getting lower in the sky, a 16-foot box truck drove up and parked in front of John's house. Ray, Lola, and Red jumped out of the cab.

"One box truck as ordered," said Lola.

"And full of gas," Red added.

"You guys are incredible," John replied.

"The ball is in your court," Red continued. "Now, all the pressure is on you, not us."

"I won't let you down," John replied. "I think it's early enough that I'll head out tonight if Jillian says it's OK."

The three from the truck laughed. John turned when he heard a laugh coming from behind him. It was Jillian.

"You think I want to be the bad guy in this town? I'll start getting your things together."

Ten minutes later, Jillian appeared with John's pack and a bag of snacks. John sought and got a long hug from Jillian before he climbed into the cab. It seemed that he was always leaving her. He hoped that no one would be in danger this time while he was gone.

The first part of the drive was easy. It was still light enough that it would be easy to spot wildlife on the road. After sunset, he had to slow down. He didn't want to ruin this trip by hitting a deer. He also reminded himself that horses and cows were running loose now.

As he arrived at the village, he saw several campfires burning. He got out his flashlight, cranked it for a minute, turned it on, and started walking toward Rob's cabin. Rob's voice came from out of the darkness ahead of him.

"Marshal Smith, I presume. No emergencies, I hope. That doesn't look like the lights of a school bus, so I'm guessing you aren't here to pick us up."

"No emergency and no pickup," John replied as he approached Rob and two other men. "I need some help from some of your guys. I discovered that I could get the town's water system running with enough solar power. I'm heading up to Max's cabin to disassemble and transport his solar system to town.

"We want to set it up and have running water before we bring your people to town. That will happen faster if you can spare three more of your people to help me tear down and rebuild the solar system. When I return to the town, I must take them with me, so they've got to be OK with that. Oh, and did I tell you that I need them ASAP?"

"Boy, you don't ask for much. What kind of skills do you need?"

"I need strength and some familiarity with power tools. It isn't very complex, just some heavy lifting and tedious disassembly."

One of the men standing with Rob said, "I'll go."

"OK, get your stuff and see if you can find two more volunteers," Rob said.

He then asked John, "So, how is everything going?"

"That's a long story for another time. We had eight convicts try to take over the town. They weren't successful, and we've relocated them to a farmer's field outside of town."

Rob chuckled and said, "It's your fault, you know. People wouldn't try to take advantage of you if you didn't look so young and vulnerable. If you looked like Fred, people would leave you alone."

Three shapes appeared out of the darkness, all carrying packs.

"That was fast," said John.

"There was a battle, sir," one of the men said. "Many of us wanted to go with you. You have quite a reputation. We had to flip coins to determine who got to go with you."

"No 'sir' necessary. We're all just workers on a job. My name is John."

The three were introduced as Dennis, Todd, and Larry. They threw their packs into the back of the truck and climbed into the cab. It was cramped, but no one wanted to ride in the back of the truck. John headed up the road toward his cabin.

"So, what do you know about this job?" John asked.

"Something about taking apart a solar system," Todd said. "Will we be sleeping in the truck or camping outside?"

John laughed. "You said that you guys were the lucky ones who won the coin toss. You just didn't realize how lucky you were. You'll be staying in a heated cabin tonight, and if you can wait long enough, you can take a hot shower."

They all laughed, thinking that he was joking. That was OK; the joke would be on them.

There was no moon when they arrived at the cabin, so it was pitch black. They couldn't see much outside of the cabin. As John opened the door and switched on the lights, they gasped. They hadn't seen this kind of luxury since the epidemic. John told them that there was one guest room. They could share it, flip coins for it, or sleep on the living room floor. He grabbed a flashlight and went outside to turn everything on. He had to charge the water system this time since he'd drained it the last time they left.

When he returned, he found them all sitting in the comfortable chairs. They hadn't had a padded chair to sit in for many months. He told them they would have hot water in an hour, but their showers needed to be brief since there were four of them to share the hot water. It was late, but John made everyone a hot meal.

Everyone got a hot shower and retired. John climbed into his bed and immediately felt something was missing... his TeenGirl.

The following day, they had a hot breakfast of scrambled eggs and hash browns from a bag in the freezer. John encouraged them to eat until they were full. This would be the last hot meal prepared in this cabin. The first thing John would do was turn off the electricity. That meant no heat or water since the water pump needed electricity. It also meant he had to remove everything from the refrigerator and freezer or face terrible smells when he returned.

When everyone was ready, John ceremoniously turned off all the breakers and the inverter. The solar panels would continue to produce electricity when they were in the sun, but it was low-voltage DC and harmless if you touched them. He then showed everyone how to unbolt the solar panels from their frames and carefully store them in the truck. With four people working, they had all 20 panels safely stored in the truck after two hours.

The next job was to disassemble the frames that had held the panels. This was a tedious job requiring the loosening of many bolts that had been tightened a year ago. The power tools helped, and all of the bolts were carefully labeled and saved in bags. The men were instructed to take their time and remember how everything was put together. They'd have to reassemble the frame in the next day or two.

Once the frame pieces were loaded into the truck, they started the last major part of the job. John had four large batteries hanging on the wall in the outbuilding. He found some old towels and cardboard to lay on the truck's floor. The heavy batteries required all four workers to carry each of them to the truck. They moved slowly and carefully and laid them on the cardboard padding. The wall brackets that supported the batteries were also moved to the truck.

The truck still had room after the significant solar system pieces were loaded. In the back of the garage were 16 boxes marked "Physics Lab." These boxes contained parts and equipment from Max's old physics hobby, which he played around with before the virus. Since the equipment needed electricity to operate, there was no reason to leave it here. As an electrical engineer, Max had always enjoyed tinkering around with electricity while trying to understand the laws of Physics. Maybe he might want to return to his old hobby sometime in the next thousand years. The boxes easily fit into the back of the truck.

It was getting late, and the sun was getting lower in the sky. They were all tired and decided to quit for the day. All that was left was to recover the electrical conduit and the wiring it contained. That wouldn't take long, and they could wait until morning.

They ate a dinner of canned goods, which was still extravagant compared to their life at camp. As John looked down into his small valley, memories flooded his brain. He'd watched as Jillian left and then returned to that valley and watched the deer graze there many times. Life was so simple when he lived in this cabin; now, many people depended upon him. In fact, the future of humanity now depended on him and Jillian. It was a heavy burden, but one he gladly accepted.

Everyone was up early. They were anxious to complete the job and head toward town. The conduit and wiring came apart quickly; by mid-morning, they were ready to leave. John drained the water system, knowing that it would never be refilled. He walked out to the chicken enclosure to ensure their feeders were full of chicken feed. His next big task would be to come out, collect the chickens, and take them to town. He and Jillian could do it and make a vacation of it.

They loaded their packs into the truck and headed back to the village. They stopped briefly at the village and told Rob about their successful task. John had cautioned the men about talking about the hot shower. There was no need to brag. It was a story best to retell in the future.

The drive back into town was uneventful, and they arrived around noon. John parked the truck in front of Red's house and was enthusiastically greeted by Jillian. Pam greeted the men from her village and directed them to their house. They were excited to be in the town finally. John told them that after lunch, they needed to begin the reassembly task.

The advance team was now too big for Red's dining room. His house had a large backyard, and someone had found enough patio tables and chairs to accommodate them all outside. Lunch was a happy event, knowing that John and the new arrivals had successfully acquired the solar system. Jillian informed him that they'd been assigned a house of their own just down the street. The house was large enough for a big family.

After lunch, John and the new men jumped into the truck and headed up to the water tank. He apologized for not having time for a break, but he pointed out to them how important it was to get the water running. The four of them surveyed the area around the water tank. They decided that the best place for year-round sun exposure was on top of the hill that hid the water tank from the town. They staked out the area, indicating where the frame should be built, and started building it.

The assembly process took longer than expected. The frame had to be level and plumb to support the panels correctly, which required leveling the ground in some places. It was hard, tedious work, but the men continued their work without complaint. They had most of the vertical pieces in place at the end of the first day and completed the frame the next morning. John started wiring the panels together once the panels were bolted to the frame. It was around noon when the wiring was complete.

Word had gotten out that the work was almost completed. A crowd had gathered as John finished the wiring. John double-checked everything and then turned on the switch. The pump started humming, and water started flowing into the tank. Everyone cheered.

Lunch was a celebration. Everyone wanted to know how soon they'd have water flowing into their house. John had to tell them that the water was still shut off to the entire town. He first had to fill the tank with enough water to create pressure in the water system. The next step required directing water to one street at a time. The first water to come through the pipes would be rusty and dirty. The lines must be flushed by opening fire hydrants on each street. He told them he'd start turning on sections near the water tank and move street by street toward their homes.

After lunch, John returned to the water tank. Fred and Red joined him to help with the flushing. They opened the hydrant closest to the tank. Rusty water came flooding out, but when it turned clear, they closed the hydrant. They opened the valve to the next street and allowed the water to flow to the next hydrant, flushing the water pipes to that point. As each new street had the water turned on, Red and Fred went into the homes and backyards, looking for any open faucets that might let their precious water escape. This process was repeated as they approached the part of town where they lived.

Finally, they turned on the water for Red's street. After the main line had been flushed, Red ran into his house and returned, shouting, "We have water! The water is rusty, but it's getting clearer."

They immediately assembled a meeting of the entire advance team. They were told to conserve water for the next few days so that the town water tank could fill. They were also advised not to drink the water until the lines were thoroughly flushed.

25

The advance team now totaled 16 people. They'd made significant progress. Houses were ready for all of the survivors. Each house had been cleaned of garbage and provisioned with at least a week's worth of canned food, and the water lines had been flushed so that clean water flowed to each house.

Mary had assigned houses for the people at the survivors' camp, and Pam had done the same for her friends in the village. Each woman had volunteered to ride on their respective buses so they could distribute housing information to everyone on the ride back to town. Everyone should know their house's location by the time their bus had arrived back in the town.

The two camps had always been separate but needed to unite. To accomplish this, Pam and Mary worked together to identify similar people and families from the different camps. These people were placed together as neighbors. The goal was to combine the original groups and form one unified neighborhood.

John and Jillian planned on driving the car to the camps the day before the move. They'd notify the survivors when their buses would arrive so they'd be ready. Each bus could hold 50 passengers, but when the survivor's possessions were included, it would only hold 25 people.

The advance team debated whether to make the move a one-day or two-day event. Each camp would require two bus trips, with 25 people on each bus. Each bus trip would take half a day, and they had two buses at their disposal. A one-day move would require the advance team to work from sun up to sun down. It would be a hard day, but they decided that getting everyone moved on the same day was worth it.

They were ready. The advance team decided that John and Jillian would drive up tomorrow, and the move would happen the following day.

It was a relaxing morning for John and Jillian. They both had worked hard to prepare the town for the survivors. They sat out on the front porch of their new house. For once, they weren't sharing a house with others. Everyone on the advance team had been assigned their own home. The group still enjoyed the companionship of meeting together for lunch and dinner in Red's backyard. It was the peak of summer, and it was still comfortable in his backyard.

They'd be visiting both camps today and then returning home. John liked the way that sounded: home. His cabin had come close to being a home, but this was better. His TeenGirl was here.

They jumped in the car and headed toward Vicki's camp first since it was the closest. They arrived mid-morning, parked the car, and walked into the camp. Vicki and Rex walked out to meet them. John knelt down to say hello to Rex.

"Are you going to introduce me to your wife?" Vicki asked. She stepped toward Jillian and extended her hand. "I'm Vicki Reese."

"Hi, Vicki, I'm Jillian. I've heard a lot about you and your dog, who knows how to find people."

"He's a good friend," Vicki said as she reached down and patted Rex.

Rex wagged his tail and let out a loud bark.

"I'm glad to meet you finally, Jillian," Vicki said. "I owe my life to your husband, which is something I'll never forget."

"He told me about how you took the place of a man during the kidnapping. You seem like an extraordinary woman. I can't wait to get to know you better."

John felt sincere warmth in the Chi between the two women. They would become good friends.

"Are we moving soon?" asked Vicki.

"Tomorrow," John replied. "The first bus will arrive a couple hours after sunup. It can hold about 25 people and their gear. Mary will be on the bus when it arrives. She's assigned houses for everyone in your group. Once that group is taken to the town, the bus will return for the rest of your group early in the afternoon. Your advance team has worked hard over the last ten days, and we have a surprise for you. Each of the prepared houses has running water."

"As I've often said, you never cease to amaze me!" Vicki exclaimed. "How did you pull that off?"

"We were lucky. The town had a gravity-fed water system. We just hooked up solar panels to provide electricity to the well pump."

"You're going to be a hero when everyone finds out. Hauling water from the river every day gets old quickly. Can you guys stay for a while?"

"I'm sorry, but we can't. We have to backtrack down the road and cross the river. We then need to drive up to Rob's village to give him the heads-up about tomorrow."

"So everyone will be moving on the same day?" Vicki asked.

"Yes. I told you that your advance team excelled. They got two buses running and houses prepared for everyone. It will be a long day, but everyone should be in town by the end of tomorrow."

John and Jillian said their goodbyes and started driving south back toward town. When they got to the bridge, they crossed it and turned north again, now on the other side of the river. John liked the idea of traveling in a car. It meant that he didn't have to wade across that river again. Within an hour, they arrived at the village. John repeated the message he'd given to Vicki, and Rob assured him that they'd be ready.

The drive back to town was uneventful. As he drove, he reached over and held his bride's hand. She looked at him and smiled.

"I'm looking forward to a time when you and I can just sit around the house in our pajamas and be lazy," she said. "You have been so busy. I miss you."

"I miss you too. Once we get everyone settled, the council can take over the responsibility of getting things done."

They arrived in town in the afternoon. Everything seemed

peaceful. Tomorrow would be another busy day.

They had a good plan, and the first buses left at sunup. John and Jillian had no role until the buses returned with their first load. Getting 50 people to their homes in a new town might require some hand-holding.

The advance team set up tables in the school and filled them with snacks and water. The buses would drop the survivors off at the school, and Red would top off their gas tanks. After the bus drivers rested and ate some food, they'd head back on the road to finish the job.

Just before noon, the first bus from Vicki's camp arrived. The survivors headed to where they thought their new homes were located. Members of the advance team helped those who needed additional directions. About 45 minutes later, the first bus from the village arrived. Willie was one of the first off the bus. He eagerly looked around until he found Fred and went running toward him. A big hug was exchanged before Fred started walking Willie toward their new home.

The first bus arrivals went surprisingly smoothly. By the time the buses headed back for the second load, everyone seemed to be settled. It was strange to see so many people walking around the town. Some were looking at the school, while others had gone down to the dock. Members of the advance team were armed just in case some wild dogs wanted to make an appearance.

The second bus from Vicki's camp arrived late afternoon. John watched as people he knew got off the bus. He looked for one in particular. The last one off the bus was Vicki, with Rex by her side. She smiled as she saw him.

"Did you get everyone from the camp?" John asked.

"Everyone is here," she replied.

"Let me walk you to your new home. It happens to be next to ours. It has a fenced-in backyard for Rex to roam and a great lake view."

They arrived at Vicki's porch and walked up the steps.

"Thank you," Vicki said, her voice tightening.

"What for?"

"For everything. You have been the glue in this valley. We may not have survived without you." She waved her arm around while pointing at the town. "All of this has happened because of you. Most people won't realize it, but I do. I want to thank you for all of the survivors."

She then stepped forward and hugged him. John could feel the gratitude in her Chi energy.

"What's going on here?" Jillian's voice exclaimed in mock jealousy. She'd arrived behind them unnoticed.

Vicki stepped back, somewhat embarrassed.

"I was just thanking him, that's all," Vicki replied.

Jillian smiled, walked over to Vicki, and reached for her hand. "I know what you mean. He's a wonderful man, and I'm grateful for him daily."

John was embarrassed and looking for an escape. "I need to return to the school and greet the last bus."

The last bus finally arrived late in the afternoon. John again greeted people he knew as they exited the bus. As the good leaders they were, Rob and Judy were the last to exit. He looked tired, but now all of his people were in town. He could rest now. John walked with them as they found their new house.

"Everyone decided to come to town," Rob said. "There's nobody left in the village. It was the flushing toilets that convinced the last holdouts."

"If we're lucky," John replied, "the solar system could last twenty years. But, eventually, it will fail, and so will the water supply."

"Having twenty years to plan for it is a blessing, and we have you to thank for it. So, what happens now?"

"The council needs to have a big meeting with everyone in the town. We're one group of survivors now, and the council needs to make everyone understand its importance. Jillian and I can help by giving the survivors some insights from our point of view."

"You're being vague and mysterious. Can you give me a hint about what those insights are?"

"I think everyone needs to hear our insights at the same time. You'll understand once you hear them. The advance team has cleaned out the local theater. It's large enough to hold everyone in the town. Let's give everyone a day to get settled in their new homes and have the meeting the day after tomorrow. I'll start spreading the word."

26

It was the first meeting of the survivors, and it was held in the only movie theater in town. It wasn't a big or fancy theater, but it was one place that could hold the entire combined group of survivors. There was a stage at the front where several tables were set up. Seated at those tables were the nine members of the survivor council. John sat at the council table, and Jillian sat off to one side of the stage.

Vicki and Rob stood up and waited for the crowd to quiet.

"Hello," Rob said. "Welcome to town. The town's old name was Lakeside, but we can rename it whatever you decide. It's our home now. With your help and the council's guidance, we can make this town a nice, safe place to live and raise your families. We all need to thank the advance team. They've worked tirelessly over the last week to prepare the town for us."

As Rob and Vicki started applauding, the entire theater rose to their feet and joined in. Once the applause had stopped, Rob continued.

"Most of you know Marshal Smith as the one who's made the valley a safe place to live. He and his wife, Jillian, have asked the council if they could address all of you with some insights on our future."

Vicki and Rob sat down, and John and Jillian walked to the front of the stage.

"Most of you know me as the Marshal of the valley," John said.

"Many of you have asked, 'Who appointed you?' Tonight, I'm going to reveal my story. Everything that I'm about to tell you is true. Most of it will be hard to believe. Please let me finish my story, and then I'll answer any questions you may have.

"First, I want to tell you about the COVID-24 virus. This virus was created in a laboratory for biological warfare purposes and accidentally released. It was cleverly designed to quietly spread among the entire population of the Earth before waking up and becoming instantly lethal. Because of that, we had no way of stopping it once it started killing people. I'm sure that you all noticed how quickly everyone died.

"You probably wonder how I know all of this. The answer will shock you as it shocked me. A member of an advanced alien race contacted me. Someone not from this planet. They've been observing humans on this planet for thousands of years, just as we observe dolphins or other species on the Earth. They meant no harm to us; they just observed us to learn about us."

A buzz of muffled conversation with an undercurrent of quiet laughter moved through the crowd. Many were not prepared to believe in aliens.

"Is this a joke?" someone asked.

"I know it's hard to believe," John replied, "but please listen to my whole story. It gets even crazier."

"They have strict rules dictating how they can interact with us. With one exception, they can't reveal their presence or interfere with us. When we study animals on Earth, we try not to interfere with them unless a species is going extinct. When the Bald Eagles were going extinct, we stepped in with massive regulations to preserve their habitat and remove chemicals from our manufacturing that were harming them. Just like we humans, the alien species was only allowed to interfere with us to keep humanity from going extinct.

"The aliens had done this for the Earth once before. Many thousands of years ago, a star briefly passed near our solar system, causing the polar ice caps to melt. The resulting flood threatened to wipe out humanity. This was the great flood described in Genesis from the Bible, and the aliens helped Noah and humanity survive.

"The alien species realized that humans had no immunity to the COVID-24 virus and, if left alone, would kill every human on the planet. By the time they could travel here and neutralize the virus, almost every human on Earth was already dead. Have you noticed how everyone in this room lived remotely when the virus struck? The only reason that we're alive today is because we were the last humans to be infected. Those who were infected first, died first. The aliens could only save those of us who were last infected and were still alive when they arrived.

"This point needs to be understood by everyone in this room. We may be the only survivors of humanity able to form a community in this area of our planet. There are other small pockets of survivors worldwide, but we're the last survivors in this area. We all need to stop thinking only in our own self-interest and work together to save humanity from going extinct forever. This is why I've worked so hard to get both groups together in one place."

"So," John continued, "the answer to your question about who made me Marshal is the alien who contacted me. Before the virus struck, I lived in a remote cabin in the valley. Once the virus started killing everyone, I just settled down and waited for it to kill me. One day, while hiking, I met an older man named Don. He looked just like every other older man I'd met.

"He said that he was a member of an alien species trying to save humanity. Of course, I didn't believe him and figured he had a sunstroke. But he convinced me in a way that you'll find difficult to accept.

"Everyone in this room knows me as John Smith. It isn't my real name. I just took it to do the Marshal job. My real name is Max Everitt."

"No way," said Rob. "I met Max several times last fall. I've been to his cabin up in the hills. He's an older man in his seventies. There's no way that you're Max."

"Yes, Rob, I'm that same Max - almost. Let me continue.

"I rejected the proposal from Don, the man with sunstroke. I figured I could dismiss him gently and told him I was too old to be a Marshal. He said he could remedy that by giving me a new, younger body, and he did just that. Using their advanced technology, he transferred all my memories into the new 18-year-old body you see today. I have over seventy years' worth of memories in this young body. In my old life, I was an electrical engineer. That's how I knew how to fix and rebuild the water system for this town.

"Don said that the valley had become a collecting place for survivors. He wanted a Marshal to protect them from harm and preserve what was left of humanity. That's how I became the Marshal of this valley."

Someone in the audience raised their hand. Max pointed at them.

"So we should call you Marshal Everitt now?" the man asked with a disbelieving smirk.

Max realized that few in the audience believed their story, but that was expected.

"Yes, but it's OK to slip up. When I first changed my name to John Smith, it was confusing for me, too."

Max continued, "There's more to tell you. About a month ago, I saved a middle-aged woman from being killed by a man named Jack, whom some of you knew. I was able to save the woman, but she was shot in the leg. That woman's name was Jill, and some of you got to know her as we visited your campsites together. When Don met Jill, he decided to give her a younger body, too. My new wife, who you know as Jillian, is Jill in her younger body. Those who have known me for the past few months must have wondered where my new wife came from. I'd never even talked about her before. Now you know the story."

A woman from the audience said, "Sorry, Jill, but I've got to ask: Why you and not me?"

There was a nervous laugh from the audience.

Jillian responded, "I was shocked when he made his offer to me. I didn't think that I was that special to be selected out of all the survivors to have a younger body. He explained that he'd determined that I had a good connection with the Chi, which was important to him."

The woman in the audience continued, "I understand why our Marshal needed a young, strong body to protect us, but why did the alien want you to have a young body, too? Was it just so that John, or Max, would have a young wife his own age?"

Jillian looked at Max, and he said, "There's another significant element to our story that I've got to tell you now. It may be difficult to hear, but I told you I'd only speak the truth today. Don told us that a serious problem occurs because of an extinction event. Since so few people are left alive, it would take tens of thousands of years for the human population to recover, if ever. To speed up the process and increase the odds of success, these younger bodies have a modification in their DNA.

"To help Noah and humanity recover, the aliens gave Noah and his wife new, younger bodies like ours, too. If you have read the Bible, you may remember that Noah lived to be 950 years old. When the aliens made their bodies, they changed their DNA to allow them to live for over 900 years. This allowed them to produce more children in their lifetime. This life-extension gene was passed down to their children, too. This lifetime extension helps the human population to recover much more rapidly.

"The aliens didn't want all future humans to have longer lives. This would lead to an overpopulation problem. What they did was to have the lifespan gene slowly reduce the length of the human lifespan with every generation. Eventually, humans would return to their normal lifespan once the population recovered. While Noah lived for 950 years, Moses only lived for 120 years.

"I know it's confusing and hard to believe, but let me make this crucial point. While Jill and I will be able to have many more children, that's not the solution to the problem. Our children cannot mate with one another. Genetic errors would result. Our children must choose mates from you, survivors with normal lifespans. The lifespan extension gene would then be passed down to their children. The alien gave Jill and me a special life extension seed that must be spread to every genetic line in this room if humanity is to survive. Humanity needs those of you in the audience just as much as it needs Jill and me. None of us is more special or important than the rest. We're just different pieces of the puzzle that guarantees humanity's future.

"I'm sure many of you may think that Jill and I are just two crazy teenagers telling a story to get attention. I might feel the same if I were in your position. Whether our story is true or not, it won't impact your life for many years and will be revealed when you see how we age. If we age more slowly than everyone else, we wanted you all to know in advance so you would know we weren't trying to keep a secret from you."

* * *

"Are there any more questions?" Max asked.

A man in the back raised his hand.

"I hear you say you don't want to be special, but you are special. You can run faster than any of us, and you know about things before they happen. We heard about how you overcame eight criminals who tried to take over our town. That's not normal."

Max replied, "Those abilities have nothing to do with the story I just told you about the alien or our younger bodies. I had those abilities before I met the alien, and that's why he wanted me to be Marshal of the Valley. The abilities that you speak of come from my understanding of life's energy, the Chi. Anyone in this room can develop the same skills as I have. It's just that, a skill you must learn and practice to master. Just as a master carpenter or master gardener has spent years dedicated to learning their skill, I've spent years learning to listen to the Chi. Jill and I can help any one of you learn about Chi, but you must put in the time and practice to become a master. Chi will help you in whatever occupation you choose. You can become a better fisherman, a better farmer, or, as I am, a better warrior. It has made Jill a better healer. I hope that in our schools, we can teach every child to listen to their Chi and make them successful in life."

With no more questions, Max and Jill sat down. People began talking and laughing among themselves, which required Rob to call for order so the meeting could continue with regular town business. The meeting went on for hours. People wanted to know what would happen now that they were in town. Schooling for the kids needed to be organized. Food needed to be collected from the town and surrounding area and brought to one central location for everyone to share. A million details were required to set up life in this new town. The survivors were excited. For once in a long time, they could dream of a future for themselves and their families, even if they had a pair of crazy teenagers living in the town.

27

Life in their small town began to take on a regular rhythm. Hundreds of tasks needed to be done, but someone was always willing to help. School hadn't started yet, and with the summer heat, the children had discovered the cooling fun of swimming and paddling canoes at the dock. They were monitored by several mothers discussing the problems in setting up a school this fall for their children. They had plenty of supplies but not enough teachers. One solution was to combine grade levels. The discussion became heated as different opinions were given. They didn't notice the young girl in a pink bathing suit getting into a canoe without a life jacket.

Jill was in the center of town setting up a medical clinic. The storefront had become the place where all the new homeowners brought any medical supplies they'd found in their houses. She was interrupted as Liz walked in carrying her newborn baby. Liz had recovered well from the breech birth. Her short, blonde hair and trim figure made her quite attractive.

"I hope I am not interrupting you, but I thought you might like to meet your namesake," Liz said. "Steve and I appreciate your help in delivering her."

"Yes. Max told me that you'd named her after me. That was so kind. She's so cute. Are both of you doing OK?"

"We're doing fine. We have a lovely new home, and Freddy and Nancy will start school soon. Did Max tell you that I used to be a pediatric nurse? I was hoping that I might be able to help you here in the clinic."

"Yes. I was going to find you later and ask if you'd help here. I just hadn't gotten around to it yet. Your skills with babies will be invaluable in our new community. Thank you for offering. Do you mind if I hold little Jill for a while?"

Before the baby could be passed between the women, Jill suddenly felt anguish in the Chi. There was a problem at the dock.

"What's the matter?" Liz asked, seeing the worried look on Jill's face.

"Someone is in trouble at the dock. I need to go there right away."

Jill left the clinic and raced to the dock, which was not far away. When she arrived, she observed a young girl in a pink bathing suit far out in the bay floundering in the water. It appeared that her canoe had capsized, tossing her into the water.

One of the parents was already swimming out to help the child but was not making good progress due to her own lack of swimming skills. Jill ran to the end of the dock and dove into the water. She'd been an excellent swimmer in high school and had made it to the State championships.

Jill quickly covered the distance to the girl, but not before the child disappeared beneath the surface. Jill dove deep into the water to try to find the girl. The water was murky, and Jill couldn't see very far, so she had to surface without finding her. She took a moment on the surface to calm herself and listen to the Chi. She felt that the girl was behind her and down about ten feet. Jill dove again, using the Chi to direct her to the girl. She grabbed the girl and brought her to the surface. Looking back toward the dock, she saw Max diving into the water and heading in her direction. He also had felt distress in the Chi.

Max met Jill halfway to the dock. They swam together to the dock and pulled the girl out of the water. With her healing skills, Max let Jill take charge of the recovery efforts. He sent Chi to the girl and prayed that she'd recover. Jill cleared the girl's lungs of water and started CPR. Within minutes, the girl was coughing and crying. The crying was a good sign. It meant that she would recover.

The child's mother, who was not on the dock initially, came running onto it. She pulled the girl into her arms to comfort her. The mother looked at Jill and whispered, "Thank you."

* * *

Max and Jill went back to their home to put on dry clothes.

"You did well in the water," Max said. "I knew you were a strong swimmer as the 'Older Jill,' but I didn't know if those skills got carried over to the younger Jill."

"I have memories of how to swim. My younger body now has longer arms and legs, which made my strokes more powerful. I used the Chi to find the girl!" she added excitedly. "I could feel her even though I couldn't see her in the murky water."

"You're getting better at listening to the Chi. It helped you save the girl's life."

Jill moved into Max's warm arms as they shed their wet clothes in the bedroom.

"I'm cold," she said. "Let's get under the covers and see if we can get warm."

Max didn't resist.

28

Fall was making its appearance. The leaves were beginning to change as summer released its grip on the valley. Things in the town had settled into a predictable rhythm now that the school was operating. Everyone in town had become scavengers, collecting food and tools from all the houses. Stores had been set up to separate the spoils by category so all items could be found easily when needed. The goats from the survivors' camp had been moved to Rod and Mandy's pasture outside of town, and bushels of apples and pears had been collected from their orchard. The survivors had found enough food to survive the coming winter.

Yesterday, the whole town showed up for a memorial service for all of the townspeople who had died from the virus. Their remains were buried just outside of town in a field that had now been set aside as a cemetery. The survivors had tried to collect as many of their names as possible from scraps of evidence left in the homes. They filed the list of names at the library in case anyone needed it. It was a somber ceremony that reminded them of their own vulnerabilities.

A desire had arisen in the town to learn about Chi. Max had taught a couple of classes about Chi and how to feel it. Someone in the town had practiced Tai Chi before and was now teaching a class on the school's playground. Fred and Willie were active participants in the classes. Fred had experienced how easily a teenage boy could defeat his years of training and realized there was something real about it. Max was more frequently hearing snippets of conversation that included the phrase "Tai Chi in the kitchen."

Max and Jill sat outside on their front porch, admiring the view of the lake.

"I have to go on a rescue mission," Max said.

"Who needs to be rescued?" she asked with a tone of concern in her voice.

She then looked at Max and saw the smile on his face, relieving her anxiety.

"My chickens!" he exclaimed with exaggerated emphasis. "They are still up at the cabin, and I can't leave them there all winter." And then, in a more loving tone, "I also considered taking you there for that honeymoon I promised you. I haven't forgotten."

"That would be nice! We could spend some time at the cabin all by ourselves. We would have to 'rough it' since there is no more electricity or water, but getting away by ourselves would still be fun. Where would you keep the chickens here in town? They won't be in our backyard, will they?"

"No. Have you met that young couple, Rod and Mandy?"

"Yes, they've moved onto a farm just outside of town. They collected some horses and cows roaming around and wanted me to look at them. Are they interested in chickens, too?"

"They are, and there already is a large chicken coup at the farm."

"When would we go, and how would we transport the chickens to town?"

"Well, chickens can be hard to catch, and I think we'll need some help. My chicken enclosure is quite large, and you and I might have trouble cornering them. We could drive a pickup truck to the cabin with Rod and Mandy. After the four of us get the chickens in the truck, Rod and Mandy can drive the truck back to town, leaving us alone to fend for ourselves. Do you think we can survive on our own?"

Jill laughed and said, "It would be fun trying. Without heat, we might have to snuggle a lot.

"That means we would walk back to town. Could we stop by your old camp and spend some time in the hot spring?"

"Of course. That sounds very romantic; it's just the kind of honeymoon I was thinking of."

"Now you have me excited. When can we go?"

"I'll ask Rod and Mandy when it fits their schedule. If they're available, we can go soon. There isn't much going on in town that needs my attention."

Rod and Mandy needed a few days to repair the chicken coup and the surrounding fence to prepare for the chicken transfer. They got Kenny to build some cages to transport the chickens, and they found a tarp to cover the cages during the trip. Once the empty cages were loaded into the truck, they were ready for the trip.

Max and Jill's packs were loaded into the back of the pickup. The truck's cab had a back seat and easily accommodated the four of them. Max made sure that Rod and Mandy remembered the route they had driven since they would make the trip back to town alone.

They arrived at the cabin without any problems. Max drove the truck over to the chicken compound and backed it up to the entrance. He removed their packs from the back of the truck and set them aside. Everyone had brought gloves, which were necessary when picking up chickens. A peck from a chicken could be quite painful without gloves.

About 12 chickens, three roosters, and a few chicks needed to be put into their cages. The process initially went smoothly, with the four of them able to corral and pick up chickens easily. It got more complicated when trying to catch the last three or four. The last chickens seem to be able to anticipate the actions of their captors and escape to an open area of the pen. Max thought that "Chicken Chi" was helping them escape. Finally, they caught the last chickens and safely stored them in their cages. Max drove the truck over to the building where the chicken feed was stored. Don had kept the chicken feed well stocked, so there was a lot of feed to be loaded into the back of the truck.

Max started a fire in the cabin's fireplace and boiled some water. As a "thank-you" to Rod and Mandy, he treated them to a lunch of freeze-dried meals that surpassed the food back in town. He also gave each of them a couple of meals to take with them. They promised to keep it a secret.

Jill thought they made a cute couple. They were both of average height and had light brown hair. She had helped them with the animals on the farm and knew they were hard workers.

"So what did you guys do before the virus spread?" Jill asked.

"I was an electrician, and Mandy managed an HOA," replied Rod. "We lived on a small hobby farm."

Mandy added, "We really enjoy working with animals. We had ducks, chickens, turkeys, and even two pigs. Moving to the farm outside of town is a dream come true for us."

After lunch, Rod and Mandy got into the truck and headed back toward town. Max and Jill moved their packs into the cabin and were ready to begin their honeymoon.

"What should we do first?" asked Max.

"How far is it to where you first met Don?"

"About a half-hour hike that isn't too difficult. Would you like to go?"

"Yes. I would like to see where our adventure all began."

They loaded up their day packs with water and snacks and headed down into the small valley in front of the cabin. Max reached over to hold Jill's hand as they walked. He couldn't get enough of sharing his love for her, and she responded with a smile. They followed a well-worn path the deer often used, winding through the trees and along a small stream. The scent of the pine trees was strong, but there was also the smell of leaves decaying on the ground. With little wind, it was a beautiful day for a walk in the woods. They were alone, only surrounded by the Chi of the forest.

They finally came to a clearing that Max remembered well. This was where he'd first met Don, the alien that had saved humanity. As Max walked over to the log where Don had been sitting, he noticed a package resting on the log. The package was wrapped as a gift with a beautiful bow of pink and blue ribbon. The paper was appropriate for a baby shower. The package was utterly unspoiled by the weather and looked like it had been placed there minutes before. Under the package was a note. It said:

"Open when appropriate, Don."

Max looked around the forest, hoping to catch a view of Don watching them. He saw nothing.

"How does he keep doing this?" Jill asked. "How would he know we would be here at this moment on this day?"

"Remember, his species is technically so far ahead of ours that what he can do seems like magic to us."

"So when do we open it?"

"It's obviously a baby gift, so I think we should wait until we're going to have a baby. His note says 'when appropriate.'"

"What do you think it is?"

"I don't know. But a gift from an alien could be interesting."

They returned to the cabin hand in hand, absorbing all the Chi that the forest would share with them. The gift from Don was left unopened and was placed above the fireplace on the mantle. They spread their sleeping bags before the fireplace and cuddled to stay warm. The bedroom had a perfectly good bed, but this felt more like a honeymoon.

They woke early the next morning and added fresh wood to the fire. They ate the last of the freeze-dried scrambled eggs and then moved to the front porch to watch the deer in the valley. They sat close together, wrapped in each other's arms with a blanket protecting them from the morning chill. It was another beautiful fall day with clear skies and bright sunshine. More deciduous leaves had turned to the golden reds and yellows of fall. The fall changes were more advanced at this altitude, which was higher than the town.

"What do we do next, TeenBoy?"

"Whatever you want. What would you like to do next?"

"Why don't we start heading back to town? There is no rush, so we could stop by your old camp and enjoy the hot spring for a few days."

"Now that does sound like a honeymoon activity! We can pack up any leftover food packets and head out later this morning. We should be able to reach the camp before dark."

"Do you think we'll see the wolves again at the top of the ridge?"

"We'll just have to wait and see what the Chi brings into our trip. I'm guessing that unless they need our help, we won't see them. They are probably miles from here by now. With winter coming, they may have moved lower in the valley where food will be more plentiful."

After loading the last food packets into their packs, there wasn't much left in the garage. They left some canned food as an emergency supply in case they ever came back. Max's survival homestead had been stripped bare. There were no solar panels, chickens, or car, and very little food was left. They secured all the windows and doors, picked up their packs, and started climbing the ridge between the cabin and John's summer campsite.

They reached the crest of the ridge a little after noon and stopped for a lunch snack. The sight from this spot was always breathtaking, with an unobstructed view of the large valley and its river running toward the lake. No wolves joined their picnic this time. They were alone to take in the view and reflect on all that had happened during the summer. Max moved to sit behind Jill, wrapped his arms around her, and kissed her gently on the neck. "I love you with all of my heart," he whispered into her ear.

"I know," she replied. "I can feel it in your Chi."

The rest of the hike was easier because it was downhill. They had to pick their way around large boulders, but Max had made this trip many times. They arrived at the camp as the sun was starting to set. The guest tent had collapsed and lay in a pile. A gust of wind or an animal must have helped that to happen. Everything else was in good shape. They put their packs down beside John's tent and collected firewood. The evenings were cooler now, and a large fire was welcome.

They surveyed the supplies left in the supply tent. True to his word, Don had not brought any more supplies. But they had more than enough meals for their stay here and the trip back to town. At least while they were on their honeymoon, they wouldn't have to go hunting for dinner.

The sun set earlier this time of year, so it was dark by the time they finished their meal. A crescent moon hung in the sky to the west.

"Hey, TeenBoy, you can do the dishes."

"That's not fair!" Max replied, again using his whiny voice.

They laughed together at that memory of when they first met. But TeenBoy did end up doing the dishes.

After the dishes were done, they walked to the hot spring pool. They stripped off their clothes and slid beneath the warm water. They leaned back against the rocks and looked up at the stars.

"The stars are so beautiful tonight," Jill said. "Without the air and light pollution, the stars are absolutely stunning."

"This would be a good time to listen to the Chi around us. Imagine the Chi flowing out from the universe and into you. Close your eyes and listen to what it's telling you. Can you get a distinct sense of the animals around us?"

Jill closed her eyes and relaxed. She focused on what was happening at this moment in the world around her. Yes, she could feel the presence of an owl in a tree not so far away. She expanded her awareness farther away from their camp and could feel other lifeforms scurrying around in the night.

Suddenly, she sat up straight and gasped.

"What is it?" asked Max

"I feel that someone is watching us."

"Very good! I wondered if you might be able to feel our 'watcher' in the Chi."

"You knew?"

"Yes, I've sensed we were being watched for a while."

"Who is it? How far away are they, and are we in danger?"

"Listen to the Chi. What is it telling you about our watcher?"

Jill closed her eyes and leaned back against the rocks. After a few moments, she opened her eyes.

"It's a man, and he's not close by. I don't know how I know this, but I know he's not nearby."

"Are we in danger?"

"No. I feel no anger or ill will. I feel a sense of curiosity. How do I know he's not close by? Can I tell distances using the Chi?"

"No, not directly. If you listen to his Chi, he will tell you how far away he is. When someone is far away, they feel safe and are calm. As they get closer, they start to worry about being seen or detected, and that worry shows up in their Chi. When they are really close and ready to attack, their anxiety is so high that they are like a beacon shining in the Chi. You only felt his calmness and knew there was no immediate danger."

"So you don't know how far away this man is?"

"In exact miles, no. Since he's not worried, I would guess he's several miles away. He must have seen our fire and is curious about us, which is what the Chi told you. This has been one of those moments when the Chi teaches you how to listen more closely to its messages. You have learned well. The Chi would have communicated to you if you were in danger. And, of course, I never would have let anything happen to you."

She snuggled into his arms.

"So what should we do?"

"Nothing. We have to let the Chi direct what happens in our lives. If we are to meet this man, then it will happen when the Chi deems it necessary. We might want to have more clothes on now that we know someone is watching. Just a suggestion."

The next morning, they were up early. The watcher had put a kink in the idea of two newlyweds being alone on their honeymoon. They ate breakfast, collected more firewood, and did some laundry. Max was always listening for the watcher in the Chi but hoped that Jill would take this opportunity to practice her listening skills, too.

At noon, Jill told Max, "Our watcher is beginning to get nervous. I think he's getting closer, but I still only sense curiosity."

"Yes, it appears he wants to contact us. Let's build a fire and plan on having company for lunch."

They built a fire and started heating water. They set out plates for three. Then, they sat on the rocks around the table and waited. The watcher was very good when he approached the camp. There was not one sound that betrayed his presence. When he was just outside of the camp, Jill raised her voice and said,

"Hello there. Whoever you are, why don't you enter our camp and join us for lunch? We have a place set for you."

The Chi rippled with his shock. He'd assumed that they would never see him coming. How was he given away? He recovered his confidence quickly, stepped out of the trees, and entered the camp.

He was a tall, well-built man in his 30s. His hair was cut short, and he had a stubble of a beard. He moved gracefully, almost cat-like. He wore a full camouflage uniform, but there were no patches or identification on it. He was definitely a military man, but not like Fred. You could sense that this man had seen action up close and knew how to survive. His face had a small scar on his cheek just above his beard. It was ragged, as if caused by shrapnel from an explosion, and had not been stitched by a plastic surgeon. While his body communicated deadly capabilities, his face radiated genuine kindness. He approached Max and Jill with a big smile.

"My name is Jill, and this is my husband, Max. You're welcome at our table."

"My name is Chuck. I must be losing my stalking skills in my old age if you already have a place at your table for me. How long have you known I was around?"

"For a while now," Max said, extending his hand for a handshake. "We have a variety of meal packs. You can have the first choice."

"I'll take whatever is offered, but I haven't had many vegetables in a long while."

Chuck took a vegetable stir fry packet and joined them at the table.

"I'm sorry to intrude on you," Chuck said. "You're the first people I've seen in months. When the virus hit, I was camping alone in the wilderness. I needed some time by myself."

He rubbed his scar unconsciously and continued, "I didn't even know how nasty the virus was until I hiked back toward Crescent City and met some people running away. They were headed to a small village in this valley, but I felt I stood a better chance alone and didn't feel like I wanted to be around many people.

"I returned to my remote camp and lived there through the winter. I found that I could survive OK but didn't realize how much I needed others to talk to. I decided to go to the village and live with them, but when I got there, the village was empty. Everyone was dead or gone. I was heading to the lake when I saw your fire. I'm sorry about talking so much; I haven't had anyone to talk to for six months."

"No apology needed," Max replied. "I've some good news. The people from the village have moved into the town on the lake. We have a community of about 100 survivors trying to stay alive. You would be welcome to join us if you want."

"So you live in the village and not at this camp?"

"Yes. We just came to the camp as sort of a honeymoon. We'll be heading back to town in the morning."

"Wow," Chuck said. "Now I really feel bad. Talk about a third wheel on a honeymoon. If you give me directions to the town, I'll just meet you there."

Max looked at Jill, and she nodded.

"You really should travel with us," Jill said. "We need to catch you up on what has happened in this valley while you were camping alone. You should know all of these things before you arrive in town."

"Are you sure it's OK?" Chuck asked.

"Yes," Max replied. "If you set up our guest tent, you can sleep there. Where is your gear?"

"I ditched it about a quarter mile away. I wanted to be quiet when I snuck up on you," he laughed. "You know how well that worked. Your wife was really good at detecting me. Maybe she can give me some advice on what I did wrong."

"That's part of the story that we have to tell you. Go get your stuff, and I'll help you set up the tent."

The next day, they closed the camp for good. They dug a hole and buried the tents and extra camping gear in a place they could easily find if they ever needed it again. Walking toward town, they told Chuck the whole story of the virus and Don and the Chi. He didn't believe much of it for now, but that was understandable. It was, actually, a very fantastic story. He would have to learn the truth at his own speed. Right now, Max and Jill were just two young teenagers spinning a fantastic yarn about aliens.

"So, were you in the Army?" Max asked. "We have a Master Sergeant in our town named Fred. You two should get along fine."

"No. Actually, I was in the Navy. We have similar camouflage uniforms."

"Well, it so happens we also have a Navy man in town. Rob started out as a sub-driver and ended up as the captain of a ship."

"Do you know his last name? That sounds like a ship's captain I used to know. His name was Rob, too."

"No, actually, I don't. With only 100 people in town, everyone pretty much goes by first names only. I only know him and his wife as Rob and Judy."

"Wow! That's amazing. The guy I knew had a wife named Judy, too. I wonder if it's the same guy."

"You can ask him when you get to town."

They made the trip to town in three days. There was no need to hurry, and the weather in the valley continued to be a series of perfectly sunny fall days. Jill offered to have Chuck stay with them when they arrived in town, but he declined, saying he'd imposed enough on their honeymoon. Max took Chuck over to Rob's house, figuring that one Navy man would take in another until housing could be arranged for him.

When Rob opened the door, both men greeted each other with surprise and recognition. Judy came up from behind Rob and warmly greeted Chuck as well. She invited them in, and they moved into the living room.

"I found this guy wandering around the valley, and he said he might know you," Max laughed. "What a small world it can be sometimes. He decided to drop in on our honeymoon. Don't they teach you Navy guys any manners?"

"Well, they don't train Navy SEALs to be polite," Rob replied. "Actually, it's quite the opposite."

Rob and Chuck exchanged a knowing look.

"So, he's a Navy SEAL," Max said. "That would explain a lot. He tried to sneak up on us and was surprised when we knew he was there. I also noticed there were no identifying patches on his uniform."

Max then turned to Chuck and said, "Thank you for your service. I know it must have been difficult for you."

"I still can't believe your wife could detect my approach," Chuck said. "I've been trained by the best to be absolutely silent as I approach my target."

"Jill detected you?" Rob asked with a chuckle. "That must be really embarrassing. I didn't know she was that skilled in listening to the Chi. She's just learning, and Max is the Chi Master."

"So you also detected me?" Chuck asked Max. "When did you first know I was watching you?"

"It was after it got dark, and we started our fire. I could feel you watching us."

"I'm sorry, but I must have been two miles from you. It was dark, so you couldn't have seen me, and you couldn't have heard me from that distance."

"Max uses the Chi to sense things happening around him," Rob said.

"I keep hearing about this Chi stuff. Do you really believe in this voodoo?" Chuck then turned to Max and said, "Sorry."

Both Rob and Max laughed.

"I know it sounds crazy," Rob replied, "but you'll have to form your own opinion once you work with Max. I've known Max for a while now and believe the Chi is real. He and his knowledge of the Chi have saved everyone in this town. I'll tell you later how he alone went up against eight convicts while rescuing Jill. We are lucky to have him as our Marshal."

Max was thankful that the conversation then changed direction as Rob explained how he met Chuck. Chuck's SEAL team had been dispatched to Rob's ship by helicopter to handle the kidnapping of a commercial ship's captain by pirates. After the situation came to a successful conclusion, Rob and Chuck had time to talk, which led to a more extended friendship once they were both in port.

It had been a long day, so Max left them as they were laughing together and returned to his TeenGirl. It was good to be home again.

29

Jill was worried because she knew she was sick. She'd always felt great since she'd acquired this new, younger body. But this morning, after Max had left the house, she'd thrown up twice. She hadn't eaten anything that could cause this, so she wondered if something was wrong with her new body. She didn't have any way to contact Don if the body was failing.

She decided to see if her Chi could tell her what was wrong. She closed her eyes and focused on bringing more Chi into herself to boost her healing energy. She directed her focus on her body to try to get a feel for what was wrong. The impression she received was that everything was OK.

As she savored the Chi in her body, she detected something strange. There was the feeling of another, separate Chi inside of her. It was weak but definitely there. Was it a tumor? As she focused on it, the answer came to her. It was another life form. She was pregnant!

Jill tried to discover whether it was a boy or a girl. Sometimes, she felt it was a boy, but other times, it was a girl. She'd ask Max; he'd know. She was so excited and couldn't wait to tell Max. But for now, until she felt better, she was going back to sleep.

Two hours later, she woke to find Max at the bedroom door with a worried look on his face. When he saw her awake, he asked, "Vicki said you missed a get-together with her. Are you sick?"

She smiled and said, "No, I don't think so. I'm just not feeling good this morning, but I have some good news."

Max came over and sat on the edge of the bed.

"What's this good news?"

"You're going to be a father!"

Max's face exploded with surprise and happiness. "Are you sure?"

"I think so. I can feel its Chi energy separate from mine. Is that what a baby feels like inside of a mother?"

"Yes. You can feel the two separate sources of Chi. It's easy when the baby is far along, but not so easy at your stage. Can you tell the sex?"

"I'm not sure. Its Chi is weak, and sometimes I get the sense of a boy and other times a girl. Maybe you can tell."

Max reached under the covers and put his hand on her belly. He closed his eyes, was quiet for a moment, and then smiled.

"I understand your confusion. You're carrying twins, one boy and one girl."

He leaned over, and they embraced. She laughed and said, "You don't do things halfway, do you, TeenBoy?"

"I just have too much love for you."

"Where is that gift that Don left for us at the cabin?" Max asked.

"It's in the top drawer of my dresser. Go get it."

Max retrieved the box and gave it to Jill. She slowly unwrapped it, wondering what kind of gift an alien would give a human. Under the wrapping paper was a box. She opened the lid and discovered two round balls, each about the size of a golf ball. One was blue, and one was pink.

"So he knew we would have one girl and one boy even before they were created?" Jill asked.

"I guess so."

Max picked up one of the balls. It was very light, as if made of foam, but it had a hard surface of some metal. It was cool to the touch. He thought it might be some sort of rattle and shook it, but it made no sound. They just seemed to be two lightweight metal balls, one blue and one pink. The colors obviously related to a boy and a girl. What they were, he had no idea.

"What a strange gift. It's obvious that Don didn't go to many baby showers," Jill laughed. "Well, they aren't a swallowing hazard, so we can just let the kids play with them. We wouldn't want to offend Don in case he's watching."

Max returned the gifts to the dresser and gave his wife another hug.

30

It was a cool November morning. The skies were clear, and the air was crisp, hinting at the approaching winter season. Jill wanted to collect pine cones to use for decorations around their house. Max was with the council members, discussing matters concerning the town. Boring! The original farmers in the town had cut down most of the pine trees to grow crops, but Jill knew of a place a couple of miles away with many evergreen trees. At this time of year, their cones should be lying on the ground.

She left a note for Max, picked up a basket, and headed out of town. It was a pleasant walk in bright sunshine with little wind. As she crossed an open field, she could see the grove of trees on the other side. She was feeling good this morning, even though she still occasionally experienced some morning sickness.

As she entered the grove, she was disappointed with the few cones around the trees. Other survivors from the town must have been here before her. She moved deeper into the grove and started collecting her cones. She was so focused on finding the best cones that she was not paying attention to her surroundings. The best cones were up the hill, where large boulders were spaced among the trees. As she moved deeper into the grove, she was rewarded when she found large, beautifully formed cones.

Suddenly, a sound broke her concentration. It was the bark of a dog. She turned, trying to locate the source of the noise. In the distance, she saw a pack of dogs coming her way. The survivors had been harassed by packs of wild dogs roaming outside of town. When their owners died from the virus, the dogs formed packs and became feral.

Jill felt foolish that she'd come out here alone. Usually, the dog packs didn't come this close to town anymore. They must have felt comfortable being inside the grove of trees. She was scared and in trouble. A pack that size could easily overwhelm her. She must get to a more defensible position. There was a huge boulder just up the hill. The dogs couldn't surround her if she could get her back against it. It would slow them down but wouldn't stop them. She picked up a large branch and broke it into a size she could use as a club.

Jill closed her eyes and focused on the Now. She then communicated into the Chi: Max, I'm in trouble. I need your help.

The council meeting was plodding along. Max, Vicki, Rob, Chet, and Red were among the attendees. Max was reporting on the local disturbances during the last week when he suddenly stopped mid-sentence.

"Max, what's the matter?" Vicki asked.

"Jill is in trouble. I've got to go," he responded.

Max jumped up and ran from the room, quickly followed by Vicki and the others. Exiting the building and into the street, he nearly ran into Fred and Willie.

"What's wrong?" asked Fred.

"Jill is in trouble north of town."

Max sprinted down the street, heading for the forested area where he knew Jill needed his help. He was thankful that he wore his throwing knife. It was now considered part of his uniform. The council decided that people wouldn't argue with a man carrying a knife, so they asked him to wear it while on duty.

As he headed out into the open fields, he could sense that others were following him. Fred, being the fittest of them all, was close behind. Max started absorbing more of the Chi to fuel his rapid pace.

Jill had moved so her back was against the giant boulder. The pack was almost there. They were all barking and growling, as attacking pack dogs are known to do. Their sound was intimidating, and Jill could feel the fear creeping into her mind. She knew she must focus on the Now to increase the Chi energy she needed in her fight. She must be like Max and be a warrior in this moment. She must protect her unborn babies. She could now feel Max was coming, but he was still miles away. She didn't think that he'd arrive in time.

Max was sprinting as fast as he could. The Chi was helping him achieve a speed he'd never done before. He looked over his shoulder and saw Fred running hard but falling behind since he didn't benefit from the Chi energy. Farther back behind him were others, with one carrying a rifle.

Max worried that he'd not arrive in time to protect Jill. This had happened once before and was still haunting him, so he increased his speed even more. This time was different. She was carrying their babies. There were now three lives that must be saved.

The dogs had arrived. Jill was focused on the present moment, waiting for the battle to begin. The dogs were inching closer, trying to gain an advantage. Jill was waving the club back and forth, threatening any dog that got close to her.

Suddenly, the dogs stopped barking and backed off a little. They became restless and paced back and forth. Their attention was no longer focused on Jill but on something above her. She stepped away from the boulder and looked up. On top of the boulder stood four wolves. One larger than the other three. One of the smaller ones had a white paw.

Jill realized that it was the mother wolf and her three pups that Max and Jill had met before. The three pups were now almost fully grown, but she recognized the white paw on one. Jill had removed a thorn from the mother's paw, probably saving her life and, therefore, the lives of her young pups.

The mother wolf looked at Jill, and Jill felt a loving energy in that look. The wolf was communicating with Chi's energy. Jill smiled and sent back her own loving energy, attaching a thank-you with it.

Max was racing through the trees, trying to reach Jill in time. He could hear a pack of dogs in an attack frenzy. His heart sank as they suddenly became quiet. Their attack must have been successful.

As he came up a hill, he observed the dog pack nervously pacing back and forth. He pulled out his knife and charged at them, determined to make them pay for what they'd done to Jill. The dogs scattered when they realized there was danger in front and behind them as well.

Once the dogs scattered, Max saw Jill standing unhurt against a large boulder, holding a club. On top of the boulder were some old friends from before. Max sent out a loving thank you feeling into the Chi energy. The mother wolf issued a quiet bark, turned, and melted into the trees behind the rock. The pups turned and followed.

Max raced into Jill's arms and held her close. Both were crying as their emotions were released. He thought he'd lost her, and now she was safe. They held each other without saying a word for several minutes.

"It seems I can't depend on you to arrive on time," she laughed.

"The Chi wants to keep you alive, even without my help."

A shot rang out, followed by a dog's painful cry. The others had finally arrived. Fred was the first to arrive and was clearly out of breath. Vicki wasn't far behind him. They both hugged Jill, saying they were glad she was safe. Jill retrieved her basket of pine cones, and they all returned to town.

That evening, Max and Jill were sitting on their porch holding hands. The day had been difficult, and it felt good to sit and relax.

"You never told me how you first met the mother wolf," Jill said.

Max began telling the story of his first meeting with his friend.

"Before I met Don, I was out on one of my regular hikes when I heard an animal whining with pain. I followed the sound and discovered a female wolf had stepped on a spring trap someone had set out. The trap was connected to a ground stake with a chain. The wolf had obviously been there for some time and was weak from hunger and thirst. When the wolf saw me approach, she growled and showed her teeth. I didn't know quite what to do. I didn't have a weapon to put her out of her misery, but I also didn't want to leave her there to die slowly.

"I removed my pack, got a cooking pail, and put some water in it. I slowly approached the wolf, careful not to get close enough that she could bite me. The ground clearly showed the limit of the chain. Her attempts to pull away from the trap had disturbed the soil in a circle around the ground stake. I sat down just outside of the circle. As I did, she backed away from me and growled. I focused on the Now and started projecting love and caring thoughts into the Chi.

"I splashed my fingers in the water to show her what was in the pail and slowly slid it over the line and into the disturbed area where she could reach it. I took a small stick and pushed it closer to her. She sniffed the pail suspiciously. After a few minutes, her thirst overwhelmed her fear of me, and she approached the pail and started drinking. When she emptied the water in the pail, I used the stick to retrieve it and fill it again. We did this a couple of times before she stopped drinking.

"I didn't know what to do next. To free her, I had to move inside the range of her chain, which meant she could attack me. I just sat there sending out my love into the Chi.

"She made the first move. She approached me as far as the chain allowed and laid on the ground. We were now quite close together. I looked into her eyes, and they didn't seem threatening. She seemed to know I might be the only one who could help her.

"I moved slowly, a little distance at a time, and crossed into her circle. She didn't move to attack me; she just watched me very closely. I was finally close enough to reach the trap. Its teeth had dug into her lower leg but seemed not to have broken any bones. If I could open the trap's jaws, she might survive.

"My next move was dangerous. When I opened the trap, she was free to attack me. As close as we were, I knew it would be fatal for me. I used my foot to push on one of the trap's jaws while pulling with my hands on the other. I did it quickly in case she'd pull on her leg before it was clear of the jaws. She pulled her leg from the trap and backed away from me.

"We just sat there looking at each other momentarily, separated only by three feet. I didn't know if she'd attack me or just run away. She did neither. She laid down and started licking her leg.

"After a few moments, she got up and approached me. It wasn't a threatening move, so I wasn't scared. She sniffed my hair and licked the side of my face. I reached out and scratched the fur behind her ears. I felt love in the Chi energy coming from her and returned it. She then turned and disappeared into the forest."

"That's some story. Now I know why she'd seek you out when she needed help with the thorn in her foot. She knew that she could trust you to help her. My first thought was how she could recognize the young John when her first meeting was with the old Max. But I now know it's your Chi she recognized, not your body. She did the same with me today. She knew the Chi of Jill and not the body of Jillian.

"I sure was grateful to our friend who showed up today when I needed her. She probably saved my life and that of our babies. I'm also glad that you came to rescue me, too."

Jill got a playful look in her eyes and said, "Let's go inside."

31

Winter had arrived along with the new year. It had been cold, but very little snow had fallen. In this area, winter was usually a cold rainy season punctuated with occasional small snow storms. The snow usually didn't stay long enough to make life difficult. The survivors in the town were thankful they had houses to live in instead of the tents of last winter. Everyone had moved to houses with fireplaces, and school was now held in empty homes with fireplaces to keep the children warm. It rarely got cold enough for the lake to freeze, so fishing as a food source could continue. Vegetables in cans were still available but would run out soon.

Next winter, they would need a new supply of fruit and vegetables. The council had already made plans to grow crops next spring, and some canning supplies were found in the town, but not enough to feed the entire town. The library proved to be a great source of knowledge when they needed to learn new skills like canning vegetables.

Jill's babies were growing, and she was now "showing" as her pregnancy progressed. She and Max continued to send loving Chi energy to the growing babies. They didn't know if it would help them develop, but it seemed to be the logical thing to do. After all, every expecting parent has loving feelings for their developing child as a natural instinct.

Max's duties as Marshal in the town were minimal. After realizing that they were trying to preserve humanity, the people in the town developed into a community where petty disagreements were rarely brought up, and the council resolved more significant issues. Max's role now was focused on using his engineering skills to solve problems in the town.

A storm was coming. Max had found a barometer that didn't need electricity and set it up in his home. Over the last few days, he'd watched the pressure reading move lower, indicating that a low-pressure system was moving their way. He did not know how big of a storm it would be, but the pressure reading was much lower than usual. Max always warned the council and his neighbors when he thought there might be a storm and earned the nickname "The Weather Man."

It was getting colder, so Max thought this might be a dangerous snowstorm and told the council to ensure the people were prepared. His car was an SUV with all-wheel drive, and it would do fine in a snowstorm. In case someone needed emergency transportation during the storm, he made sure the battery was fully charged.

The next morning, he felt unsettled when he woke up next to his TeenGirl. When he checked his barometer, he found it was even lower, and when he looked out of the window, he saw it was snowing lightly. Something was bothering him, but he didn't know if it was just worry about the storm.

That morning, he had a council meeting scheduled, so he headed to the meeting after breakfast. He was informing the council of his weather readings when suddenly he felt tension in the Chi. Someone was in trouble. He tried to locate the person in town who needed his help, but he felt that the person was north of town.

"Has anyone left town recently?"

They looked at each other and shook their heads.

"I feel that someone is in trouble north of town. I'll jump in the car and head that way to see if I can find them."

"Let me go with you," said Vicki. "I can brush off my Search and Rescue skills and maybe offer some help."

"I'll get the car, and we'll leave in a couple of minutes. I need to stop by my house to let Jill know what's happening and pick up my gear. You can meet me there when you're ready."

When Max told Jill that he was leaving, she wanted to go.

"What if you need my medical skills? I should definitely go."

"Sorry, but I'm not taking my pregnant wife out in a snowstorm. Vicki has some medical training, and we won't be gone long unless the car breaks down. I'll drive you to the medical clinic, and you can wait there for us to return."

When Vicki arrived, they all got into the car and headed toward the clinic. The snow was increasing in intensity, and the wind was getting stronger. Before they got to the clinic, they saw Steve walking toward the docks, so Max stopped the car to warn him of the storm.

"I hope that you're not going fishing today. There is a big storm brewing."

"No, I was just going down to ensure all the boats are tied up securely."

"When you're done, could you ask Liz to join me at the clinic?" Jill asked. "We might need a nurse there later."

"Sure. Is there an emergency, or can it wait until I check on the boats?"

"Take care of the boats first. Max and Vicki are just now heading out of town to check on someone who might need help."

They dropped Jill off at the clinic and headed north on the old road. The snow and wind were really increasing now. Max had to drive slowly due to the poor visibility. He could clearly feel a man in distress about five miles out of town.

"How can you see to drive?" Vicki asked.

"I'm just watching the tall grass on either side of the road and driving down the middle."

"This is hopeless! We'll never be able to see anyone, let alone rescue them."

"I can feel someone in the Chi. We are close now."

Max suddenly stopped the car.

"He's close. Somewhere off to our left."

Max and Vicki got out of the car. Vicki tied a rope from her rescue pack around the car's door handle and gave the other end to Max.

"You lead, and I'll follow. Don't let go of the rope."

It was a total whiteout. They couldn't see two feet in front of them, but Max slowly and confidently walked into the storm.

They walked for about 40 feet, and suddenly, the view in front of them changed from snow-white to gray. They had reached a grove of trees. As they got closer, the shapes of the individual trees appeared. Underneath one of the trees was a man in a red jacket curled up for protection. Max walked up to the man and touched his shoulder. The man looked up at Max, but his eyes were glazed over, and he seemed unaware of his surroundings.

"Let's get you out of here," Max told the man. "Can you walk?"

When he didn't respond, Max tried pulling him to his feet. The man rose slowly and showed some stiffness but was able to stand. Max put his arm around the man's waist, and they made their way back to the car. By this time, several inches of snow were on the ground, but it was blowing into drifts almost a foot deep. They needed to get back to town before the road became impassable, even for the SUV.

Vicki tended to the man in the back seat as Max carefully turned the car around and headed back to town. They had to plow through several snow drifts that tested the SUV's limits. The town suddenly appeared out of the white cloud of snow in front of them. Now, Max had buildings to give him a reference as to where he was, and he headed for the clinic. The buildings in the town also provided a buffer for the wind, and the visibility was better.

When they arrived at the clinic, two men came out the door to help move the man inside. Max was happy that his wife did not venture onto the slippery street. Inside the clinic, a group of people had gathered. The word had spread, and people had arrived to help. Jill and Liz took charge, had the man lie on a table, and then put warm blankets over him. They then shooed away the others and pulled a privacy curtain around the table.

Chuck walked up to Vicki and Max.

"It's getting really nasty out there. I was worried that you wouldn't make it back, and I would have to come and rescue you."

Vicki initially smiled at his comment but then realized he was serious.

"I wasn't concerned," Vicki laughed. "I had a Chi Master with me."

She looked at Max and smiled, but her comment produced a scowl on Chuck's face.

"You shouldn't joke about things when your life is at stake,"

Chuck scolded her.

Max could feel that the tension Chuck was radiating, was rooted in his worry about Vicki. He seemed to really care about her.

"Easy, Chuck," Max started but was quickly interrupted by Vicki, who needed no one to defend her.

"It's OK, Chuck. I know you don't have a lot of faith in Max's abilities, but I've seen him in action and totally trust him with my life. He saved me from a certain death, so don't be too quick to judge him. I would go anywhere with him and not be worried."

Chuck did not reply but just looked at Vicki. The tension in his Chi was gone, and his look now was one of concern for her well-being.

Jill came out from behind the curtain.

"The man's name is Alfred, and he will survive. He was mainly disoriented from the cold and dehydration, but we have another problem.

"It seems he and his wife Emma were living on a farm north of here. When they finally ran out of food, he decided to try coming to the town to find food. I guess that Emma was weak from hunger and couldn't travel. The storm started after he'd left, and he wasn't prepared. He thought he could wait it out under the tree where you found him. It appears that another rescue is required."

"There is too much snow for the car. I'll have to find some skis and go on foot," Max said.

"I'll go with you," Vicki added. "I have some alpine rescue experience and know how to ski. We must take some sort of rescue sled to bring her back."

"Wait a second!" Chuck exclaimed. "You can't really be considering going out in that blizzard on foot. You may have been lucky the first time, but the storm is only getting worse."

"I have to go," Max said. "It's my job, and I feel comfortable that the Chi will guide me."

"That's fine for you, but do you really want to risk Vicki's life?"

That last comment touched a nerve in Vicki.

"It's my decision to make, not Max's. I am qualified to go, and I am going."

Chuck was silent for a moment and then seemed to have come to a decision.

"Max, I'm also very qualified and an excellent skier. I want to come too."

"I know you're qualified, Chuck, but you're used to being in charge of your team. I'll be in charge of this rescue, and since you don't seem to trust my leadership, it might be best for you to remain here."

"I was in the Navy for 20 years. I know how to follow orders. I'll promise to follow your lead even if I disagree with it."

Max could tell that this was more about Vicki than him. Chuck was scared that Vicki might come to some harm unless he was around. It was obvious that he didn't know Vicki. This might be an opportunity for him to get to know her better and recognize the respect she deserves.

"It's OK with me," Max replied. "What do you think, Vicki? Do you want to add risk to the rescue by taking an unknown team member with us?"

Chuck bristled at Max's last comment but said nothing. Vicki looked at Chuck.

"Do you promise to listen to Max? I don't want any division on the team. As someone who has led a team, you know how dangerous that can be for the entire team."

"You have my word," Chuck said. He was surprised by her question. It showed a key understanding of team leadership and the importance of a team working together as one unit. She was more experienced in rescue operations than he initially had thought. It seemed he only had to worry about the kid getting them killed.

"Well, it seems that we need to find three sets of cross-country gear somewhere in this town and have them fitted to our sizes, Max said. "Who do we know that could do that for us?"

"Kenny!" Max and Vicki said simultaneously and laughed.

"What's so funny?" asked Chuck. "I've seen Kenny around town, and he doesn't look like an Olympic skier to me."

"Kenny is our Jack-of-All-Trades," Vicki replied. "If you need anything built or repaired, then Kenny is who you want to go to. He seems to know how to do anything."

True to his reputation, by early the next morning, Kenny had acquired and adjusted three sets of cross-country gear for the rescue team. He also had made a lightweight rescue sled that could be pulled behind the team with a rope.

After dropping eight inches of snow, the storm showed no signs of abating. The drifts were now reaching three feet in height. The team reviewed the gear that they were taking, and Chuck, true to his word, was working smoothly with everyone.

It was a very qualified team, and Max wasn't concerned they might fail. Vicki had received training on alpine rescue operations, and Chuck, as a Navy SEAL, should have received intensive rescue training. They left early in the morning, following the old road. The man they had rescued earlier told them where the farm was relative to where they had found him. He hadn't gone far when the storm forced him to take shelter. The difficulty would be seeing the landmarks he described in the middle of a blizzard.

Vicki had insisted they were tied together with a lightweight rope so nobody would accidentally wander away. Max took the lead, with Vicki in the middle. Chuck brought up the rear and pulled the rescue sled. The first part of the hike was slightly uphill as the road climbed up away from the lake. There was less wind here, and the visibility was OK. Once they crested the ridge, the road leveled, and the wind was unrelenting. The visibility was poor; all they could do was follow Max's lead.

Max again just tried to stay in the middle of the road. He opened himself to the Chi, hoping to feel the woman's presence. After an hour, Max halted so everyone could rest and drink some water. Chuck seemed to approve of the rest stop and its timing. Evidently, Max was doing a good job so far, according to Chuck.

"How do you know where to go without landmarks or a GPS map?" Chuck challenged Max.

"I'm just trying to follow the road to the point where the man said his driveway was."

"But how will you know when to leave the road? With the snow, I've seen no indications of any driveways along the road."

"I'm hoping to be able to feel the woman's Chi when we get close to her."

Although the wind made hearing difficult, Max thought he heard Chuck laugh under his breath. But he didn't need to hear Chuck's doubt; he could feel it in his Chi.

After another hour, they stopped again for rest. They were now past the location where they had rescued the man, and Max felt they should be close. He closed his eyes and opened himself to the Chi. He could feel the little animals close by struggling against the storm, but no human. He expanded his awareness, and then he found her! She was weak but still alive.

"I've found her," Max told the others. "She's a little farther ahead of us."

They continued another 100 yards, and then Max stopped. He walked to the side of the road and started scraping the snow with his boot. He asked the others to begin searching for the driveway. Ironically, it was Chuck who discovered a fallen mailbox under the snow. Max could feel Chuck's doubts about his skills slowly starting to fade.

The visibility was still poor, but they blindly followed a fence that appeared to run along the side of the driveway. At times, the fence was obscured by large snow drifts, but it would reappear as they kept pushing forward. After half a mile, they came to a collection of buildings that looked like a small farm surrounded by large trees. The trees reduced the wind and improved the visibility. Max could feel that the woman was close now.

The snow was still blowing, but it wasn't snowing as hard. It seemed like maybe there was a break in the storm. The wind had plastered the house with snow, but a thin wisp of smoke from the chimney hinted at life inside. They untied their ropes and removed their skis, and Chuck grabbed a nearby snow shovel and started clearing a large snowdrift from the steps. Once clear of snow, they climbed the steps and entered a screened-in porch.

Max knocked at the door and shouted, "This is Marshal Everitt. We were sent to help you."

After a few moments, the door slowly swung open, revealing a woman wrapped in blankets.

Turning to Chuck, she asked, "Did my husband send you, Marshal?"

"Yes," Chuck replied, enjoying the mistaken leadership role. "He's resting in our town, and we're here to take you there, too.

"My name is Chuck, this lady is Vicki, and the young man is Max, our town Marshal."

She smiled at Chuck and said, "Come inside. I have a fire, and it's warmer inside. I'm afraid that I'm almost out of wood. I didn't want to risk going outside to bring in more."

"I'll bring some in," Chuck said, and he disappeared back out into the storm.

After Chuck reappeared with an armful of logs, the rescue team brushed as much snow as possible from their clothing and entered the house. It felt good to be out of the wind and snow. Chuck took the logs over to a wood stove to build up the fire.

The team removed more of their outer clothing as the house heated up, and the woman removed her blanket. She was petite, in her early 70s, with gray hair and blue eyes. Behind her gold-rimmed glasses, her eyes had a flirtatious spark when she looked at Chuck. He seemed to enjoy her attention.

Vicki talked to the woman privately to determine her health status. When Vicki returned to the others, she announced that the woman seemed to have no other health issues except malnutrition.

Max decided to break out their food supplies and make a hot meal for everyone. After everyone was fed and rested, they would head back to town. Again, Max sensed that Chuck approved.

The woman's spirits seem to lift after the hot meal.

"How are you going to get me to town?" she asked. "I'll try to walk, but I don't know if I can walk too far in the snow."

Vicki smiled at her feisty, overly optimistic nature and replied, "I've done Search and Rescue for years, and I know how to bundle you up on a sled we brought with us. All you have to do is lie in the sled, and we'll take care of the rest. We brought this big, strong man with us to pull you to the town."

It was obvious that Vicki was trying to encourage the woman's infatuation with Chuck. Vicki winked at Chuck, who smiled at both Vicki and the woman.

"I won't let anything happen to you," Chuck said.

Max went outside to start preparing for the return trip. Vicki saw Chuck watching him from a window, so she walked over to him for a talk.

"Chuck, be honest with me. If you had led this team, could you have found this house in the storm?"

He turned to her. "Never in a million years."

"Neither could I," she replied. "Max has unique skills that you and I don't have. Whether you understand them or not, you must learn to trust them. Someday, they could save your life like they saved mine. Don't fight him. Learn from him. He claims that anyone can learn the skills he has. He's made me a better leader, and he could do the same for you. He's willing to teach you if you can overcome the fact that he appears to be a teenager."

"He told me a tale that he's actually an old man. Do you believe that?"

"I do. Talk to Rob about that. He knew both the old man and the young kid. He believes they are one and the same."

Max came through the door and announced they were ready to pack up and leave. The storm was lessening, and the visibility was better. Another advantage during their return was that since the wind was blowing from the north, they would have the wind at their backs instead of in their face.

When they reached the crest of the hill above the town, they untied the ropes between them and tied additional ropes to the sled. With three of them tied to the sled, there was less chance that the sled would get away from them while going downhill.

When they reached the clinic, a small group was waiting. Chuck unbundled the woman, lifted her into his arms, and carried her into the clinic. Max thought he heard her giggle with the experience. The woman's husband, Alfred, was waiting there and had recovered enough to sit in a chair. He also looked to be in his early 70s and had an average build. He had a full head of gray hair and a neatly trimmed mustache and beard.

Vicki talked with Jill about her observations of Emma's health and feisty spirit. Jill then closed the privacy screen to do her own exam.

Alfred struggled to stand and approached Chuck.

"I want to thank you and your team for saving us."

"I'm not the team leader. You need to thank Max. Without his help, we could never have saved you. He's our town Marshal and a good man to know."

Chuck then turned to Max and nodded.

32

A few days later, Max was resting at home while Jill was at the clinic. Looking out his back window, he could see into Vicki's backyard. He heard Rex bark and then saw him go racing across the yard chasing a ball. As he watched, Chuck came into view, walked up to Rex, and patted him. It appeared that Vicki and Chuck were growing closer. A knock at the door interrupted his "nosy neighbor" activities.

He opened the door to find Fred and Willie standing there and asked them to come in. Neither of them was smiling, and Max felt from their Chi that they were both uncomfortable with this visit. He directed them into the living room, where the fire would keep them warm.

"Hi, guys," Max said. "Why so serious? Is there something wrong?"

"Willie has something to ask you, but he is a little nervous. He won't even tell me what this is about. It seems your reputation intimidates some of the younger children. He asked me to come along."

"There's nothing to worry about, Willie. My job as Marshal is to help everyone. How can I help you?"

Max started projecting calming feelings into the Chi, and he could feel Willie and Fred relax a little.

Willie looked down and began in a soft voice, "I heard how you found that man in the snowstorm even when you couldn't see him. You and Rex also found that boy who was lost. I wonder if you could find my family?"

"Well, I don't know," Max replied. "Can you give me any details on how you became separated? Is there any chance they might be close by?"

"I was bad and didn't do what my father said, so he just left me in the woods." Willie started to cry.

Fred was shocked! He now knew why the boy had been so troubled. Being abandoned as a child can leave long-lasting emotional scars.

Max could feel the boy's pain in his Chi. He'd always noticed how his Chi was full of guilt, but Max couldn't fix that. To heal, the boy needed time to process what had happened. It seemed like Willie was finally able to talk about his experience.

"What did you do that was so wrong?" Max asked softly.

It took a moment for Willie to compose himself again, but then he began his story.

"We were visiting my Uncle Bob at his cabin, which was always a lot of fun. My dad and Uncle Bob were twins, and they laughed a lot when they were together. My uncle was a doctor, and when people in the city started getting sick, he said we should stay at the cabin until things got better. Uncle Bob's house was big, and he had a lot of food stored in the basement. In the beginning, it was fun. I could go out in the woods and explore and didn't have to go to school.

"One day, Uncle Bob didn't wake up. My mom and dad said something about his heart. My dad was really sad, and I saw him crying. After that day, my dad was different. He never smiled anymore, and he always seemed angry. He started yelling at my mom all of the time, and he even hit her. When I told him to stop, he hit me and told me to shut up.

"It wasn't fun anymore being at the cabin. I told my dad that I wanted to go home. He got really angry and said we were never going back to the city.

"We stayed at the cabin during the winter. My dad was angry all the time and was sleeping a lot. My mom and I tried to stay away from him, but every so often, he would yell at us, saying it was all our fault. I didn't know what to do. Every time I did something, he told me it wasn't good enough and would hit me. If my mom told him to stop, he would hit her."

Willie started to cry again and was shaking uncontrollably. Max could feel pain in Willie's Chi as he relived the experience of being abused by his father. This was an experience that could affect him for the rest of his life. He'd bottled it up for over six months, but it was now being released. Fred moved next to the boy and put his big arms around him. Willie didn't resist and moved closer to Fred. He needed someone to love and protect him now more than ever.

After several minutes, Willie's crying subsided, and he looked ready to continue his story.

"We were slowly running out of food. My dad said it was my fault because I was eating too much. He said I was a burden to the family because I didn't do anything but eat. He started giving me less food, and I was always hungry."

"How many were in your family?" asked Max.

"There were just my mom, dad, and little sister."

"When it started getting warmer, my dad said we should drive to our family cabin on Sloan's Creek near Indian Lake. He said more food was stored at the cabin, and we could drive there in a couple of hours. We got into the car the next day and started driving to the lake. After an hour, I asked Dad if we could stop so I could go to the bathroom. He got very angry again because I didn't go before we left. He stopped and told me to go into the woods to pee. He yelled at me and said I should hurry because I was holding everyone up.

"I went into the woods, but I heard my mom cry out before I could finish, and the car drove away. I ran as fast as I could after the car, but it didn't stop."

Max was astonished! How could a father abandon his son in the middle of nowhere where he knew he would die? The only explanation was that the strain of losing his twin brother and the desperate situation with the virus had caused the father to have a mental and emotional breakdown. He wasn't thinking rationally anymore.

"I walked down the road," Willie continued, "hoping to catch up with them, but I never did. After a couple of hours, I saw a sign that said "Sloan's Creek," where a creek ran under the road. Dad had said the cabin was on Sloan's Creek, so I knew I must be close. I found a trail that ran along the creek and started following it, hoping it would take me to our cabin.

"A couple of hours later, I saw Fred's camp."

Willie hesitated at this point and looked down.

"Why didn't you ask me for help?" Fred asked.

"You were so big and strong that I was scared of you. You were like my dad and never smiled, so I hid and just started taking your food when I was hungry."

Over the years, Master Sergeant Fred Maldonado had to project an image as someone not to "mess with." This image helped him as a leader whose orders would not be questioned. But what had he become that caused children to be afraid of him? He decided that he must work harder to let go of that gruff Army personality. Isn't that what Marshal Smith had asked of him when they first met? The Marshal knew it would be difficult, knowing how hard it is to change your personality, but Fred was deeply disturbed by the idea of Willie being afraid of him. Willie needed him to be an understanding father figure rather than an Army man. He must change for Willie; along the way, he needed to learn to smile more.

"Marshal, can you help me find my family? I miss my mom and sister."

Max noticed how he didn't mention missing his father, but he wanted to be part of a family again. Unfortunately, while Max could welcome Willie's mother and sister into the town, he couldn't say the same for his father. Willie's father had committed child and wife abuse and had left his son to die. A person with this history could not be added to their community.

"Willie," Max said. "What can you tell me about your family's cabin? Do you know the address or what it looks like?"

"I never went there. My father bought it last summer and made trips to put in furniture and supplies. All I know is that he said it was on Sloan's Creek near Indian Lake."

Max knew the valley well, and there were no cabins along Sloan's Creek. The boy must have misunderstood the father's description of its location. The cabin was probably somewhere around Indian Lake, but there were hundreds of cabins around the lake. They would find it, but it would take some time.

"We'll have to wait until the weather is better," Max said. "I'll ask Mary to help Fred find any records in the town offices or the library that might give us the address of your parents' cabin. It might take a while, but we'll help you find your family. We need to know your father's and mother's names so we can search for records."

"My father's name is William Carpenter. I was named after him. My mother's name is Eloise."

After Fred and Willie had left, Max sat by the fire, thinking about the problem. This was no longer just a search for a missing person. Willie's father had committed crimes, including abandoning his son to die. It had become a problem that only he, as the Marshal, could resolve.

Mary took charge of the search for Willie's parents. Fred and Mary first went to the town offices, but unfortunately, since this town was not the county seat, very few property records were stored there. They next went to the library, but again were unsuccessful since it only had historical records for the town. Their third stop was the local post office, where, after a tedious search, they found no record of mail delivery for Willie's parents. No mail delivery had been set up since they weren't living in the cabin.

Their next focus was in the real estate sector. If Willie's parents had used a local realtor, some records might have been in one of the local offices. They identified five realtors in the town and started visiting the offices. Three of the offices were locked, but Red was able to open the locks to gain entrance. However, after several days of sifting through their files, Mary and Fred could find no record of his parents purchasing a cabin in this area.

After a week of effort, Mary and Fred met with Max to report their results.

"We came up with nothing," Mary said. "We searched every resource in town and found no records of a purchase. They might have used a realtor in Crescent City. I'm sorry, Max, but I did the best I could."

"That's OK. I was hoping we might get lucky, but now we just have to work harder. We know that the cabin is somewhere around the lake. It's a big area to search and may take some time, but we'll find it. I've talked to the council, and they've agreed for Fred to use the car for short trips when it isn't needed for something else. Just make sure that it gets plugged in when you're done to keep the battery charged.

"The cold winter weather and snow will limit our initial search to the local area. Fred, why don't you take the car when it's available and drive around looking at the cabins north of town? The snowdrifts aren't too bad there, and the SUV should be able to handle them. Have Willie give you a description of his family's car, and maybe you'll see it in a driveway."

"Why not take Willie with me?" Fred asked.

"I need to handle the law enforcement aspects of this situation before we reunite Willie with his family. His father has committed crimes that I need to deal with first. If you find the cabin, don't make contact with the family. I'll need to speak with the family first to determine what is best for everyone. I don't want to bring Willie back to a father who will continue to abuse him."

"That's something that worried me too," Fred replied. "I've formed an attachment with Willie, and I don't want to see him hurt again. The weather is good, so I'll start my search after lunch."

After they left, Max started thinking about the search. There were hundreds of cabins spread out over many square miles around the lake. If Willie's parents were still alive, they would come out of their cabin when anyone drove up in a car. If, however, they had not survived the virus, the searchers would have no way of knowing which cabin was theirs unless Willie recognized their car. Without the car as a clue, they would have to search every cabin around the lake before concluding that his family was dead. This search could last well into the summer.

Mary had found a street map of the town in the library that showed not only the streets in the town but also the streets north of town. The map showed 57 cabins, and more could have been built since it was printed. Fred brought the map to Vicki's house and, with her help, was creating a search plan for the northern cabins.

"Most of the area will be easy to reach with the use of Max's car," Fred said. "This area is hilly," he pointed to the map, "and will be impossible to check out with the snow on the streets."

"I can check that area out for you using the skis I have," Vicki replied. "I was looking for a good excuse to do more skiing while the snow is here. If Willie can give me a good description of the car, I can look for it at the houses in that area."

They were interrupted by a knock at the door. When Vicki

answered, she saw Chuck standing there with a big smile.

"I was in the area and thought I would stop by and say hi."

"Well, come on in. Fred is here, and we are creating a search plan for finding Willie's family."

Chuck greeted Fred and started looking at the map. Vicki pointed out the hilly area that she would search on skis. Then, addressing Fred, she described her route to cover the area.

"Why are you going that way?" Chuck asked. "You should start at the bottom and work your way uphill."

"I thought about that but ruled it out as being more difficult and tiring," Vicki replied.

"But you're wrong!" Chuck responded with an assertive tone. "It would be much more efficient to work your way uphill, one house at a time."

The sharpness of his tone surprised both Fred and Vicki, and they looked at one another.

"I think my route is the best for me," Vicki said.

"Well, I'll go with you and show you that my route is much more efficient."

Vicki grabbed Chuck's arm and started leading him toward the front door.

"I appreciate your offer, but I think I can handle this alone. I'll talk to you another time."

She opened the door and gave Chuck a slight push out the door. She then closed the door and walked back to Fred. Chuck stood there for a moment, trying to process what had happened. Why wouldn't they listen to him? He knew he was right, and his route was better. He now wished he was back in the Navy, where people would just follow his orders.

"That was a little tense," Fred said. "He's used to people obeying him without question, and I can understand that somewhat. The military is very structured, and orders can't be questioned."

"That's OK; I'm used to some men believing that I am not capable just because I'm a woman. When they say 'My way or the highway,' I take the highway."

She looked at Fred and gave him a smile and a wink.

* * *

Chuck was still trying to process what had happened with Vicki as he slowly walked down to the docks to think. Would her route have worked? Of course, it would; only his way was better. That thought triggered a memory of his wife's words when they divorced. She said, "You won't let me live my life." His response in anger was, "That's because you want to do it wrong." At that moment, he realized he was the common denominator in both situations. Why couldn't he just let people do what they wanted to do?

As he walked onto the dock, deep in thought, he didn't notice that Max was sitting on one of the boats with his eyes closed. As Chuck finally noticed him, Max opened his eyes and nodded.

"Sorry to disturb you," Chuck said. "What are you doing out here, sleeping?"

"No, just enjoying the warm winter sunshine and practicing my 'voodoo,' as you call it."

Chuck looked uncomfortable with that remark.

"What brings you out here today?" Max asked. "You look upset. Is there anything I can help you with?"

"I just realized that I'm a jerk; I'm a good soldier but 'broken' when it comes to interacting with civilians."

"That's a real kick in the gut. I remember when I first realized that I was a jerk. It's not a fun experience to see yourself as others see you. We all have flaws, but we usually fail to admit to them. The good thing is that you first must see your issues before you can begin to fix them. It's like an alcoholic having to first admit he has a problem before he can change. What has triggered it for you?"

"I just told Vicki she was wrong on something, and she politely kicked me out of her house."

"Come over here and sit with me out of the wind, and I'll tell you what I've learned about right and wrong."

Chuck found a chair and pulled it up next to Max. He understood why Max had picked this spot. It was pleasant, out of the slight breeze yet exposed to the full winter sun.

"The first thing I've learned is that right and wrong are relative, not absolute. What is right in your eyes can be totally wrong to someone else. The people who started every war truly believed they were in the right, yet the invaded country believed the invasion was wrong. So, who is correct? Was the invasion right or wrong? It depends on each person's viewpoint.

"You have spent most of your life in the military, where you're trained to believe that everything can be judged as right or wrong. This is necessary to make the command structure work. You must believe your leader is doing the right thing, or you won't follow their orders. As a leader, you must believe you're leading your group to the right objective. Good leaders are never unsure of themselves because their team will pick up those feelings and not perform well.

"So you're not 'broken' just because you always believe you're right. You've been trained that way so you could be a successful military leader. The fact that you kept being promoted shows that your decisions or intuitions are usually right. But I think you'll admit that you've made a few wrong decisions."

"Yes, there have been some, and it has caused the loss of life."

"That's why you're having such a difficult time changing. In your world, being wrong leads to death. The problem you're having is common for many who leave the military. You came from the military, where being right must be your central focus. But now, you live a civilian life, where many people make mistakes daily. Mistakes are usually easily fixable in civilian life, but they can lead to death in the military. Even though you may know the best way of doing something, you have to learn to let us fallible people make those little mistakes."

"But why can't I save them from a mistake before they make it? Wouldn't it make their life better?"

"Because you take away the control of their own lives. When you demand that everyone must follow your instructions, you've put yourself in the role of being their master. The key difference is whether you give them a suggestion or demand that they follow your instructions. When you give them a suggestion, they remain in control of the decision, and it will be the 'right' decision for them whether they follow your suggestion or not. When you pressure them to follow your idea because it's the 'right' thing to do, you've taken control of the decision away from them. They must do as you tell them, or they will be 'wrong.' Everyone wants to be in control of their own lives."

"But it's so hard for me not to say anything when I know they are doing something wrong."

"Is it really wrong, or is it just something you would do

differently? Are their goals and capabilities different from yours?"

"So you're saying it isn't always right and wrong; sometimes, it's an apple vs. an orange?"

"Actually, I think you'll find that most decisions in civilian life involve a preference rather than a life-or-death choice. Your life in the military has daily life-or-death decisions, so you have been trained to ensure the 'right' decision is followed every time."

"So how do I change? How do I reprogram myself? You said you once were a jerk, yet now you seem fairly normal now. Were you in the military, too? How did you change?"

"You must remember that I am 78 years old in this young body. It took me most of my previous life to slowly reduce the number of times I acted like a jerk. It isn't easy to change your personality.

No, I wasn't in the military. I acted like a jerk because I was insecure and tried to bring attention to myself by doing thoughtless things. It took me years to develop enough self-confidence that I didn't feel it was necessary to draw attention to myself. So, my path was totally different from yours. I was a jerk because of a lack of self-confidence, while your problem is that you're highly capable and, therefore, over-confident. You genuinely believe that you're always right, even when you're wrong. This is a problem for many leaders, even those outside the military.

"I'm sure you've noticed that our town is governed by a council and not a single leader. We chose that method to minimize wrong decisions that a single person can make."

"But as a Marshal, you must make life-and-death decisions like I did in the military. How do you know what the 'right' thing to do is?"

"I listen to the Chi to guide me, and then it isn't my decision anymore. People have died because I didn't arrive in time to stop it, but not because I made the 'wrong' decision. I've learned to trust that the Chi will place me where I need to be. The harder thing is learning to accept the outcome when someone dies or is hurt."

"So this Chi is your master and tells you what to do? That makes you its slave."

"Not really. If you're a slave, then you're punished or 'wrong' for not obeying your master. The Chi is constantly guiding us through our intuition and feelings. It's more like a trusted friend. How much you listen to your friend depends on how much you trust their opinions. If you ignore your friend's suggestions, your friend will still be there for you when you need them. Since I trust the Chi completely, I listen to every whisper from the Chi and have mastered that ability. When I do, I've found that my life is happier, and I can help many people around me.

"I would like to offer a suggestion. I'm not saying this is right or wrong, but it's just a thought. As you have heard, I'm going to be a father for the first time. I've been reading books at the library about how to be a good parent. One book talked about the concept of 'tough love,' where you must allow your child to make mistakes so they learn how to handle adversity when you aren't around. Now, you don't let them make life-or-death decisions, but you do allow them to make bad decisions to help them learn. The key here is the 'love' part.

"As painful as it can be to watch your child fail at something, you allow it because you love them. You might try to look at the people in this town not as people under your command, but instead as friends you love. You won't always be around to protect them, so you must allow them to learn from their own mistakes. Save them from life-and-death mistakes, but allow them to choose an apple even though you know an orange tastes better. If you can change your personality from being a military leader to a loving parent, you might have some success in acting less like a jerk. It's just a thought."

"Thank you for the suggestion. As I talk with you, I see the wisdom of a 78-year-old man. I'm sorry if I've disrespected you in the past. Please feel free to pull me aside and tell me when you see me acting like a jerk. I'm sure that I'll need a lot of reinforcement. I hope that I haven't ruined my relationship with Vicki."

"You need to see Vicki for who she really is. She's strong like you in many ways and doesn't need your protection. While you both have great survival skills, she may prefer an apple while you prefer an orange. Get to know who she is; don't try to control her, and you'll be fine."

It had taken Fred almost a month to search the northern cabins. His search had been hampered by cold weather, which reduced the charge of the car's batteries, and cloudy weather, which prevented him from charging the batteries. Unfortunately, he'd not found a cabin that he could definitely say belonged to Willie's parents.

The snowdrifts were now gone, but the cold, cloudy weather restricted how much time they could use the car. Fred had put the map up in their house and, with Willie's help, slowly crossed off cabins as they ruled them out. This process kept Willie involved even if he could not go with Fred. Fred and Willie attended a council meeting to report their results.

"I'm sorry that you haven't been successful," Vicki said. "But don't get disappointed. I've been on many search missions that ended with a happy result after a long search. You have eliminated the northern area and now need to devise a plan to continue searching. I can help you with that if Mary can find us a map."

"One complication," Rob added, "is that we can't have you use the car for extended periods during your search. It's a resource we must have here close to town in case we need it in an emergency."

"I can go on foot," Fred said. "I'll just take one search area at a time and return for supplies when needed. I won't stop until I find Willie's family and will start as soon as it warms up a little."

"I want to go too," Willie said.

"I'm sorry, Willie, but it's too dangerous for you to go too far from town. I can search faster if I go alone. I'll keep you up to date as I search around the lake. You'll be in charge of having supplies ready for me each time I return to town."

Fred knew that Max still wanted to make the first contact with the family if he found them. Having Willie along would only complicate that first contact.

"Well, there is another issue," Rob said. "Fred, you're one of the strongest men in town. We need to get seeds planted in the ground if we are to survive next winter. We need everyone's help to get our fields plowed and planted on time. We can't spare you until the beginning of June. If you help us this spring, then you have our blessing to spend the whole summer searching for Willie's parents."

"I understand," Fred replied.

Willie understood but was not happy. He would count down the days until June arrived.

33

It was time. Their babies would wait no longer. Vicki and Liz arrived at their house to help Max with the births. Yes, there would be two born today. All three helpers had birthing experience, so the delivery should go smoothly. Max and Jill had set up a nursery in one of the spare bedrooms. He was excited but not anxious. Jill's Chi energy was strong, and he felt only happiness in it.

There were no difficulties with the deliveries. When Don had built Jill's new body, he'd made it strong enough to deliver babies for hundreds of years. Once the babies were delivered, the house was filled with the sound of two babies crying, one louder than the other. That would be the boy, making his presence known. It was a "guy" thing. Jill was lying in the bed and looked radiant. Happiness was flooding into the Chi around her, even surpassing his own happiness. She'd told him when they'd first met that she loved being a mother. You could tell.

As Max held his babies, he could feel the Chi radiating from them. It was unusually strong for newborns. He and Jill had been constantly sending Chi energy to them as they developed. Max wondered if they were born with a greater ability to listen to the Chi because of that. He couldn't wait to watch them grow up and grow into the Chi.

Max had finished doing the dishes and was sitting on their front porch, looking out over the lake. He held a baby, tightly wrapped in a blanket, in each arm. Jill was getting some much-needed rest. Max had learned that by sending out calming feelings into their Chi, the babies were quiet and happy.

It turned out that the gifts that Don had given the babies were more than they seemed. When his son held the blue ball, it glowed softly, but nothing happened if he held the pink one. The pink one glowed only when his daughter held it. The balls fascinated the babies when they glowed, and they smiled as they looked at them. Max had no idea what the balls did. When glowing, the balls remained cool to the touch. How a metal could glow like that confounded him. He didn't imagine that Don would give his babies something that would harm them, so he continued to let the babies play with them.

It had been almost exactly a year since he first pulled Jill out of Sloan's Creek. So much had happened. The town had organized and made it through a brutal winter. New babies were born, and many others were on the way. Humanity was alive and thriving.

He thought of Don and wondered if he was watching. Were we just a species for him to study, or did he really care? Receiving the gift for his babies surprised him, and maybe Don had more feelings than he thought. At least it felt good to know that someone was watching over humanity.

Everyone in the town had taken to heart the observation of how one person in control would eventually lead to failure. The council worked well to resolve any issues that came up. Could they keep the idea of shared control, or would someone eventually convince enough people that they should put them in charge? Probably a man with a huge ego. For humanity, this was a new beginning. He hoped they wouldn't screw it up.

It started to rain lightly as Max sat on the porch, looking at the lake. The porch's roof kept him and his babies dry, but he was reminded that:

Spring in the valley again meant warm, wet weather was Max's constant companion. Recent rains enhanced the scent of the earth and the evergreen trees that dominated the valley.